ALSO BY BETOOL KHEDAIRI

A Sky So Close

Absent

Absent

A Novel

BETOOL KHEDAIRI

Translated by

MUHAYMAN JAMIL

RANDOM HOUSE TRADE PAPERBACKS

NEW YORK

2007 Random House Trade Paperback Edition

Published in the United States by Random House Trade Paperbacks, an imprint of The Random House Publishing Group, a division of Random House, Inc., New York.

RANDOM HOUSE TRADE PAPERBACKS and colophon are trademarks of Random House, Inc.
READER'S CIRCLE and colophon are trademarks of Random House, Inc.

Originally published in Arabic as *Ghayib* in 2004. This English translation was published by the American University in Cairo Press in 2005.

ISBN 978-0-8129-7742-4

LIBRARY OF CONGRESS CATALOGING-IN-PUBLICATION DATA

Khudayri, Batul.
[Ghayib. English]
Absent: a novel / Betool Khedairi; translated by Muhayman Jamil.
p.   cm.
Translated from Arabic.
ISBN 978-0-8129-7742-4 (pbk.)
I. Jamil, Muhayman. II. Title.
PJ7842.H685G4813 2007
892.7'37—dc22   2006050439

Printed in the United States of America

www.thereaderscircle.com

2 4 6 8 9 7 5 3 1

To my late mother and father

THANK YOU

Sami Finan for lending me your eyes to see.

My sister, Raneen Khedairi, and her husband, Dr. Omar Sammaraiee, for being my family.

Dr. Layla Naim and Dr. Fadia Faqir for showing me the way.

Dr. Muhannad Younis, Dr. Mehdi Hammadi, Dr. Alaa Tahir, Dr. Fehmi Jaddan, Atta Abdul Wahab, Abdul Razak, Abdul Wahid, Mohamad Aref, Abdulelah Al Sammaraiee, Mohamad Saed Al Saggar, my Arabic language publisher, Maher Kayyali of The Arab Institute for Research and Publishing, for your support.

Zuhair Abu Shaib, Mohammad Al Shammery, Mohamad Al Jazairy, Agnes Bashir, Jamil Awad, Maad Fayad, Kotaiba Al Janabi, Mai Muzaffar, Barbra Nimri Aziz, Khalid Wahal, Jackie Sawiris, Malik Athamneh, Ali Kassay, Ali Maher, for your valued notes.

Dr. Muhayman Jamil for being my neurosurgeon-translator cousin.

Deborah Garrison, Alice van Straaten, Clare Gittins, Laetitia Rutherford, Samar Anqud, for your creative editing suggestions.

My agent Toby Eady for not giving up.

Ahmad Albeer for watching over me.

My friends: Mayada Akram, Usama Al Naher, Omar Saadi, Outor Abdul Jabar, Ali Naji, Rana Mamish, Abbas Touqmachi, Hana Sadik, Anita Gallo, Tariq Hashim, Niran Naji, Mark Jones, Madian Al Jazeera, Ali Zayni, Basil Alissi, Majdoline Gazzawi, Manar Jamil, Bayan Barak, Muna Jabali, Nadia Kahtan, Assil Bakki, for believing in my work.

My nephew Yezen Sammaraiee for being my youngest critic.

I found the following two books helpful in my research for this novel: *Iraq Under Siege: The Deadly Impact of Sanctions and War*, 2nd edition, edited by Anthony Arnove (Boston: South End Press, 2002), and *The Scourging of Iraq: Sanctions, Law and Natural Justice* by Geoff Simons (London: Macmillan Press Ltd., 1996).

CHAPTER ONE

ACCORDING TO THE medical report and the police statement, my father, an oil refinery engineer, died half an hour before my mother, a house-wife. It happened as we were traveling by car from Baghdad to his new job in the Sinai desert. Witnesses confirmed that a small bundle was ejected from the front-seat window; the cause: an exploding landmine left over from the 1967 War. The bundle settled in the sand; it was me.

A police officer said, "Praise to God; the baby doesn't have a scratch on her." He handed me over to my aunt. I was four months old. Her bedroom is next to mine. She still has the swaddles in which I was bundled and the eagle-crested death certificate in her bottom drawer.

Her husband is infertile yet he refused to change his name. He didn't follow the custom that dictates parents be named after their firstborn child. He didn't wish to be referred to as the father of his deceased sister-in-law's child. Instead, he insisted that he should be called Abu

Ghayeb, the father of the absent one. My aunt conceded and accepted that she would be known as Umm Ghayeb, mother of the unborn child. It was her way of returning the favor—she would be labeled a barren woman in exchange for his consent to raise me. Growing up, I could never understand this arrangement, so against tradition, I decided to call him "my aunt's husband" instead of *amou*—uncle.

Sometimes, when we're alone, he calls to me in a soft voice, "Babati"—my little daughter. He sounds like someone who's lost his voice, and is trying out his vocal cords by calling me.

❈

She makes her way toward him, with the broom in her hand. She is silent this time. She brushes the warm tiles around his bare feet. She clutches the wooden handle firmly as she sucks in her lower lip. She tries as hard as she can to control her tongue.

He makes no movement as she sweeps the thin white scales from around him. Some cling to the bristles of the broom. Some of yesterday's fall away. Last week's scales now lie on the soil, nurturing the vine as it attempts to reach new heights. The plant ascends laboriously from the mustard-colored pot sitting beside the sofa. Its wilted leaves lift up their greenery lazily toward the fingers of sunlight that tickle playfully at the sides of a restless curtain.

When my aunt's husband throws himself exhausted onto the sofa, its seams gape, like little mouths saying "boo" in slow motion. The color of the fabric has recently started to resemble the color of his skin. She will annoy him by taking her time sweeping up. Before he loses his temper, he inserts his finger into the slit sides of the middle cushion, and starts picking at what remains of its sponge filling. A few soft tufts gently drift onto the floor.

My aunt continues to sweep.

❈

He bought her the sofa in the Days of Plenty. She wanted an onion-colored sofa. Instead of paying for it in installments, he deferred our trip to Moscow till the following summer so that she could plunge into a leather sofa the color and texture of pine. He ran his hand up and down my aunt's thigh, patted the treasured new item of furniture, proud to have acquired them both. His salary then allowed him to do that. For her birthday, he brought her the vine. Its pot was bright yellow. She sang to the plant and to him.

After blowing out the candles on her cake she went to the cloth market in Naher Street. She chose a cream-colored French curtain. It was embellished with soft brown knots made out of shiny nylon threads. It looked as though the tailor had scattered raw sugar cane crystals onto the fabric, and the crystals had dissolved, clinging to the cloth wherever they'd landed. She said, "I've got good taste, haven't I?"

The problem with the scales hadn't yet started.

✦

Many years have passed by this big window. Today, my aunt draws back the curtains. The knots no longer sparkle, and the edges are now frayed.

She shrieks, "My God, what's this black grime?"

Black lines trickle down the sides of buildings, walls, and houses. Stripes of varying thickness dribble down from top to bottom. The city is wearing a jailbird's pajamas, like a scene in a Disney cartoon from the days of black-and-white television.

Her husband says, "It's the black rain. I didn't want to worry you. They're saying that Baghdad is wearing eyeliner today. Eyeliner provided by the Allied forces."

She replies with a drawn-out wail, "What eyeliner is this? We're all going to die!"

I join her at the window to share her amazement. The smoke from the bombing over the past few weeks has combined with the rain from last night, painting bars of loathsome solution everywhere. The local weather forecasters failed to predict the sudden downpour. Its smell is like a mixture of burnt engine oil and the stench of a rat that had died a while ago. Its death had gone unnoticed until the smell of putrefaction began to emanate from a remote cupboard. I said to myself, "Waterproof Lancôme!"

He says, "If the birds are still alive, then we too will survive."

With a movement of her hand she grumbles, "You and your birds! Who's going to clean up all this filth?"

"You." Then he adds, "And the Baghdad City Council, obviously."

I walk away from my aunt and her husband. Every window I look through mocks me, singing out, "Black, black, made of tar; this jumping pig, near and far."

I prepare the hot water for him to soak in. He has to follow the instructions. He must mix one cupful of ground oats with warm water. The solution helps to loosen his flaking skin. He must also remember not to rub too vigorously, as that can worsen the inflammation.

While waiting for the water to bubble up in the big pot, I decide to boil an egg for myself. I peel it quickly before they finish arguing. Ouch! A small splinter of the hard shell gets embedded underneath my fingernail. I pull it out quickly and place the shiny beautiful hard-boiled egg on the plate. Its thin skin is perspiring.

The pregnant cat wanders back in. I trip over her. The smooth egg slides off the plate and lands on the floor. It breaks open and the yellow yolk falls, disintegrates as it rolls, then collides with the foot of a nearby chair. It reposes there, releasing its steam.

I lash out at the cat, hitting her head. I could cry. It is the last egg we have in the house today. I yell at her, "You horrid little animal!"

I pick up the dusty yolk. I try to squash it back into its rubbery white socket. I shove it into my mouth and it quivers with no salt.

I take a sip of water to get rid of this feeling that I've swallowed a mouthful of doughy straw that tasted like a boiled egg.

The electricity is due to be cut off at any moment for the next three hours. My aunt's husband refuses to buy amperes from those who have generators. The current price is two thousand dinars for an ampere. Ten amperes is just enough for the fans; forty amperes will operate the fridge, the television, and possibly a fan as well.

Whenever my aunt uses her hair dryer, the lift stops between the floors and one of the people trapped in the lift calls out, "Abu Ghayeb's family, for God's sake, switch off your hair dryer, we're stuck!"

This time it's the thin teacher from the first floor. I leave the heat of the kitchen behind me. The wire netting on the window no longer lets the air in. My aunt often used to douse it with water to cool the breeze as it came through. Eventually the tiny squares became clogged up with a soft filling of rust. The teacher is lucky; the lift stops at our floor.

I open the metal grille for him. He breathes in deeply from the corridor air. His work is very demanding and he's developed high blood pressure. When his car stopped working he started giving private lessons in social studies to secondary school students in his flat. Every time he bends forward to tie his shoelaces he gets dizzy and starts to sway. To save his eyesight from the effects of the high blood pressure, he resorted to selling all his shoes with laces, replacing them with ones he could slip on. Eventually, he sold all his other shoes as well.

He says to me, "Thank you, Dalal."

❈

Before she became a seamstress, my aunt taught arts and crafts at a primary school. Abu Ghayeb used to be an employee at the Ministry of Tourism and an amateur artist. He is now, like all his colleagues, professionally retired. In his youth he wanted to become a painter. He enrolled at the Academy of Fine Arts. Two years later, his teachers called him in and advised him not to waste any more of his time. They told him, "Your eyes can see the beauty of true art, but unfortunately, the lines that your hand draws are flawed." His dreams went up in flames. He'd hoped to become one of the artists that made up the "Group of Pioneers" who led the Iraqi art movement in the 1940s. That was when the failed student had to accept the offer of a job as a tourist guide after he'd been sent to London on a course to improve his English-language skills.

My aunt continues to pursue him relentlessly. "You wouldn't listen to me, refused to become a trader, and look at the state we're in now!"

He answers from his bath, where he's having his soak, "It was I who asked you for your advice in those Days of Plenty. I wanted to invest our salaries abroad. You were the one who was adamant that we shouldn't. You were the one who said, 'Darling, how could we possibly send our money away?' Wasn't it you who accused me of smuggling our dinars out to foreign banks? And all I was doing was saving up to buy a small property abroad that we could go to for the summer holidays."

Whenever they start this argument, I'm reminded of my first-ever reading book at school. The Khaldouniya reading book started with the words, "One house, two houses, many houses. One fire, many fires. One dinar, two dinars, many dinars. . . ."

My aunt's anger is reaching a crescendo, "You're talking about dinars when the official exchange rate was three dollars to one dinar, and now when the rate is nearly three thousand dinars to one dollar, you're blaming me?"

"Yes, because all you wanted to do was keep the money there, in front of you. Accessible, in your hands! It's true that I was never a trader, but still I sought out other people's advice. But you, you were never convinced."

"And so, in order to punish me, you started buying a painting every month. Or were you just doing that to compensate for your feelings of inadequacy because you could never become an artist yourself?"

"I agree, I'm not a painter, but these artists have been my companions for so many years. I immerse myself in each painting in order to forget. Can you understand that? To forget."

"And what benefit have we gained from these splashes of color on our walls, huh?"

"You wanted to keep the money from our salaries in your hands, isn't that right? So I converted it into paintings. In this way, I've accommodated both your wishes and mine. I enjoy my paintings during my lifetime, and when I die, you can do with them what you will."

He then added with a heavy breath, "How could I ever predict this damn blockade?"

In the corridor overcrowded with paintings, my aunt paces up and down. Her voice resembles successive beats on a worn-out drum, "In 1980, we became involved in an eight-year war with our neighbor Iran. We'd barely celebrated the ceasefire, when in 1990, the government decided to invade Kuwait and the Gulf War started. My God, first the foreigners bomb us, then they crown their operations with an open-ended blockade? Can anyone believe that this is happening to us?"

She heads toward her husband and me, reaches over and gives him an article she's clipped out of the paper. Behind her is a row of portraits painted by local artists. He refuses to read so she says, "The glass factory was hit and several thousand liters of liquid gas were released into the atmosphere by the explosions."

He answers her, watching out the big window, "I know that."

"They've also bombed the fertilizer factory."

"I know."

A little later she adds, "Which caused ammonia to leak out into the river."

"I know that too."

"Did you hear that, every month, unbelievable amounts of raw sewage are dumped into the Tigris River?"

"I heard."

She stops beneath the photograph of her father that hangs from the wall. It's a photo of my grandfather; I mean my dear departed grandpa. Her head remains immobile as she faces him for several minutes. She goes through the ritual, "Oh, where have those days gone?"

She puts half a cigarette in her pocket to smoke it in the afternoon. She mutters, "The days of the embroidered flowing dresses that my mother used to wear when we went for walks along the riverfront. Those were the days of sweets and chewing gum, and balloons on the swings at Eid time. I remember the beauty of the silver earrings my father gave me when I graduated from sixth grade. The lovely ringing tones the house keys made when they jangled against the key of my upstairs bedroom still sound in my ears. My girlfriends would come to visit me, and we'd hide up there to smoke Rothmans. I asked them how they'd learned to inhale the smoke. One of them said, 'It's simple, just repeat after me with a gasp, *Oh, here comes my father!*'"

She smiles at the photograph, and says, "I made sure they never found out that I used to smoke!"

❦

This morning, my aunt is using a damp cloth to wipe the black mask. It's a dark image of a face erupting from its ebony background.

The mask frightens me. It has silver creases around the eyes and mouth. The brow is metallic. It thinks. Bright veins bulge around the skull. She cleans between the aluminum furrows. How she wishes that her husband would sell it before it falls apart.

When she stands facing it, and blows vigorously into its shallow crevices to disperse the accumulated dust, her face wrinkles; she starts to resemble it. She grumbles at it, "Protocols! Protocols! Isn't starving civilians considered an unethical and inhuman form of warfare? What're they doing to us?"

The mask doesn't answer.

Her husband goes out to look for work. She steps back from the sculpture. She's a short woman; her body appears compressed, shaped like a pear with a large behind and narrow shoulders. She always wears shoulder pads, soft spongy pillows permanently attached to her tight shoulders. On one occasion she forgot to put them on, so her handbag slipped off. Her husband laughed loudly and called out, "Come on my sweet pear, don't be upset."

I'm taller than she is, like my late mother, or so they tell me. My aunt's nose is very large. I don't like to look at her as she stands at the big window, watching her husband as he makes his way from the building to the street. Her face is bathed in the sunlight that illuminates her smooth oily nose. I catch a glimpse of the small hairs germinating inside it. She's always picking at her nose, as if she's trying to remold it into a smaller shape. Wasn't it she who said to me—after my illness—that our appearance is determined by the will of God?

✳

When my aunt's husband was working, I used to enjoy his business trips more than he did. When I was little, he used to take me with him to many places around the world: Madrid, Paris, and Tunis. Had he known that we'd be unable to travel in the days ahead, we might have tried to visit other capitals. On the way back, he would always say, "Dalal, never forget that no matter where we roam in this world, our country is the source, the cradle of civilization." He would tell me, in the plane heading back home, about the first Iraqi artist, who'd lived in Tal al-Sawan, six millennia before Christ. Then he would tell me all about the Office of Plastic Arts, where he'd taken on the responsibilities of an official. His duties involved liaising between the Directorate of Artistic Exhibitions and the National Museum of Modern Art. His favorite pastime was telling the foreign air stewardesses with great animation that human beings first started to write in Iraq, using Sumerian mud tablets. It was here that the first library had been set up, the first school, the first epic. . . . He'd go on and on, until they eventually offered him more fruit juice to calm him down.

✳

I've decided to keep these old photographs of me when I was ten. My aunt's husband took me with him to Denmark for three days, where he photographed me outside the Tivoli Gardens. In another shot I stand beside the statue of the Little Mermaid. The lyrics "Wonderful, wonderful Copenhagen, nice little town by the sea" resonate in my head when I look at it. I peer closely at the photograph. I was more beautiful than Copenhagen. My perfect mouth gobbled an ice cream as I stood by the seaside.

Two years later Abu Ghayeb took me with him to see his friend, a professor of plastic surgery in Turkey. He examined me, and then told him, "Bring her back in a few years time. She has a facial palsy, proba-

9

bly due to a small stroke. This isn't the right time to operate. She's still growing and her features will continue to change. If we operate now, she'll still have facial asymmetry as the muscles on the healthy side of her face will continue to grow."

In Istanbul I learned to avoid ice cream . . . and cameras.

❖

I walk out onto the balcony. I look down at the people below me. In the distance are queues of men and women, all carrying their ration cards, waiting for rice, sugar, and tea at the food distribution points. The intensity of the heat raises a gray mirage that trembles between us. They eventually appear to me as masses that gradually melt away in vertical shapes. Their outlines coalesce into forms that look like crowds of Bedouins attempting to cross a road, but their bodies are dissolving into each other. They stay rooted to the spot and can't get across.

A pigeon, the color of cement, is sheltering in the shade of the balcony's parapet, oblivious to my presence. The schoolchildren are preparing for their exams. Some of them will study on the rooftops tonight; others will settle down in the central median between the two lanes of traffic, making use of the powerful streetlights. The boys dream of falafel sandwiches and a bottle of Pepsi. The girls dream of chocolate bars. They will pass their exams in exchange for a top quality pair of English nylon stockings, which must be offered as a gift to their teacher. The boys pass in exchange for a stolen Parker pen.

I go back inside. My aunt is praying on a straw mat imprinted with the image of a peacock. She inherited it from her mother. It used to hang on the wall. My aunt has been praying more frequently since she made the acquaintance of Umm Mazin, who told her to make use of my grandmother's blessed prayer mat. Every time she lays her forehead on the mat to recite "Glory to God high above us, glory to God high above us," she kisses the peacock's blue beak.

I watch her as she prostrates herself. In the Days of Plenty, she used to wash her blond hair, and then drown it in Wellazid conditioner imported from Germany. She would then comb it out, making it shinier and blonder. Now I can't help noticing the state of her hair, streaked with white and drooping like an overripe mango. When our water supply is cut off for several days the streaks become greasy and cloudy.

There's an oily stain on the back of her veil.

✦

In the Days of Plenty, my aunt was enraptured by the color red, and a magical creation: ruby-red lipstick. The walls of her bedroom are red, as are the curtains, the bedspread, and the small rug. Her favorite shade of red is the hue of the spongy center of the watermelon as the season approaches its end. Her problem was that she was allergic to lipstick. Every time she applied it to her lips, she'd sneeze violently a minute or two later. That would make it smudge, and she'd be forced to wipe it off and start all over again.

But eventually she came up with a way of getting around this. Before it was time to go out, she would uncap her lipstick and hold it close to her nose. She sniffed it vigorously. Two minutes later she'd sneeze, wait a while, and then apply the lipstick with no further hesitation. She'd congratulate herself in the mirror with a slight nod.

My aunt would walk past me, her face like that of a tortoise who's imbibed a glass of thick pomegranate juice from Jabbar's Juice Bar. She would lick her lips as she waved goodbye to me. One night, she was going to Abu Ghayeb's lecture at the Artists' Association Hall. He showed slides from the latest excavations undertaken by the Directorate General of Archaeology. They'd uncovered priceless treasures, hidden architectural features, and historic finds from the ancient civilizations of Nimrud, Nineveh, Hatra, and Ctesiphon. She left me in her bedroom, alone, and went out with her husband, happy.

Nowadays, she pretends that lipstick no longer has any significance in her life. She's trying to be considerate of my feelings, yet I know that she goes out to get dayram, the traditional Arabic lip color based on walnut extract, since imported makeup has become an extinct species in our markets. But she never found out what I used to do with her lipstick when she went out.

When I was struck down by my illness, my mouth became crooked. My lips were drawn across to the right side of my face as though someone were pulling them with an invisible string. It may be that I'm attached to my guardian angel, who mocks me, by means of this invisible link. I tried to be like other children; I tried to convince myself that I was normal. My sad attempts to whistle always failed. I'd cry in front of the mirror that echoed back the sound *phht, phht* instead of a long elegant whistle.

I would draw myself in the mirror, using the lipstick as a crayon. It crushes as I press it onto the smooth surface and follow my perimeter. I start at my head, then mark out my body until the circle is complete. Suddenly the electricity is cut off. The red oily frame goes out. I abandon my pose, leaving behind me a map tracing out my figure hanging in the middle of a mirror in a darkened room.

❖

Yesterday, my aunt's husband spent most of the afternoon scratching himself. He has spent months looking up articles about his condition. He's become obsessed with seeking out the cause of his illness. He used to think that his pillow might be a factor. He was convinced that the chicken feathers were a breeding ground for a type of mite that bit his face while he slept, thus infecting his skin. He would then awake the next morning complaining of a new inflammation and a terrifying itch.

He calls me to have dinner with him. He is chewing on a tender potato as he speaks. He brushes away a few scales from his clothes to stop them from falling onto the dinner table. He says, "Psoriasis is a disease that can't be predicted. It can affect the skin of men or women at any age."

He removes a scale from his plate with the tip of a fork. "Would you believe that I actually sought out the oldest surviving member of our extended family to ask him if we're of Circassian origin? They say this race is most susceptible to this condition."

I ask him, hoping his conversation won't drift into scientific jargon, the way it usually does, "And are you of Circassian origin?"

"No. Anyway, this inflammation of the skin leads to periods of redness and itching, and the appearance of these thick, dry, silver-colored scales on the surface of the skin. Am I annoying you with these boring details, Dalal?"

I think to myself, "Where's my aunt? Why does she delegate the task of listening to her husband's woes to me? Or doesn't she want to join us because she's no longer prepared to dine on potatoes alone!"

I say to him, "Then, we could all be struck down by it."

He echoes my words, "Yes, all of us, certainly. Even though it's not contagious."

He passes me a plate of potatoes. A sprinkle of salt tumbles from his fingertips onto a crust of dark bread. He bites into it. He says, "Briefly, our skin renews itself more rapidly than it does in others, and even more rapidly in the affected areas."

At that moment, his wife appears in the doorway. As she passes the table, she comments, "At least there's something about you that renews itself!"

I swallow. The potato takes the shape of my gullet, chokes me. My aunt pats me on the back on her way out of the kitchen as though nothing has happened.

Her husband says in a pitying tone, "Your poor aunt thinks that the blockade is our only problem."

Without saying a word, I agree with him. My problem precedes his by several years. He is still trying to deal with the shock of having contracted this illness, whereas I see in him an echo of my affliction. He says, "How am I going to get hold of another course of the medication I need? All the pharmacies are restricted to selling standard medication and nothing else."

"What is it you're looking for?"

"They're tablets of shark cartilage extract. What I have will only last me for another few months."

❈

His primitive fears remind me of my torment. I waited many long years for him to take me back to Turkey. I was due to have plastic surgery there, but no one made a move. Everyone was too busy with his or her daily routine. What about my mouth?

My aunt paid no attention to my predicament; she was too busy with the embroidery classes she taught in the summer. Abu Ghayeb used to go out on expeditions to the north and the south accompanying foreign delegations and archaeological teams, in winter and summer. That provided him with an additional income, and enabled him to acquire more works of art. He'd recently gone out on visits to the plain of Shahrazur. That was where they'd found the site of Arbat. Excavations there had revealed a seven-story building from the Islamic era, and the remains of a palace that had been the administrative center of the city. I imagine Abu Ghayeb announcing how this indicated that these structures were from the period between the fourth and fifth century of the Hijra.

His mind registers all these places and dates, but when it comes to me, he's oblivious to the passage of time! When he was unable to contact his doctor friend in Turkey, he assumed that the phone must have been disconnected. He decided that we'd have to go to his address directly. Each year he deferred my operation. He wanted to combine traveling for my surgery with a family holiday for the three of us. Then the war started. And then we found out that the best time to operate is when the patient is in their younger years. After that, it's too late.

It has now been too late for twenty years. One war followed another, punctuated by a watertight blockade of twenty-two million people. That included everyone who lived in our block of flats. The north and the south are no-fly zones, and no one can travel abroad. The hyper-inflation is terrifying, the poverty is degrading, and the economy has collapsed. Social structures have crumbled and unemployment exceeds all logical limits. Is this all happening because we have the world's second-largest oil reserves after Saudi Arabia?

That's what the media tells us.

❖

Did either one of them feel any less guilty when they would accompany me to the Alwiya Club? They would leave me alone to spend endless

14

days by the swimming pool, not returning until the evening. They sacrificed a part of their salaries and took out a lifetime membership at the club that they paid for in installments. I considered it a form of compensation; a substitute for the second trip to Turkey that never happened. This club was one of the city's bourgeois features. In its big halls the members played billiards, bingo, and darts. In the corners, women played bridge. People gathered for afternoon teas, barbeques, and held shipwreck parties, where people pushed each other by surprise into the water in full clothing, around the pool. They read books and newspapers in its library and once a month couples would enter the ballroom dancing competition. My aunt liked her friends to know that we were members there. Her husband always reminded everyone that it had been built by the British in the 1920s, and that Agatha Christie used to write in its gardens, underneath a leafy tree.

I tried to use swimming as a means of forgetting my reconstructive surgery.

CHAPTER TWO

I CHANGE THE sheets on my aunt's bed. My household duties are clear. Abu Ghayeb's pillowcases must be changed every day. I suck on the sweet in my mouth, a square, strong mint tablet; white with small flecks of green on both sides. It feels as though I am licking the wall tiles that pave the entrance to the Haydari Hospital. They too are white with flecks of green. My aunt tells me that it was in Room 18 that I first emerged into this world.

The local magazine *Alif Ba* that came out today has a cartoon about hospitals. Instead of having a patient in a bed in his hospital room, there's a huge cat stretched out on the bed. It's eyeing the patient disdainfully as he enters the ward, and is saying to him, "Shoo!"

I'm attracted once again to the painting hanging above the bed. It's the image of a human eye that has been painted by an ear, nose, and throat doctor. I never tire of contemplating it no matter how many times

I have to change the bed sheets. It speaks to me as it hangs there surrounded by an area of harmonious colors. It is a collage in equilibrium, as though the eye had pierced the painting, so that it could look out through it.

※

I remember that doctor well. Abu Ghayeb used to take me to see him whenever I developed an ear infection. His clinic was at Nasir Square. It sometimes took us more than half an hour to find a parking space there. I disliked the narrow alleyways leading off from Saadoun Street, where all the medical clinics are based. The street got its name from the statue that stands there of a former Iraqi prime minister from the days of the monarchy. My aunt's husband explained to me that he opposed the British who ruled us for forty years and eventually committed suicide when he was accused of being a traitor. I jump across a puddle of stagnant water. The street sweeper approaches to displace the water with his large broom made of palm fronds. He pushes it toward the rectangular grille covering the drainage pipes. I wonder how many people have accidentally dropped their car keys through one of these metal grilles?

The doctor sat me down in a leather chair that spun around. He probed my ear and my nose without asking permission; but my mouth was a different matter. Initially, his warm hands sought permission before lifting my upper lip. A few moments later he struck a metal instrument against the arm of the chair. The sound of metal striking metal startled me. He said, "Don't be afraid, show me your teeth." He drew the base of his tuning fork toward my teeth, and my head drowned in resonance. I looked up to my aunt's husband for support, but all I saw was his back.

This morning he smeared his face with Soulaf shaving cream. The phone rang and he went to answer it. The head of the archaeological team on the western sites called to tell him what the excavations had revealed. They'd found several structures at right angles to the wings of the Crusaders' Dome; and they'd also located the boundary wall of the Friday mosque. My aunt's husband thanked him for the information. As he walked past me, the froth on his face was drying and blowing away in all directions. White flakes dancing like tiny butterflies.

The doctor asks me, "How do you feel?" I don't answer. The ringing in my ears is competing with my prayer that my mouth will go back to the way it was. There's a painting over his head with the word "Allah" printed on it. It's surrounded by fluffy pink clouds shaped like a tuning fork.

❊

This week, there are no car tires available in the local markets. People are in a quandary about protecting their cars. Car wheels disappear from cars parked in private garages in spite of their owners' vigilance. Last month, Oldsmobiles were targeted; now it's mainly Japanese cars. People are selling their cars before they get stolen.

They say that a car thief died yesterday while trying to steal a car. The owner was a clever electrician who was fed up with the gangs' attempts to take his car. He extended a cable out to his car in the night and connected it to his electricity supply. The thief was electrocuted and died instantly; the car owner handed over his body to the police. They turned up on foot, as the ignition had been stolen from their patrol car. The ambulance arrived without its usual sirens. They had run out of spare parts.

The people in our building tell the story of a thief who was removing the wheels of a car when he realized that another thief was undoing the wheels on the other side. He shouted to him, "You keep the ones on your side, and I'll have the ones on my side. They're not worth fighting over!" I tell myself, "Rumors, nothing but."

Disabled. The infrastructure and industries have been damaged. Electricity generators, water purification plants, and petrochemical refineries have been blown up. Communication networks have been blown away and bridges have fallen into the rivers. The roads and highways are full of craters. The rail tracks, along with the carriages on them, loaded with foodstuffs, have been destroyed. Aluminum and textile factories, and the centers for manufacturing electrical cables and drugs, have been wiped off the map.

In the Days of Plenty, when my aunt heard the sound of the orange Volvo with its distinctive purr, she'd get ready to welcome her husband home. His return every afternoon had special clamorous sound effects. The brakes squealed, the garage door slammed shut, and his shoes clattered. His keys jangle constantly. He starts to read al-Thawra—the revolution newspaper—while she prepares his glass of cool fruit juice. She gently holds up the glass that she's chilled, attempting not to disturb the layer of condensation that has formed on its outside. When Abu Ghayeb comes in and sits down, she quickly brings him his comfortable slippers and takes away his outdoor shoes, and withdraws with complacency, as if tucking away the noise of his elegant shoes in her pocket.

She reaches out with a smile and takes the bag of shopping he brought back with him. She knows that he'll comment about the way she stores things in the fridge. He used to argue with her at length about her purchases. He'd accuse her of being an unenlightened consumer because she only bought pretty looking items with shiny packaging, without checking the quality or the price. He also used to complain that she had no sense of order and that she piled up her shopping in a haphazard way. He said to her, "Don't you sense the importance of empty space and filled space?"

Today, the fridge doesn't get filled, not even halfway, and the car is no longer in the garage.

She's no longer bothered with her husband's return or his absence; she's busy polishing her unusual collection of buttons. Her present concern is to acquire a varied selection of buttons that she can apply in an artistic way to the dresses she makes for customers. She has run out of polishing liquid, so she steals some of the ointment that Abu Ghayeb uses for his psoriasis. She reads the label, "Does not leave a greasy residue." She squeezes out a bean-sized globule saying to herself, "This'll do."

She no longer chills fruit juice for him. Nowadays, when there are two oranges in the house and she has to share their juice with him, she squeezes them both and then divides the juice in half rather than squeezing each one into a separate glass. This way she shares the good and the bad fruit with him saying to herself, "If I do it like this, no one can tell the fresh from the old orange!"

❖

Everything has been tampered with these days, from building materials to tomato paste that turns out to be a mixture of old potatoes and red coloring of indeterminate origin. Two days ago, the bathtub fell down from the flat above us. The dampness had eroded their bathroom floor, and because of the exorbitant price of repair, they were unable to deal with it properly. They used poor quality materials that didn't support the weight of the bathtub. Now half of it is still in their bathroom; half dangles over our dining room table. Our ceiling forms their unstable floor. My aunt is about to have a nervous breakdown.

After several attempts, we managed to get hold of Aziz, the Kurdish repairman. He promises to come straight away to return the bathtub to its rightful owners. Kaka Aziz cuts off the water supply to the entire building. He's a large man, gentle and hardworking. He refuses to eat his lunch until he's finished his work. He mispronounces his own name with a Kurdish accent, calling himself Kaka Asees.

During the several days it takes to make the repairs, our water supply is cut off. My aunt refuses to go to our neighbors' flat to use their toilet. She prefers to use a large tin can that she empties every evening when all the building's residents are asleep. She creeps stealthily down to the ground floor and spreads it over the plants.

❖

A young woman has come down with blood poisoning and was admitted to hospital last week. I will accompany my aunt to visit her family. We don't take a taxi; we worry that the driver might ask for a thousand dinars. They say that a lizard had crawled inside a sanitary pad at a small shop where the shopkeeper had started selling them individually. The small reptile had entered the young woman's body and she fell ill. Officials from the Ministry of Health closed down his shop and sealed it with red wax. The shopkeeper is in prison, and the girl's mother is seeking compensation. Pretty Lady Tampons, Cinderella Sanitary Pads, Virgin Tampons, and now Lizard Sanitary Pads!

We sit down in the living room. The poisoned girl is in her bedroom. Her mother offers us a glass of water. She looks down at her tray as she serves the water, apologizing because she has nothing better to offer. As she moves away, I grow aware of the painting hanging in front of me.

The woman in the painting appears coarse, like a solid figure decorated with a grainy coat. There are purple, pink, and blue squares. There's a breast in one square; the other breast is in another square. A face is in one square, and the rest of the body is in another. The woman is distributed in squares.

As we leave, I drag my hand along the gypsum wall surrounding their house. The artist would've enjoyed painting on these surfaces. I ring a front door bell that is out of order, I press down on the nipple of one of his ladies with my finger.

❋

I have no wish to return to our apartment. My aunt will give me a headache with her tales of buttons and shoulder pads. In days gone by, our block used to be known as "the teachers' flats," as we lived in a building that was allocated to teachers. Now my aunt collects buttons, immerses herself in her fabrics and threads; and I'm being labeled as the seamstress's daughter. As for Abu Ghayeb, the former Mr. Tourism, he will become the seamstress's husband.

She has a huge number of square, see-through plastic boxes, where she keeps her precious buttons. No one is allowed to approach her possessions. Each box has a small sticker indicating its contents. Plastic buttons, wooden buttons, metal buttons. She has an unusual collection of ivory buttons, and another set made out of compressed cork. Sometimes she writes on the box the type of button it contains: teardrop, circular, cuboid, reed. On others she writes in a clear hand the occasion the type of button would suit: wedding, graduation, mourning.

She became more attached to the boxes when people started buying old clothes. They can no longer afford to buy new items, so we've now entered the age of darning, patching, and mending what we already have. Trading in secondhand clothes has become an everyday occurrence. Some families only do it in the evening, away from prying eyes. They hide under the cover of darkness as they rummage through the racks of secondhand clothes.

Younger people head out to the used clothes market after sundown. The items are piled on top of each other. Odors of people who once had homes emanate from between their folds. They are laid out on a metal bed frame in the "rummaging section." The other clothes are in the "hanging section." A weak light from a battered lamp gives off the resigned smell of kerosene. The faint beam filters through the little holes in the dangling clothes. A man shouts at the top of his voice, "A curse on all this poverty; come and get it for next to nothing."

My aunt insists that need is the mother of invention as she attaches buttons to her clients' worn-out clothes, announcing proudly that the clothes are now as good as new. Her husband gets fed up with her prattle on one occasion, and thrusts a handful of melon seeds at her saying, "Here you are; dry them, paint them, and make buttons out of them!"

My aunt takes offense very readily from Abu Ghayeb's comments. Her shoulders tense underneath her shoulder pads. The spongy pillows become inflated and protrude upward. When his teasing oversteps the limit, especially when he calls her "Little Beady," she throws a box of buttons at him, one that might contain colored glass penguins or little ceramic fishes. If one of them breaks, she pretends not to be bothered, but the tone of her voice rises until it sounds like the hum of a helicopter engine that's hovering in the distance above our block of flats.

He says to her, "We're drowning in a sea of beads, buttons, and thread."

She replies, "It's better than drowning in the sea of scales that you shed regularly every three hours; like the timetable of the power cuts."

My aunt laughs, "Ha, ha, ha"; then her laugh deepens within a few seconds to become, "Hu, hu, hu."

❖

I slide toward the kitchen to make myself a cup of Nescafé. I am looking forward to a few moments of clearheadedness. I was unable to sleep well last night. I always sleep on my left side. I hope that my cheek will dangle down as I sleep and maybe that will help straighten the crooked angle of my mouth, even if only a fraction. When I was taught at school that the center of the earth was the source of tremendous gravitational force, I imagined it as a huge magnet in the form of a horseshoe. How I wished that magnet could pull my mouth back to its proper shape.

I bought the jar of coffee a month ago from the nurse, Ilham, who lives on the second floor. We did an exchange. I gave her two tins of sliced mushrooms that were close to their expiry date.

I plunge the spoon into the coffee jar and scoop out a generous spoonful. An errant breath of wind blows in through the open window near me. The coffee granules become dislodged, landing on the wet tabletop by my cup. They fall onto the shiny surface and melt like instant brown teardrops. I watch them spreading out in an irregular fashion on the table. I wipe them away and close the window. I spoon out a smaller scoop.

I sit down to relax as I drink. My aunt and her husband are still angrily exchanging buttons and scales.

I pick up the telephone to check once again whether our faulty lines have been fixed. We hear a lot of weird and wonderful tales from the crossed lines. Some people say that it's the cheapest way to pass time.

A woman is telling her friend, "My son has managed to emigrate."

"Where's he gone to?"

"He's arrived safely in New Zealand."

The woman listening at the end of the line gasps, "What? How could you send him to New Zealand? What about the hole in the ozone layer? Don't you care about his well-being?"

"My dear, if you manage to get out of Saddam Hussein's hole, who cares about the hole in the ozone?"

I replace the receiver. End of conversation.

CHAPTER THREE

Between 16 January and 27 February [1991] some 88,000 tons of bombs were dropped on Iraq, an explosive tonnage judged equivalent to seven Hiroshima-size atomic bombs. Thus *for a period of the war Iraq was subjected to the equivalent of one atomic bomb a week, a scale of destruction that has no parallels in the history of warfare.*

—Geoff Simons, *The Scourging of Iraq: Sanctions,*
Law and Natural Justice, 4–5

THE ECONOMIC BLOCKADE seeps into our block of flats. The building overlooks the Mosque of the Unknown Soldier in one direction, and the tennis courts belonging to the Alwiya Club in the other. When I was a child, a Jewish family lived in the top floor of our building. They had three daughters—Gilda, Iris, and Valerine. I adored Iris because she would meet me on the balcony at night with magic sparklers that she'd smuggled out for me. We'd light them and wave to each other with the little suns that hissed delightfully, smelling of gunpowder.

They called their grandmother "Grumma." Her big toe had a large corny growth that got bigger every day until she was unable to walk. Iris's father Moshi had a mole on the back of his neck. Three hairs grew out of it and Grumma would cut them off for him every month. I remember going over to their flat every Saturday to turn on the lights for them or to light their cooker. Her mother had told Iris that when their God finished creating the world, he sat down on the Saturday and put his feet up. That's why they don't do any work from sundown on Friday till Saturday evening. They don't even switch on the lights because they avoid anything resembling lighting a fire. Grumma, with hair like white cotton wisps, used to say to me in broken Arabic, "Thank you, thank you. May the Lord switch off your light just like you do for us."

I once played with Iris underneath the bed. We found an open tin of effervescent Vitamin C. We managed to salvage a few tablets soiled with dust. We placed them in our mouths; they tasted like solid rounds of a medicated orange mixture that had dried up in a solution of 7UP. They boiled on our tongues releasing a bitter tang with a fizz.

The family's departure left an aftertaste like those Vitamin C tablets. Unexpectedly, they emigrated, leaving their flat, which was taken by an instructor at the military academy. Iris whispered in my ear, "Mama is very upset, she doesn't want to go. They're sending us to a country called Israel."

❖

I saved the last magic sparkler in the drawer beside my parents' death certificate.

I remember Iris whenever I go past the old calendar that still hangs in the corridor. It's a promotional agenda for Iraqi Airways. Their emblem is a trendy design of a white airplane, like the side view of a chunky fork. The pretty air hostess in the picture swallows to bring down the pressure in her delicate ears. The vomit bags are on her right; the instructions for the oxygen masks are on her left.

Today our airplanes are stranded, distributed at random in the airfields of various Arab countries. Most of the pilots have emigrated. Those who were unable to go are working in the airline's kitchens, which now prepare pre-packed meals, with compliments of the airline, in green and white.

The military instructor had no daughters. He lived alone without a wife. He had two thick bushy eyebrows with tapered hairs. They remind me of sprouts from chicory seeds sown together and planted carefully underneath the skin in two graceful arcs above his eyes. He was a dark-skinned man, almost completely bald. The skin of his scalp shone through between the tufts of hair scattered across the top of his head. It looked as though he'd covered it with small mounds of crushed coal here and there. He never spoke to anyone; he read a lot, even in the lift—when it was working. One of his jobs had been to accompany the Jewish family to the door of their plane, but his civilian duties also included reminding everyone to hang up shiny decorations in the corridors to commemorate anniversaries of national political events, and to light a candle outside each flat when the president's birthday came around in April.

That was a while before he sold his flat to Umm Mazin.

❦

In time, people stopped calling our building the teachers' block. It came to be known as Umm Mazin's building. We met her for the first time as she was coming up the stairs, with some difficulty. She was a short, stout woman. Her head was covered with a black veil that blended into a black dishdasha and from her shoulders dropped a black abaya. She looked like a dark seal moving heavily under layers of matte material. In her right hand she held a bundle of papers; in her left she was carrying a large see-through carrier bag containing a number of plastic ablution jugs. They had handles like large ears and spouts like rigid rods. Some of them had perforated the bag. Halfway up the stairs, the bag could no longer tolerate the pressure of the jugs inside and it burst.

The colored jugs tumbled out, bouncing from one step to the other on their way down. *Tick, tack, tack, tock, tick.* They ended their descent unharmed. Umm Mazin called out at the top of her voice in a rural southern accent to a woman at the bottom of the stairway, "Badriya, gather the jugs on your way up."

We assumed she was a trader in plastic goods.

❖

My aunt's husband refuses to let me work at the nearby private hospital run by the nuns. They were advertising for cleaners. He said, "You will not be a cleaner while I'm around to provide for you."

I would have walked there, passing by the statue of Kahramana, the heroine in Ali Baba's tale. This lady-shaped fountain had dried up since the imposition of sanctions. The jars containing the forty thieves were now covered by a layer of greenish rust. I remember when I was a little girl, Abu Ghayeb took me to meet his friend, assistant to the sculptor. He was working on another sculpture at that time, of Shahrazad. She was in two halves; he hadn't yet welded her torso to her lower half. The assistant received us in the studio and greeted Abu Ghayeb by saying, "Welcome to the friend of all artists." He was too polite to greet him as "Our friend, the failed artist."

I climbed a spiral staircase made of black metal. I paused halfway up, and found myself standing beside Shahrazad's body. Her extended hand was by my side. Her enormous eyes were next to mine. They took a photograph of me standing there. I wanted to climb into her, to wander around inside her chest and abdomen. My lollipop fell into the gaping hole that was her eye.

If my aunt's husband had allowed me to work at the hospital, I would have made my way back along Abu Nuwas Street by the Tigris River. It would have taken me past the statues of Shahrazad and Shahrayar whispering to each other. I could have stopped for a few moments to admire them and wonder to myself if my lollipop stick was still inside Shahrazad. Then I'd leave them behind to their privacy, and walk along bombed-out pavements that resembled dislocated shoulders.

Why does everything remind me of my aunt's shoulders? Last week an old woman said to her, "For God's sake, Umm Ghayeb, can you put the padding in the chest rather than the shoulders? Some of us need the enlargement at the front!"

Umm Ghayeb answered her, "I don't think I'll have the time. I have to complete two shrouds, may God preserve you. I have to finish them straight away."

She was talking about a father and son who'd committed suicide together. They had fallen on hard times, finally giving up when they were both unable to get any work after three years of trying.

I imagined that family a few days before they perished looking like a small painting on our wall: men made of cloth, a sun of worn-out threads, an acidic background, a large void.

We learned at school that sound travels faster through solid objects. I place my head against the wooden edge of my bed. I bite into a carrot and try to listen out for the echo of the crunching inside my skull. I'm the opposite of Abu Ghayeb who has a loathing of all noises.

Our street has become truly unbearable. In the Days of Plenty we had the Electronic and Miniature Instruments Sales Center, which is now a garage for car repairs. The young workmen drive the customers' cars at top speed then slam on the brakes to check them. Because our building is almost at the end of the street, the brake testing usually takes place outside our front door. The sign that reads WARNING—SPEED RAMPS is now useless.

The noises from the street drive my aunt's husband crazy. *Screech* or *dummm*, from the workshops nearby. He goes down to the street with a can of black paint and a paintbrush in his hand. He crosses out the word WARNING and writes instead, CURSES—NOISY BUMPS. When he comes back up, the fireworks that I imagined inside his head settle down. We are then both startled together. *Crash*. One of the mechanics has crashed straight into the entrance of the building.

My aunt isn't concerned with what's happening in the street, or at the entrance to our apartment block. All her attention is now focused on the new occupants of the flat upstairs. She suggests, "Why don't we go and visit our new neighbors?"

Before we leave our flat, I straighten a painting that has tilted notice-ably to the right. I often straighten out the paintings and restore them to their horizontal position after my aunt has been cleaning them. She never manages to hang them up correctly. Sometimes she hangs up a painting where another one should be. That upsets her husband who insists that each painting belongs in its own special niche. He treats the paintings as though they were his children. When he hangs them up himself, he places each one in its appropriate nest.

Abu Ghayeb will start snoring soon when he sinks into his deep after-noon sleep.

Badriya, Umm Mazin's servant, answers the door. She doesn't seem surprised that we have come to visit; it is as though she is expecting us. The hues of her complexion are inconsistent. Her forehead is darker than the rest of her face. Underneath her eyes are two weary crescents of wrinkles like ground Basra lime. Either her body is thin or her dish-dasha is very wide. She says, "Welcome," and takes us through to the sitting room.

There is another woman waiting; we sit down and wait with her. The woman is sitting directly in front of me, her hair the same brown as the frame of the painting behind her. It is a landscape in watercolors. Her dress matches the green of the field in the painting. It is dark and crushed in its lower half; lighter and more dewy higher up. The woman is nodding off in her seat, unaware of our presence. Her hand is curled up into a fist as it supports her fleshy cheek. Her head rests on its strut for a few moments, immobile.

The woman is startled from her sleep by the sound of Badriya's voice announcing that the lady of the house will join us after midday prayers. Her ring has left an impression on her cheek. The woman says, "How do you do?" with sleepy eyes and a cheek embossed with the imprint of the stone in her ring.

A little later, she asks, "Is this your first visit?"

My aunt answers, "Yes."

The woman releases the abaya from around her shoulders. "I'm sure you'll be satisfied with her services. Umm Mazin is a wise woman, and her prices are reasonable."

I exchange glances with my aunt. The woman continues, "What's your problem? I hope you're not having problems with your husband, like me?"

Her questions intrigue us, but she continues, regardless, "Anyway, there are no secrets here in Umm Mazin's house. We like the way she does things. She lets all the women listen in to the tales of the others. We sit in a circle around her while she tells each woman's fortune from the patterns in her coffee cup. The others will be here."

She has barely finished her sentence when the doorbell rings twice. The room is soon full of women who seem to know each other, or at least, each other's problems.

One of the women, Umm Ali, asks another, also called Umm Ali, "Umm Ali my dear, what's wrong?"

"You can't imagine, Umm Ali! They've all been vaporized."

"What's been vaporized, Umm Ali?"

"More than four hundred souls: women, men, children. They bombed the Amiriya shelter, Umm Ali, at four-thirty in the morning. A laser bomb blew up the metal gates that weigh six tons. The explosion generated temperatures of several thousand degrees, and the people inside were just vaporized."

The first Umm Ali covers her gasp with her hand and moves toward the door. The second Umm Ali calls out to her, "Umm Ali, where are you going?"

"To Amiriya, I have relatives living in that vicinity."

We are amazed. My aunt turns to a woman who seems calm in the face of this exchange, and asks her, "Excuse me, why are those two women talking about the bombing of the shelter in Amiriya that took place many years ago, as though it happened only yesterday?"

She answers, "You must forgive them. They both lost loved ones in that tragedy, and it made them lose their minds. They now come here every month to relive that trauma, unaware of what they're doing. One of them still thinks that if she hurries there, she might be able to save some of those who were in the shelter. It's pitiful; their illness is like a tape being replayed again and again."

Umm Mazin makes her entrance. She will probably have to abandon some of her weight at the earliest opportunity, lest life abandons her. She says, "May peace be upon you"; her greeting fills the room. Her flat is the same size as ours, but her walls are totally bare except for the painting. In our apartment, the walls of Abu Ghayeb's home are almost completely covered by oil paintings.

Her face is surrounded by a *fouta* that overheats and stifles her. It's made of brocade that she's pinned underneath her chin with a fake diamond brooch. Her brown-skinned face is centered around her distinctive big mouth that has a character of its own. It's molded into an everlasting smile, her large yellowed teeth protruding forward. It's almost as if someone's hand had tried to pull them out, then decided against it. She has a reduced number of teeth, an increased number of gaps, and her purple gums bulge out.

She glances toward us saying, "Welcome to our first-time guests. Let us prepare for the session."

She calls out to Badriya, "Bring us the coffee, Bidour."

We don't interrupt her; we sit down on the floor with the other women, wrapped in their abayas.

It appears that she is not really looking at anyone, but she gazes intently at each woman's face as she speaks. Her voice rasps like burnt wood, "I use my abilities to help people. I'm not a fortune-teller or a soothsayer. I wasn't trained by gypsies, and what I say isn't set in stone. What I possess is a gift from God. I can sense other people's problems, but I don't interfere with them. I do, however, have the cure for the tired soul and the drowning inner self."

She adjusts the way she's sitting, as though she's rearranging the folds of fat she sits on. "My sister Ghaziya also had this gift, but unfortunately, she abused it. She woke up one morning with an imprint on her hand of a star and a crescent the color of apricot jam. She should've used that blessing to heal the sick. Instead, she was so delighted with it, she started talking about it and showing it off to all her visitors."

One of the women interrupts her, "Who said this was a miracle? She could have used henna to draw the star and crescent on her palm."

Umm Mazin continues her tale, "A month later, hair started growing within the star on her right palm. God Almighty was providing her with confirmation. The poor fool was overjoyed; she continued to display it proudly until all the hair gradually disappeared, then the star itself faded away completely. It was then that my sister regretted her actions. By declaring it, she failed to preserve her gift. That's why we must operate in total secrecy. No one must know about our work, otherwise all will be lost."

Over by the door, Badriya tells another servant who has come along to accompany her mistress, "Have you heard?"

"What?"

"Basra has been bombed. A hospital, a nightclub, a coffee shop, a clinic, and a lawyer's office have been razed to the ground. The employment agency nearby for maids had its windows blown out, but is still standing."

The servant replies, "Thank God for that, my cousin is looking for a job."

Umm Mazin notes that my aunt and I are exchanging glances. She calls out for us all to be served coffee. We wait our turn with the other women.

At this moment, one of the other women leaves the circle without seeking permission. She starts to make preparations to pray on her own, aside from the group. Umm Mazin glances at her briefly through her small slitlike eyes. Her entire eye appears to be just one narrow, turbid pupil.

The lady is about to pray without a prayer mat; she takes a piece of double-layered tissue paper and separates the two halves by blowing onto it. She places one of the two pieces on the floor in front of her so that she may lay her head on it when she kneels down to pray; the other half she saves in her pocket for tomorrow, just in case there's no tissue paper to be found.

She starts praying, just as Umm Mazin is about to start telling someone's fortune by reading the first coffee cup.

She asks the lady to blow into her coffee cup, then to whisper into it the problem for which she seeks help. Umm Mazin places her hand over the cup to trap the woman's whispers inside it. The cup disappears beneath her chubby hand. The dimples between the knuckles make it look more like a fat teenager's hand.

She opens her mouth, "The cup tells me that you're weary. You're troubled by a problem that relates to your husband. He no longer comes to you or approaches you, is that right?"

The woman answers promptly, "It's true. What can I do?"

"You must be patient. This isn't the first time that your husband has rejected you."

The woman becomes agitated, "But he was wonderful with me until our situation worsened with the blockade. After that he started to ignore me completely, turning his head to the other side."

Umm Mazin asks her in a serious tone, "Have you tried a love spell?"

"Of course, but it was useless."

"You mustn't discuss the spell, nor when it was cast. If you do, its effect will be lost."

"I know that, so I never mentioned it to anyone."

"Fine, so did you try a passion potion?"

"I did, I made my husband drink it without his knowledge, but it made no difference at all."

"Do your neighbors have a pretty daughter?"

"No."

Umm Mazin's diamond falls from her veil into the coffee cup. Her questioning stops for a few moments as she reclasps the veil to cover the short white beard underneath her fatty double chin.

She continues, "Your problem is very simple; you don't need to go knocking on the charlatans' doors. Your coffee cup has revealed a bowl of stale tea and a few drops of soured milk. This is the smell of your breath. When was the last time you brushed your teeth?"

The woman bows her head in shame, "Toothpaste has become so expensive, Umm Mazin. Imported brands are impossible to get hold of, and local brands taste like car-repairing putty."

♦

"I have a solution for you."

Umm Mazin offers the woman a tube of imported toothpaste in exchange for a bag of disposable Bic razorblades. Probably she uses them to shave her little beard.

After that day, we never saw the woman with the ring imprinted on her cheek.

I wonder if Umm Mazin can read the news in the coffee cups? Did they tell her about the bombing of the baby milk factory? Can she see a red cross and hungry children sucking their thumbs in vain?

The second woman approaches Umm Mazin, her face displaying obvious signs of distress. Her fingers tremble as she offers up the empty cup into which she has whispered her dilemma. Umm Mazin starts to analyze the situation. She peers into the woman's face; the tremor in the woman's hand worsens.

Umm Mazin tells her with confidence, "It appears to me that you're here on somebody's behalf. The woman concerned has problems and great sorrow. She's suffering from something and is greatly affected by it, yet she's fearful that she'll be blamed for it, or that other people might gloat at her misfortune. I can also see a water fountain and a pretty young girl."

The woman breaks down, saying, "Yes, yes Hijjia, the girl is my daughter; the water fountain was the way she lost her virginity while still in the first flush of youth. She's my only child. I raised her alone with my sweat and my tears after her father was killed in the war."

She wipes her dripping nose with the cuff of her dress and resumes her tale, "We'd gone out to visit some friends; my daughter needed to use the toilet. Moments later we heard her screaming and rushed in to find blood flowing from her. She hadn't known how to use their western-style toilet so she mistakenly used the bidet. The jet of water gushed out at full strength and she lost her virginity in their toilet. What can I do Hijjia, what can I do?"

Umm Mazin sighs heavily, reflecting at length; she only glances at the cup briefly. I recall a long forgotten lesson in mathematics. The variable x (Umm Mazin's breathing) is directly proportional to the variable y

(Umm Mazin's reflection); and since the variable y is also proportional to the variable z (Umm Mazin's reading of the cups), then x must be proportional to z. That's how Umm Mazin operates; her behavior conforms to the laws of transgression in modern mathematics.

She pierces me with her hazy eyes, willing me not to cross her path while she's thinking.

The black stone in her ring reminds me of the man who sold me a few books yesterday. His ring looked like hers. I was cruising through Sarai Market looking for some novels. I came across this gentleman, this 'uncle,' in the street of booksellers that's gradually becoming a greengrocers' market. Nowadays, books are sold by the meter. They're arranged horizontally, measured, and offered at wholesale prices. I gazed at him for a few moments from afar, wishing that one of Abu Ghayeb's artist friends would sketch him in charcoal.

He was the classic image of an elderly man sipping tea in one of Baghdad's markets. He sits on a wooden box, his feet set slightly apart. His back is gradually curving into a slight hump as he extends his head forward to sip his tea. He has poured the tea from the beaker into its saucer to let it cool. His lips tremble forward as he draws in the cooled tea from the saucer. His head is covered by a charawiya and he wears the jacket from a suit over his dishdasha. His beard is white; he's thinking of nothing other than the taste of the tea.

When I got home, I found a dedication on the first page of each book I'd bought. "To my beloved daughter, Samia," "To my dearest friend, Najwa," "To Father, with my love."

My conscience troubled me. How could I have bought other people's treasured possessions when they'd fallen on hard times and were selling their books on the pavement?

Umm Mazin asks the distressed woman, "How old is your daughter?"

"Twenty."

"Then give her this potion of gazelle's corn and ginger twenty times to calm her soul. When a groom comes forward seeking her hand in marriage, take her to a cousin of mine who lives in Irkheita. He'll perform a simple operation on her. You must be discreet. Can you keep this a secret?"

"Of course Hijjia."

"I can't give you his real name, but we call him 'The Night Bat.' You must not go to visit him till after dark. He'll be able to reconstruct your daughter's virginity. He was a capable doctor who's now retired. He'll replace her hymen with the membrane from a bat's wing."

"May God bless you with a longer life."

"By the way, you and your daughter needn't fear the numerous cages by the entrance to his house where he keeps his bats. He only uses them for his operations. But don't delay the wedding night more than a week after your daughter's operation. Do you understand?"

"I understand."

"May God be with you. You can pay Badriya in the kitchen on your way out."

Umm Mazin starts writing down the doctor's address for her, while continuing to involve, in a spiral motion, the other women in social chitchat, "In 1912, my father used to write using a reed pen. The ink he used was a mixture of pomegranate peel soaked with rusty nails, and soot generated by burning a candle underneath a metal plate. He'd write on the metal casing of kerosene cans; when he made a mistake, he had to lick the wrong words off with his tongue because there were no erasers in those days. His handwriting, however, was amazing. He could stun a bird in flight with one fell swoop of his pen."

She shakes her head to the right and to the left as she adds, "Today, I find our circumstances ridiculous. The whole world tries to prevent us from acquiring pencils for our schoolchildren because they claim that they could be used to make weapons! I may soon have to sell the secret of my father's ink mixture to the people of this country."

One of the seated women says while rotating her wrist, causing her hand to move in circles, "Those days are gone—when we had compulsory education, free stationery, and uniforms."

She then asks with enthusiasm, "Umm Mazin, can I ask you how you acquired this ability to find out about people's problems from their coffee cups?"

"I was eight years old when I started reading fortunes for grown-ups from coffee cups. I see writing in them instead of coffee dregs. Drinking the coffee is just an excuse. When I start assessing a cup I recite to myself, 'In the Name of God and His Prophet; Peace be upon Him.'"

The women repeat after her like an echo, "Peace be upon Him."

Umm Mazin resumes her tale. "I then see phrases and images that indicate to me their owner's problems. Spells and magic are something totally different. I only operate with good intentions and do not deal with evil. I use readings from the Qur'an in my work, and I forbid the use of any other means. I derive great satisfaction from helping those who've lost their way, the victims, and those who've suffered in this world for whatever reason. I have a special affinity for women who've lost their husbands as a result of evil magic cast by others."

Another woman asks her, "How do you do that?"

"I annul their spells by casting a white light on them. It's the power of true faith that overcomes evil. They employ the jinn, and we battle against their evil acts. And of course, as God tells us in the Qur'an, 'Everything was created for a reason.'"

The women repeat after her, "Verily spoke God Almighty."

Umm Mazin adds, "The world revolves my dear. If you've been a wealthy person all your life, then you won't know the tragedy of poverty. And if all the world was full of just kindness and love, then we wouldn't know how to fight evil when we encounter it. Isn't that so?"

The women answer her from every direction, "Certainly."

"Yes, of course."

"Undoubtedly."

Umm Mazin repositions herself once again, rearranging her folds of fat, and says, "I can also read people's palms, but I only do that until midday. I beg of you, don't ask me for that service too often, because I don't condone foretelling the future. 'The soothsayers have lied even when they have been truthful.'"

And all the women respond, unthinkingly, with one voice, "Verily spoke God Almighty."

Had she looked at her own palm this morning? Her lifeline would tell her that life expectancy has dropped by twenty years for men and eleven years for women due to environmental contamination by radiation after the Atomic Energy Center was bombed.

It is now our turn. My aunt becomes a little agitated for a few moments, then says, "I'm sorry to disturb you. We simply came here to get to know you. We live on the third floor."

Umm Mazin asked her, "And why not? There's no reason why my guests from the third floor can't join me for coffee, and now I can tell you your fortune."

My aunt has no choice but to whisper into her cup. Umm Mazin gazes at me intently all the while. I am eager to find out what she will see in my aunt's cup.

She says, "So many spots, and colors flying about in the air."

I almost burst out laughing, but I do not dare. My aunt's face becomes as small as the saucer she's holding. Umm Mazin carries on, "You've waited many years to achieve something you've longed for, but it hasn't happened."

I was thinking to myself, in total secrecy, "Well done Umm Mazin, you're getting warmer. . . . I'll give you a clue. Scales. Singular: a scale. The coverings of a pearl or similar. Crustaceans. Small creatures that have no bones and live in the sea, they have a thick muscular coat. Psoriasis: the illness. The patient is afflicted with a skin disease. I am afflicted with this visit today. Come on now, dear aunt of mine, I want to get out of this place right now."

But Umm Mazin will elaborate no further in her analysis other than to say, "Anyway, your cup is drowning in a big sea pulling down its symbols and images. Come to visit me once again sometime soon and I'll reread the signs in your coffee cup for you."

She then announces to the seated ladies, "By the way, I don't accept visits from men, nor will I receive any Christian or other non-Muslim women; so please don't embarrass me."

Before she has even finished her sentence, I find myself by her front door, tugging on my aunt's hand. A blue ceramic palm hanging in the entrance attracts my attention. A number of small eyes swim around within the palm, and in its center are seven perforations. Underneath it is a strip of protruding writing, "May you be protected from all evil eyes, mine, your parents', and from your closest neighbor's."

CHAPTER FOUR

MY AUNT SIGHS, "Where are we now from the good old days?"

This is her usual introduction to a new phase of whining. I learned that from her husband who can predict the onset of another one of those episodes that he calls 'her nagging routine.' He's convinced that she's a person who can't adapt to new circumstances and insists on living in the past. I learned from him how to understand her moods. I also learned from him a little bit about paintings. He classifies his wife as 'an expressionist' when he feels like a witty critic. She can see no justification for his teaching sessions about art, as she wants me to be her assistant, to sew shoulder pads.

I hold a piece of colored cellophane up to my eyes. I look over at my aunt through the wrapper of an extinct Macintosh toffee, "My aunt, you're pistachio-colored in my eyes." Her gaze flits between me and the piece of cloth that one of her customers has left behind. She's been asked to embroider some Arabic calligraphy on it.

She rarely changes her seat when she works. She always sits underneath a painting of a man who resembles a Buddha; he's bald and his eyes are closed. A builder's plumb line hangs down over the priest. When she lifts up her face to look toward me, the Buddha appears to be sitting on her head.

I say to her, "Ilham, the nurse from the second floor, will ask you to make a dress for her."

"Does she still live alone, or has she now got somebody with her?"

"What does that have to do with the dress?"

"So that I can decide whether to put the buttons at the side or at the back."

I gaze down at the ground beneath my feet. My aunt's words make their way toward me navigating around the strangely shaped outlines etched on the floor tiles. I imagine them to be creatures from another planet. I see the outline of an apple in the tiles, and that of a fish. This spot resembles a face; that one looks like a canary. If I borrow those two circles from that nearby tile and merge them with the rectangular shape on this tile, I'd end up with a funny-looking car.

"Solitude is such a difficult thing, Dalal. The wars have snatched away so many of the men. My customers keep telling me that. One of the women told me that sometimes when she feels lonely, she likes to listen to her bedroom curtain, billowing in a gentle breeze as it makes a soft rustling sound. She closes her eyes and imagines it's the sound of her husband's dishdasha as he approaches her bed in the darkened room; yet her husband died a few years ago."

❁

As we chat, I feel a sudden yearning for Amjad. We used to play together when we were in second year at primary school. After the midterm holidays, I decided that he could be my fiancé. I can't stop thinking about him since Abu Ghayeb put up that bronze sculpture on the pillar outside the sitting room.

Amjad and I used to look out at the world through the bottom of a glass. We would drink rosewater juice that his beautiful mother Nawal made for us. Then we'd use the glasses as telescopes to see each other as deformed images: disfigured, with huge crooked noses. When we looked at his twin brothers, we'd laugh even harder. Yasir and Nadir weren't yet three; milky white creatures. They smiled at us placidly from the other side of the glasses: two pairs of hazelnut eyes gleamed as they waved to us. Then we'd go out to ride on his bike in their garden.

Amjad was no longer there when we started our third year at primary school. His mother wasn't around either, nor were the twins. The news was reported in *Al-Jumhuriya*—the Republic newspaper. The plane heading from Vienna to Baghdad had exploded when it crashed into a mountain in Syria. The older students in the senior classes were dismissive of the newspaper article. They whispered to each other saying, "The plane didn't crash into the mountainside; it was a planned assassination to take out Amjad's father because he worked for the Palestinian resistance." The news item was followed by a list of passengers unaccounted for in the explosion. I read their names, then I got a glass and read the report a second time, then a third time, through the bottom of the glass. The first set of twins I'd known in my life had been blown up. Yasir—*boom* . . . Nadir—*boom*. . . .

I remember how Miss Suhaila, the Arabic teacher hit me one day for fooling around in the classroom with Amjad. Now he was dead, along with his beautiful mother and his two brothers. I wanted to be the one who hits her this time. Miss Suhaila wouldn't explain the word 'assassination' to me, and told me to stop asking too many questions. She never stopped fiddling with her ugly breast underneath her shirt during Arabic lessons. She talked about the rules of grammar, tugging at her chest. That was in the 1970s.

The sculpture is still, yet animated. An angel floats in a space made of bronze. It's carrying two children. The angel is a lady, embracing the heads of the two children to her chest like breasts. Each breast is one of the children's heads. Her hair of bronze billows in the breeze. Her shoulders are bronzed; and behind each shoulder, a wing glints. When she reaches her destination, she'll give back to each child its head and remain breastless. Soon after that, she'll snap off her wings and give one to each child. The twins will then fly. They'll soar away leaving their mother behind, dying on the bronze mountain.

I wish that Amjad would get on his bike and cycle off, far away from my memories.

❈

My aunt's voice brings me back to where we're sitting, "As for the woman who sells me the embroidery threads, she's so afraid of being alone that she won't place her slippers underneath her bed."

"Why?"

"She worries that she'll start imagining there might be someone under her bed, and that it's this person's feet sticking out from underneath the bed's edge. She says that it's the bit of the slipper sticking out that frightens her."

"Why doesn't she leave them outside her door when she goes to bed?"

"Because she worries they might get stolen."

A moment later she resumes her conversation. "I have another customer who repeatedly hugs her pillow with all her might before she goes to sleep to warm it up. She then leaves the room to get herself a glass of water. When she gets back into bed again, she cuddles her warmed up pillow and says to it, 'Goodnight, darling.'"

"Who's her darling?"

"Her husband, missing in action, lost on the battlefield."

I say jokingly, "Why don't we take these problems to Umm Mazin, maybe she'll have a solution or a cure for them?"

The embroidery needle slips from my aunt's fingers and dangles from the red thread on her lap. Her eyes gleam as she says, "By God, that's a good idea, my dear niece."

❈

It seems that my aunt didn't get a good night's sleep last night. She's usually a very light sleeper, and the slightest movement in the house can wake her. She's so sensitive that she synchronizes her breaths with her husband's breathing. She tries to breathe in with his inhalation and breathe out when he expires. She tries to harmonize their breathing so that she can drift off to sleep. The other reason is to avoid having to breathe in his expired breath that smells like a fig that has ripened on the bough for too long then fallen from the tree onto decomposing soil.

Her husband is well aware of her sensitive nature. He reminds her laughingly how her weak body was struck down with a cold the previous winter because she opened the freezer door in December without putting a camisole on. On another occasion, her husband had opened the door of the little fridge in their bedroom at night. The gentle light woke her and she was unable to get back to sleep till the morning.

She has strange moody habits. She places the box of tissue paper inside the drawer, insisting that it's too ugly to leave lying about. Sometimes, she'll place the phone behind the sofa because she's convinced that its presence distorts the harmony of colors in the sitting room. When it rings, she tells it harshly, "Be quiet, you annoying thing."

But what really drives her mad is her husband's scales, which fly about in all the rooms. She shakes her head, which is out of proportion to her shoulders, in fury. Sometimes I think it's her head that is too large, at other times, I'm sure it's her shoulders that are too narrow. Even her nightdress has thick shoulder pads.

❖

We don't resemble each other in this family. The only hereditary connection to my aunt is her little toe. She can't bend it; its joint has been absent since birth. Before I go to sleep, I lift my leg up, and stretch out my right foot. I bend it forward and backward, but just like her's, my little toe doesn't bend.

As for Abu Ghayeb, he has huge broad shoulders, like a champion swimmer. He attempts to paint, and that's when his wife will try to provoke him. As he is getting ready to paint, she starts stripping the hair from her legs using a homemade sugar paste. Nevertheless, he does his best to enjoy listening to *The Four Seasons*. He ignores her movements for a while, then says to her, "I met Umm Mazin at the entrance of the building. What a gross creature! We barely know each other, yet she had the insolence to tell me that she'd send me her cure for my condition."

My aunt replies, "Yes, it seems that she's very capable in what she does. We heard that she treats large numbers of women in her flat."

"I'm not happy about you visiting this woman. She makes me feel uneasy."

I ask my aunt's husband, "Did you hear anything about the boy who lived in the house next to our block of flats?"

"No, why?"

"They say he died. He choked on his chewing gum as he laughed. He was joshing with his friends and fell onto his back. The gum ended up in his windpipe. It was too late by the time the ambulance got there."

"What a horrifying tale!"

"Is it true what the other kids say, that it takes the gut four years to digest chewing gum?"

"Maybe that's so, Dalal; I'm not sure."

"And is it true what they're saying about his mother? That she was so overcome by her emotions, all the freckles fell off her face?"

My aunt's husband strokes his forehead with his hands. I continue, "His father is in prison because his friend informed the authorities that he had a satellite dish hidden away on his rooftop. He installed it late at night, under cover of darkness, so that he could watch the news from around the world on the satellite channels. They say that the informer was given a reward when the dish and its cables were confiscated."

"Where do you get these stories? Wouldn't it be better if you spent your time learning how to paint?"

My aunt gets up to turn off the television. The image of the president bestowing medals for bravery to a number of army officers vanishes from the screen, and the sound of applause that was emanating from it ceases abruptly.

She adds her suggestion, "Or you could do some embroidery."

❁

Badriya knocks on our door. In her hand is a letter from Umm Mazin. I ask myself, "How could she possibly call her son Mazin? Isn't she aware that the dictionary's definition of Mazin is ants' eggs?"

My aunt reads out loud, "For the skin and its diseases. Take a handful of the green fleshy layer that covers the wooden shell of ripe walnuts. Slice it, and then boil it in a liter of water until half of it is gone. Filter it through a fine cloth, and then add two large spoons of honey to it. Stir until it dissolves totally in the water. The resulting ointment is used to treat a variety of skin conditions including ulcers, scabies, patchy hair loss, and bleeding gums."

They both stand there in stunned amazement. Badriya is thunderstruck by the sight of the paintings that surround her in every direction while my aunt is overwhelmed by the contents of the letter. Badriya is standing underneath a pen and ink study of two women. The woman on the right bears a large platter on her head shaped like half a crescent. The woman beside her wears a veil that is simply a collection of half crescents cascading down from just below her brown face. The two peasant women are exchanging gossip that tumbles from their chins. It trickles downward filling in the crevices between the crescents that make up their veils.

Badriya exclaims, "I'm merely the messenger bearing these tidings."

Her barefoot voice accompanies her on the stairway up to the last floor.

❖

Abu Ghayeb opens up a shiny poster and spreads it out on the table, there's an apprehensive girl in her bedroom bearing on her shoulders an old woman's head. A yellow snake is insinuating its way from underneath the doorway. Numerous eyes, like glass globes, are scattered around the segments of the painting. Oil pipelines extend toward infinity. A soldier is shouting out numbers, his lips are rounder mouthing "NO." The other parts of the painting are celebrations of depression and plucked doves.

He looks up at me and says, "It's titled *The Blockade*."

The edge of the poster slips from beneath his fingertips once again and reverts to its natural state. It wraps itself up into a long cylindrical shape.

My aunt's husband picks up a sewing basket and places it on one end of the poster. At the other end, he places a small sculpture. At that moment, the electricity is cut off. Abu Ghayeb lights a candle and leaves it beside the poster. I remain in my seat, and gaze at the wall in front of me. The cars pass by in the street. Their headlights brighten up the wall. I entertain myself by watching the areas of light sweeping across the wall every now and then as the cars go by. I glance at my aunt, who's peering through the darkness. She gathers her threads and disappears out of sight.

I approach the candle. I decide to be different by putting it out. I trap my breath within my lungs and contract my chest muscles. My breath spouts out forcefully from my nostrils rather than from my mouth and the candle goes out.

The darkness spreads out until the dawn.

❋

My aunt's husband cries out from the bathroom, "Attaaack!"

I run to where he is standing. He examines his body from every angle and says, "What's happening? My ears have been affected."

I stand there watching. As he rubs his ears and ruffles his hair, he says, "From now on I'll have to wear light-colored clothes so that these scales don't show up on them when they fall."

Suddenly, he bursts out laughing. I see a demonic gleam in his eyes reflected in the mirror. He asks, "Dalal, what happened to the chicken that used 'Head & Shoulders' shampoo?"

"What?"

"It started laying eggs without shells!"

He gives me a medical report, and asks me to read out its appendix for him. I put the toilet seat down and sit on it, "The cause of this disease is not known. It is a unique condition that is related to the individual's genetic makeup. However, some doctors have postulated that high daily stress levels are a significant contributing factor. It is usually not possible to eradicate this illness completely."

We do not stay long. He kicks the door open and takes me by the hand, saying, "I can't stand it anymore. Let's go."

"Where to?"

"We're going to buy a queen!"

❋

We go out into the street and head toward Karrada Dakhil. He walks as if he's in a race. He doesn't stop for any reason, as if he's trying to reach his destination before anyone else. He leads me, still clasping my hand tightly. I observe the people passing by. I wonder, "Why do cats and women wearing abayas behave in the same way? They start to cross the road without looking. When they get halfway across, they decide to look in the other direction to see if a car is coming. They're then surprised to realize that there's indeed a car coming toward them. Instead of hurrying quickly across the road, for some strange reason, these two creatures start heading back to the pavement, and quite often get run over."

We go past a shop that used to sell sweets. Sugar is scarce, so the shop has been converted into a dry cleaner's. We are in a lane called Traders' Alley. One night on this street, a group of merchants amazingly disappeared. They were accused of destroying the national economy by forming a price-controlling cartel for basic commodities like sugar and wheat flour. They were eventually pardoned, but by then it was too late. They had already been executed!

At the entrance to a bank, employees are lining up, carrying stacks of cash known as the Swiss print. They have been ordered to exchange them for the newly released notes. Other employees are already leaving from the back door with shopping bags full of bundles of the locally produced notes. This new government cash reminds me of the paper money we used as children at the Alwiya Club. The one hundred fils piece was pink, and the fifty fils piece was green. We used to call it Monopoly money.

A few moments later we pass a large hall that used to be an art gallery. Such an establishment is considered inappropriate in these times, and it has become a store that sells alarms and other security equipment. I don't like the sounds that modern alarms make to scare away car thieves and house robbers. I call that shop "Shabateet's" after the children's "long breath" game where whoever was able to continue chanting "shabateeeet" for the longest time was the winner.

We reach a small garden center hiding behind a half-deserted pharmacy. An agricultural engineer called Fathi comes out and greets Abu Ghayeb warmly. His speech is labored, his breathing rattles. I imagine his lungs are full of fine tubes passing solid oxygen instead of air. We sit down on low wooden seats amidst several plants.

My aunt's husband asks him, "Shall we start?"

"Yes, by all means."

He calls out to his wife, asking her to serve us tea.

"To start with, we have to understand the difference between the various types of bees. Yellow bees are found in the Mediterranean basin. They're aggressive and have a tendency to swarm."

"What do you mean?"

"I mean that the bees leave their colony to form a new one."

"So how do we get them back?"

Fathi laughs, exhaling as though throwing his voice aloft, "Don't rush brother, this is still our first session."

The tea arrives and he continues, "As for gray bees, their original habitats are in Eastern Europe. These are the Caucasian honeybees."

Abu Ghayeb is keen for more information. I observe the engineer's wife decorating a giant candle for a local wedding. Shiny red ribbons wind themselves around the candle and converge into a ruffled skirt made of bright blue nylon.

"The third type, the black bees, are found in Northwest Europe and North Africa."

"And which type would you recommend for me?"

I leave my seat and approach his wife. Suddenly a small child runs out, holding his arm out in front of him as he chases a hen that scurries away. It looks as if the boy is trying to stick his finger into the bird's bottom. His mother explains that he has been watching his father. They had a pair of delicate finches. The female was unable to lay her eggs, so Fathi helped her by gently introducing the tip of his finger into the bird's bottom.

Her son runs off. She continues, "We were so pleased with the eggs, but it turned out the birds were calcium deficient. They ended up eating their own eggs. The problem is, my son now thinks that putting his finger up the hen's bottom will make her lay eggs straight away. He'd love to eat some eggs. It's been a while since we've had any."

Her husband is still talking to Abu Ghayeb, "The breeds that have become popular recently are the Carniolan honeybees. The workers are strong and the queen is a vigorous egg layer."

The man coughs suddenly, and spits something out into a handkerchief he took out of his back pocket, "This breed is renowned for its minimal consumption of honey in the winter. They withstand the cold, and they won't steal."

He returns his crumpled handkerchief to its place. Using his moist index finger, he points at Abu Ghayeb, saying in all seriousness, "They have a placid temperament. They only sting to defend their home."

I follow the child's footprints in the dust. I find him peeing into a little hole in the ground. He doesn't pay any attention to me and doesn't appear embarrassed by my presence. He glances at me as he holds his little penis in his hand and says, "My mother says that I've drunk too much water today."

I smile. The hen makes its escape through a small gap in the wooden fence. The boy turns around to face me once again, saying as he points to his little member, "My father's also got one, just like this, but bigger."

I can think of nothing to say other than, "Is that so?"

He replies matter-of-factly as he tucks it away inside the fly of his dirty trousers, "Yes, but my Daddy's has lots of eyelashes on it."

I retrace my footsteps. When the engineer goes on too long about different types of bees, I imagine the little cotton crocodile embroidered on Abu Ghayeb's shirt starting to yawn.

Eventually, they shake hands, "Thank you for the information. I'll come back to see you once again in the near future."

50

I look around me. Outside, the sun licks the walls of the houses. Russet tongues slither through the black-and-white lines of the pedestrian crossings, fading from frequent use. It's many years since they were last repainted.

The eucalyptus trees that my aunt's husband calls "sticks of dust," as in the local dialect, cast their shadows across the sign that reads BUDS OF THE REVOLUTION NURSERY SCHOOL. I recall my schooldays when, at nursery school, we were taught to recite, "I am an Arab soldier . . . I hold my rifle in my hand . . . I'll use it to protect my land . . . *bang, bang, bang.*"

Later, during my days at primary school, the children would arrive in the morning wearing their ordinary clothes, and leave in the afternoon wearing the uniform of the Vanguards. The uniform was a military style khaki suit with a map of the Arab world imprinted on the jacket, the trousers, and the hat. Every Thursday we attended the flag-raising ceremony and shouted in unison, "Palestine is an Arab state; it must be freed." Our teachers always reminded us that training with the Vanguards would make us more intelligent, especially if we also spent more time playing chess.

In our teenage years, we had to join the National Union of Students. There we were told that our aims were "Unity, Freedom, and Socialism," and that we had to strive for "One unified Arab nation . . . with an eternal message." That would prepare us to join the ranks of the Arab Baath Socialist Party when we grew up, provided that the party members were assured that we merited that honor. We had to attend the meetings unfailingly, maintain secrecy, and learn the president's quotes by heart. We also had to study the articles of the Seventh National Congress in order to be considered grown men and women, who would become worthy citizens in our society.

❁

I preferred the Guides. Their uniforms were blue. And an unpleasant boy called Abbas couldn't follow me there. I had to flee from him at Vanguard training. He followed me around wherever I went and made fun of my mouth. I was unable to escape his cruelty so I decided that he would be Ibn Firnas.

I imagined him to be the character portrayed in the statue of Abbas Ibn Firnas that'd been erected on the road to the airport. It depicts a young boy, standing on a tall platform, preparing to take off. His wings are made of wax and feathers. He is about to fly and hover high above the earth. But the sun will melt his wings and he'll fall into the parking lot leading to the suburb of al-Shurta and I'll be rid of him forever.

That was my reverie when I stretched out on the back seat of Abu Ghayeb's car as we returned from the airport at the end of one of his trips abroad. I amused myself by counting the number of lampposts from the arrivals lounge all the way to Jadiriya Bridge. As I stretched out onto my back on the backseat, I remembered my math teacher. She was always telling me, "Dalal, if you don't pay attention, I'll hang you from the ceiling fan." I imagined myself dangling upside down reading the mathematical equation on the blackboard $(A - B)$. In the car, in the back-seat, I realized that everything could be seen upside down, except the sky.

Many years later I understood that people who were hung from fans by their feet were being tortured to extract their confessions.

CHAPTER FIVE

A CRISIS RESULTS in compromises. This is what I learned from our visit to see Fathi, the agricultural engineer. My aunt's husband is going to buy a swarm of bees. He's going to start beekeeping so that we can survive on the income from the honey they produce. But how will he come up with the cash for this project? It is obviously from the money that has been set aside to reconstruct my mouth. The U.S. dollars that were supposed to pay for the plastic surgery to realign my face have become the family's only savings.

The equation is clear; my mouth in return for our survival.

In spite of her husband's warnings, my aunt takes me with her to visit Umm Mazin. Entering, we find a group of women sitting in semi-darkness. They look like an X-ray image. Their upper halves have the indistinct shape of females, their lower halves have the feet of wild birds. On a side table, there is a handwritten sign that reads, "Please do not bring men with you or boys over the age of seven."

Umm Mazin is dealing with a complaining woman whose husband is no longer having sexual intercourse with her. She asks her if her husband suffers from any illness, "Does your husband have diabetes or heart disease? How old is he? Was he active when he was younger?"

She assesses his frame of mind, his age, and their financial status. When she is convinced that there's no illness, and everything is normal, she declares, as if she's announcing the winning prize in a competition, "Therefore logic indicates that it's seduction, pure and simple. You must have a specific defect, which is why another woman has seduced him and he's left your home."

The woman collapses in a heap when this conclusion is pronounced. Umm Mazin, reassures her that a solution is available, "I advise you to burn a handful of peppers in a saucepan with some oil and recite your husband's name out loud. You must burn the peppers until they're dry. The peppers will burn away at his heart, and he'll develop a prickly yearning for you and a desire to come back. Eventually, he'll declare his love for you within two days."

An elderly woman is listening intently. Umm Mazin surprises her, "What about you? What's your problem? You appear anxious."

"I too want my husband to do it with me more often."

"How old are you?"

"Sixty."

"And how old is your husband?"

"He is sixty-five."

"And how often does he have sexual intercourse with you?"

"Once a week."

Umm Mazin taps one palm of her hand with the other and says, "That's a blessing. You must thank God who created you for this grace, and not be so greedy. As the saying goes, 'If your friends are sweet, don't eat them all up.' Have a safe journey home, and you can pay Badriya on your way out."

The old woman doesn't object. She is probably trying to remember the recipe for the burning peppers that was given to the woman who preceded her.

Beside me is a young woman immersed in a newspaper. I inch my way closer so that I can share the news without disturbing her. She isn't annoyed; on the contrary, she opens up her paper to help me see. I delve into its pages gratefully. "When the city of Basra was bombed in the early days of the conflict, a large number of people died underneath the rubble of their homes. Many inhabitants choked to death in the thick toxic fumes. The cloud of pollutants covered an area of 1.5 square miles annihilating all plant and animal life beneath it. It eventually seeped through into the underground wells of drinking water."

Umm Mazin lifts up one of her clients' cups and addresses the woman who had been drinking from it, "In here, I can see two windows, and fear."

"Yes, they must be my husband's glasses. He's so weirdly attached to them; he even wears them when he sleeps."

Umm Mazin's reading slows down as if interrupted by a comma in the coffee cup. She makes her apologies, saying her energy levels are dropping and nibbles on a Marie biscuit. She munches on the rest of the biscuit pausing for a full stop. She then carries on, "Your husband is afraid of evil spirits."

"He sleeps in them, washes with them on, doesn't even take them off when we're having sex. You may not believe this, but on our wedding night, he told me that it would be grounds for divorce if I lost his glasses."

Umm Mazin gets up to go to the toilet. Her fat belly bulges out from underneath her dishdasha and the biscuit crumbs roll down over its curvature. For a moment, I think I can hear the sound of their impact as they land on the ground. She treads on them as she returns to her seat and resumes her analysis. "Your husband believes that a cloud of evil follows him around wherever he goes. He believes that his glasses give him greater weight and prevent him from floating up and becoming part of that interminable haze. That's why he wears them twenty-four hours a day."

"What can I do?"

"Go to Badriya, she'll give you a potion to banish his delusion. When your husband drinks his tea, does the steam not rise from the cup and condense onto his glasses? Is that what usually happens?"

"That's it exactly."

"Then you must add the potion to his tea. It'll rise with the steam and settle on his glasses. That way the spell will work. His fears will soon calm down."

A woman heading toward Umm Mazin attracts my attention. Her armpit has been eroded by an extensive fungal infection. The woman is illiterate, and unknowingly sprayed wood polish onto her armpit thinking it was a deodorant. One puff burnt away her skin. She is followed by another woman who has come to Umm Mazin because she is losing her hair.

Umm Mazin says to her, "My dear, your hair is falling from the inside, not on the outside."

The woman becomes animated as she replies, "No, Umm Mazin, I swear to God, it's only the hair on my head that's falling out."

Umm Mazin tut-tuts with impatience. "No, no, what I meant was that this is due to emotional distress."

Her energy level drops again. Badriya brings her a sweet from the kitchen then asks the two women to follow her. Umm Mazin tosses the colored sweet into her mouth. It catches the edge of the largest of her teeth. The noise of the impact sounds painful. The rest of her mouth, however, ensnares the sweet with no difficulty. She sucks on it without bringing her lips together. She mutters underneath her breath, "She can't read, she can't write, and she uses a deodorant spray!"

It feels to me like the amount of oxygen in the room is decreasing. I pray silently that Abu Ghayeb won't get back to the flat before us; but my aunt insists on lingering in order to offer her services to Umm Mazin. She wants to send some of her clients for Umm Mazin to treat. I never thought she'd taken my suggestion seriously; yet here we are. Everybody is looking for possible means to earn a living. Does my aunt really think that Umm Mazin will pay her commission for every coffee cup she reads? I expect she will probably thank her, and offer her a modest discount on future readings, nothing more.

The bulky woman on my left looks so tough. I imagine that if I shouted at her, the sound would bounce back as a harsh echo. Her hands look as though they are cast out of wet, heavy mud. Badriya keeps coming in and out, twirling amongst us like a sandstorm. She continuously hums an old television soap powder commercial, "Your pants, Abu Zaid, will only be cleaner with Tide."

The curtains remain drawn; this gaggle of women smell like fermented Italian cheese. The scene transforms itself into a roll of photographic film that has yet to be developed.

❖

Back at the flat, Abu Ghayeb explains to me, "In order to appreciate it; you must live within the painting. Don't merely look at it."

I stand in front of a painting of a naked woman the hue of drunken seagulls. Her entire body is drawn in the style of a Moroccan tattoo. She's wearing bead necklaces around a neck that bears no head. A man stands behind her. His head stretches out to gaze inside her severed neck. But nothing active seems to be happening in the painting. Whereas a lot of things have started to happen in our building since Umm Mazin moved in.

With the worsening of the economic situation, the flat residents have tended to venture out less often, but for some reason, their movement between the different floors has increased.

❖

The Alwiya Club is deteriorating. The number of paid-up club members has dwindled to the extent that it has become doubtful whether any of the cultural and social activities will continue. They closed down the swimming pool when the weeds started growing in the cracks as a result of persistent neglect.

A short while later, the club's administration announces that it is prepared to rent out the unused areas at the back to anyone who wants to use the facilities, provided no construction or excavation work is involved. This is Abu Ghayeb's opportunity. He can rent one of the tennis courts. Behind the first tennis court is a grove of palm trees with ripe dates hanging down beneath the palm fronds.

The second tennis court has already been rented out to a government department.

As we wait to cross the road, a large loaded truck goes past. A sign on its side says HIGHLY FLAMMABLE. At the back, another sign reads, BLESSED AND PROTECTED BY THE BRAVE AND HOLY MAN OF DUJAIL. Abu Ghayeb doesn't notice. He thinks of nothing but his honeybees. When my aunt asked him yesterday why he didn't sell his huge collection of paintings, he replied, "What madman would spend his money on works of art at a time like this?"

We reach the club. There is a tanker parked outside the rear entrance to the restaurant. A large hose stretches from the tanker to the water containers on the roof. One of the workers leans against the lettering on the side of the tanker, which says DRINKING WATER. Tap water is no longer safe. Everyone complains of intestinal symptoms these days: cholera and typhoid.

I don't know why Abu Ghayeb has brought me here. I could have seen everything from my bedroom window: the swimming pools, the tennis courts, the large wall where they used to show foreign films, even the children's playground.

Maybe he took me with him to demonstrate to me that my money was being invested wisely and wasn't being wasted!

❖

Through the haze of smoke from her cigarette, Ilham says, "Don't you believe what they tell you, Dalal; that this is a military operation. We're the real targets."

"Who are you talking about?"

"I mean the women and children. I know that very well, and I won't let anyone try to tell me otherwise. The hospital where I work is full of sick women and babies dying in their mothers' arms."

She sits in front of me, her back rigidly erect. She hardly moves at all when she smokes. She looks like a portrait, with her round white face and pointed European nose. Her thin lips barely cover her rabbit's teeth. She always applies lip balm to them between cigarettes and says, "It is to stop the butts from sticking to my dried lips."

I can't understand why she wastes all her wages on cigarettes and learning French! I eventually find out that she calms herself down by smoking. Learning this language will help her to face her French mother—if she ever finds her.

I ask her, "Why don't you change your job?"

"I have no choice. I live alone, and I can't ask for leave from the hospital to go looking for another job. Where would I go? Rents are exorbitant and earning a living is almost impossible. In spite of that, I thank God that I don't have to support a child, like the women I come across every day."

She crosses her legs. The smoke seeps out between the locks of her curly black hair. The layers of hair are shaped like the letter C. When she shakes her head to chase the smoke away from her eyes, the Cs dance about in all directions.

She shows me a picture of her mother who abandoned her when she was a six-month-old baby. The French bride had been unable to forge a lifelong bond with this land. Her Iraqi husband had promised her that her visit would be temporary, to meet his parents, but he didn't keep his promise, so she abandoned him, leaving him his daughter. She took her divorce papers and returned to her country. She then married one of her own kind, and forgot everything about her daughter. Ilham's father was a renowned lawyer. He died when she was five years old, but even then her mother hadn't wanted to be reminded of anything.

She says, "The emergency cases remind me of her. How could she leave me to my fate with no mercy?"

"Why do you still think of her so often, when she shows no interest in you?"

"Because she's my mother in spite of everything. I look at the people who don't even have enough money for a burial. I often think of her when we take the bodies of dead babies and send them off to be incinerated to prevent the spread of diseases."

She takes a long drag from her cigarette. "No matter how bad things get, I know in my heart that I'll meet her one day. I know it."

I interrupt her, "Can I come with you to the hospital to do some volunteer work?"

"I wouldn't advise it. That kind of work needs experience and a heart of stone. Staying underneath your aunt's wing would be so much better. I wouldn't encourage you to see what's happening."

"I'm willing to do anything for the children."

"The problem is that there's nothing we can do to help these people. In any case, maybe raising bees will turn out to be a better source of income."

"How did you find out about the bees?"

"Nothing remains secret in this building."

✦

She is right. Even Uncle Sami on the fourth floor knows all about it, although he only leaves his flat when it is time for his dialysis. Ilham keeps an eye on his health, and accompanies him to the hospital. I sometimes see her going up to his flat. She says jokingly, "It's a wash and dry day today." She never complains about having to look after him, as she considers him to be one of the most pleasant inhabitants of our building.

I meet him for the first time in his flat. Ilham is in a rush to get off to work, so she asks me to take him some painkillers. I knock on his door. I wait several minutes. The door is eventually opened by someone who looked like the fourteenth grandson of Father Christmas.

I ask him with a smile, "Uncle Sami?"

He replies, but his smile isn't crooked like mine, "Yes, Uncle Sami, come in."

He hooks his cane onto his wrist and asks me to follow him. He sits me down on a comfortable armchair and chooses a high-backed chair for himself. A few moments later he heads off toward the kitchen. He comes back with some tea. He offers me a cup, and adds a spoonful of sugar to it, without asking me if I wanted any.

He says, "You've taken your time."

I readjust the way I am sitting. "I'm sorry, but Ilham only gave me the medication this morning."

"I wasn't talking about the medication."

I look up at him and he smiles. "Don't look at me like that as if I've frightened you. Calm down and enjoy your tea. What I meant to say was that I've been waiting for someone like you for a long time."

"What do you mean, Uncle?"

He doesn't reply. He gets up from his chair and says, "Excuse me, I have to go to the other room for a moment. Please feel free to look at a few magazines."

He shuffles across to the room next door. A notebook with a shiny, wine-colored cover catches my eye. It lies on top of a pile of magazines and has the words "Umm Raid's Diary" printed on its cover. On the first page I read, "Twenty thousand houses, flats, and residential complexes were destroyed and one hundred thousand palm trees were killed by the bombardment. I heard that a woman had to have a Caesarean section without an anesthetic." I turn the page and read what the diarist has written. The factory that made household cleaning agents had been bombed. Ninety kilos of insecticide had seeped out. Another page described how the plastics factory had been bombed: tiny fragments of polyethylene had been dispersed into the atmosphere where they mingled with paint, industrial glass, solid and liquid wax, black graphite, and burning rubber tires.

I hear Uncle Sami's heavy footsteps coming back, and I slide the notebook back to its original place. He points to a small metal cage with two white mice playing about inside it, and says, "I see you've met my friends. The female mouse is called Cerebrum. Her husband's name is Cerebellum."

His giggles tumble all around me, and I can't stop myself from joining in. He says, "Yes, laugh girl, enjoy yourself. That's what those two balls of warm fur do. They provide me with great joy."

He puts his hand inside the cage and tries to grab one of the mice. His hand wriggles about and creates a ruckus on the floor of the cage. His fingers strike the metal bars like the hands of a blind man seeking something in the dark. Suddenly I gasped, "He really is blind." At that moment he manages to grab hold of Cerebellum by his pink tail and puts the mouse in his lap. He caresses the small head like a dear friend's, and says, "It's my diabetes. Insulin became almost impossible to get hold of in this country, so inevitably, the disease ended up affecting my vision. I can no longer differentiate colors. I can only make out shapes in black-and-white. What color are you wearing Dalal?"

"Green."

"I thought it might be green."

"Why do you say that?"

"I can sense gentle vibrations coming from you."

Cerebrum, alone in her cage, starts to get agitated on my behalf. Uncle Sami is becoming increasingly calm. He says, "Nurse Ilham told me about you. She suggested that we should meet. I am pleased that this has happened."

"Thank you."

"Do you want to play with Cerebellum?"

"No, thank you."

"You're a polite girl. This mouse is going back to his cage, and I'd better get back to the other room for a few moments."

He disappears. I watch the two rodents celebrating their reunion. They make contact using their transparent tails and whiskers. Uncle Sami gazes at me.

I ask him, "Would you like me to get you something from the room next door? Do you need any help?"

"There's only one thing you can do in the room next door to help me."

"Of course, what is it?"

He bursts out laughing. "If you could get rid of the wind from my tummy for me!" He pats my shoulder. "Fate can be so cruel, dear neighbor. These diseases destroy us gradually. Forgive me my candor."

He then adds, "Anyway, I must point out that you are late."

"For what?"

"I hear that you're learning about art and colors."

"Yes, with my aunt's husband."

I sip what is left of my tea in order to leave. Uncle Sami bids me farewell. He says, "What I'll teach you is that human beings come in different colors."

❂

Abu Ghayeb wishes that he could emigrate and settle on the shores of the Dead Sea. He's convinced that his skin needs to be treated with natural minerals. He has started scratching again. He brushes away the flakes that have descended from his scalp and settled on his shoulders. A few soft scales have come away from his left ear.

He gazes at a scale that he's pierced with the tip of a pencil. I ask him, "Is it possible to say what caused your disease?"

He laughs. "I thought that Pepsi Cola might be the cause of dandruff, but we haven't had any for years now because there isn't any of it around. So that's the first possible cause that we can cross off the list."

"But I'm asking you a serious question."

"And I'm telling you in all seriousness that the stuff I now drink tastes better than Pepsi. It's a gelatin solution. I have to drink half an ounce of gelatin dissolved in water every day without fail, to promote the growth of my fingernails and strengthen the flesh beneath them. It helps allay my fears that I might be afflicted with psoriasis of the hands. They say it affects the nail beds and is very painful."

"What are you saying?"

"That's it exactly. Psoriasis is exacerbated by anxiety, and flare-ups are likely to occur as one lives in a constant state of anxiety. When the disease flares up, the anxiety worsens as a result, and so on. It's a vicious circle."

"My God!"

"And apparently the only protection is avoiding anxiety!"

❂

He starts pacing to and fro in front of one of his paintings. He stops and gazes at it and says, "How do you think we can measure beauty?"

"If things aren't distorted, they may be more beautiful."

"I'm sorry Dalal. Please try to be less sensitive when we study art. Appreciating beauty is more important than understanding it."

"How can you expect me to appreciate what I've been deprived of?"

"I'll give you an example. A splodge of yellow, hanging on its own in the air may appear ugly, but as part of a painting, amidst other colors, it can be very beautiful."

I head toward a painting that is a cacophony of loud colors erupting from a volcano in their midst. I stand in front of the center of the volcano with my back toward the painting.

"Then tell me now, husband of my aunt, do these colors make me look beautiful?"

CHAPTER SIX

I RECEIVE A MAGAZINE from the fourth floor. Uncle Sami now sends me the ones he's finished reading, or rather the ones that somebody else has finished reading to him. I flick through its pages as I wait for Abu Ghayeb to get changed so that we can go together to the club. The first headline reads, "Experiments in Western Europe: Tomatoes Injected with Fish Chromosomes to Protect Them from Frost."

Abu Ghayeb calls out from the bedroom. "What's the latest news, Dalal; what are they saying?"

I read the second headline out loud to him, "The United States declares that the war it waged in early 1991 was a 'clean war.' 'Smart weapons' were used that struck their targets accurately."

Abu Ghayeb laughs as he says, "Yes, 'intelligent missiles.' They stop at a red light on their way to the explosion."

A moment later, he adds, "Truly smart weapons. They destroyed communication centers, sewage plants, and electricity generators. And they remembered to wipe out the water purification units as well. With their intelligence, they deprived a whole nation of clean drinking water."

"This is an article about the latest trends in genetic engineering. Look at this picture in a lab of a human ear growing out of the back of a mouse."

"They want to grow ears? Our fields are full of human limbs and appendages of all varieties. Some people try to grow limbs while others are born without them!"

He starts combing his hair and says, "By the way, have you heard that dried flies are being sold in the local markets?"

"Is this a joke?"

"Not at all, there's a group of young men outside Feydhi Hospital selling packaged dried flies labeled 'Animal Feed.'"

❈

As we make our way from the flat to the club, Abu Ghayeb starts explaining to me with enthusiasm some morphological points of his future career. The distance from his home to his new workplace consists of a pavement—a street—a pavement. The result would be a significant saving on travel expenses.

The lift isn't working, so we walk down the stairs. He says, "Bees have a social structure. That's what attracted me to them, Dalal. They live in groups known as colonies, and in structures called hives."

"What does my aunt think of all this? Has she agreed?"

"Your aunt dislikes all animals, so how would you expect her to approve of raising insects?"

"Then she'll object."

"She can't visualize any success except in terms of cash."

"So, will these insects provide the money she desires?"

"Time alone will tell."

The sewage draining from the ground floor flat has overflowed. We jump in synchrony across a pool of rotting lettuce leaves. He says,

"Anyway, let me tell you about the daily routine of these colonies whose lives are organized on the basis of the distribution of duties amongst various members. The group consists of the queen, the males, and the worker bees."

His foot lands in the stagnant water. He stops for a few moments and hits his shoe on the ground, trying to get rid of the dirty froth that sticks to it. On the pavement by our block of flats I learn that the queen is the largest individual in the group. She has short wings, out of proportion to the size of her body. This reminds me of my aunt. She has a curved stinger to use against other queens. As we cross the road, the conversation is about the male bees. They have shorter bodies and no stinger. On the other pavement leading to the club, my aunt's husband explains that worker bees are equipped with a trunk that they use to collect pollen, which they carry on their hind legs.

❦

The swimming pool supervisor gives Abu Ghayeb the keys to Tennis Court No. 1. The supervisor then disappears as he makes his way between heaps of wood, cork, and water pipes awaiting installation. Abu Ghayeb wastes no time. He signs a long-term lease to avoid having to vacate the premises. He wants to avoid having to move his colonies from one place to another.

"We must think long term as far as possible, Dalal."

He opens the tall gate made of heavy wire netting and admires its quality. "English workmanship."

We enter the tennis court. He stands in the center stretching his arms out wide. He looks like an actor in a play, introducing himself to the audience. He turns to me and says, "This will be our apiary."

He examines the fence surrounding the court. He paces around it to measure its dimensions. Its length is adequate; its width is adequate. The wire netting consists of openings shaped like medium-sized baklava. The bees will be able to fly easily in and out of the court without hindrance. He points out the date palm grove just beyond the club's perimeter fence, "And from there we'll gather the pollen."

His project isn't off the ground yet, but he's already started referring to himself and to his bees in the plural. I ask him, "Will the bees be able to gather enough nutrients from dates alone?"

"There are other sources of nectar and pollen underneath the date palms; fruit trees, and beneath them are the rows of vegetables."

He checks the planks of wood that he has ordered, then examines some other items. He blows forcefully into a length of plastic tubing. A fluorescent green fly emerges from its other end. His foot collides with a pile of heavy ropes that'd been stacked to one side. He gazes at it and says, "We'll have a problem though. There are a lot of red bees in the date palm grove, and they're the honeybees' worst enemy."

I have a feeling that my aunt is watching us. I look up and there she is, observing our movements from my bedroom window. She'll leaf through the books on apiculture and the instructions for beekeeping. She'll then toss them aside as she complains disdainfully, "What a waste of time. We'd have done better if we'd opened a shop selling cloth." She may have been right, but as her husband often says: time alone will tell.

Their concept of time has started to differ. She looks at time as two different seasons: one for sewing summer dresses and one for sewing winter clothes. For him, time now means the season for gathering nectar and the season for collecting the honey.

We walk away from the Alwiya Club once Abu Ghayeb has identified the work site, the food source, and the enemy.

❀

I make friends with the sound of our refrigerator. Tchik—it switches itself off, tchok—it switches itself back on again. The properties of the dual metal piece in the fuse result in the disconnection. This is what we were told in our physics lessons. The metal expands thus disconnecting the generator in the fridge from the power supply. When it shrinks, the connection is restored. As for the little light that's supposed to go on when the fridge door opens, it no longer works. At night, I sometimes have to use a candle to identify its meager contents.

I no longer watch the tennis courts from the kitchen at night, and we no longer eat a heavy meal after sundown, the way we used to. My aunt justifies this by saying that a light supper promotes calm, light sleep during the night and a feeling of lightness the next day. She says nothing of the long hours in between! The fridge has become just another item of furniture: rarely used, but still a source of tedious noises.

For my part, I could do with a light day tomorrow, in order to be able to face the physics teacher. I don't like science subjects. I find it difficult to understand their logic. The physics teacher often chides me for failing to grasp the logic of things. Yet it's she who doesn't understand me. She explains the Archimedes theorem: when an object is immersed in a fluid it displaces the same volume of fluid as the volume of the object. They should also have the same mass. Her eyes settle intentionally on the angle of my mouth, as she says the word 'displaced.'

I look at her name, which she wears in yellow gold around her neck. Kurdish people love their gold jewelry. I read her name, Parween. I imagine her surname to be Parwana, the Persian word for propeller blade. A moment later I come up with the nickname "the family of electric fans." In secret, I've got my revenge. Eureka!

My refusal to comprehend any of the sciences has persisted throughout my years at secondary school. I have no difficulties with languages, social sciences, or the arts, but getting a passing grade in the other subjects is always a struggle. I can never understand why in geometry, the area of the triangle equals half the base multiplied by the height. I would prefer to draw a flower in the triangle or fill it up with a song.

The only exception in the science subjects is biology. I am fascinated by the life of the amoeba, the movement of its pseudopods, and the growth of the fetus inside the womb. I will never be able to understand how to measure the speed of light, but I spend long sessions looking for living organisms under the microscope. The teacher used to pronounce it "micro-scooop."

I never join the other students as they scramble to book the magnifying instruments a week in advance. My instrument is different from everybody else's. Basically, it is just a low glass table. I deposit all the insects and other creatures to be studied on it. I then lie down underneath it, placing my hands behind my head, and observe. From there, I scrutinize their movement and their behavior.

At once, I become engrossed as I watch a pair of damp frogs attached to each other. The female frog blows into the ear of the male frog. Two lumps of meat, the color of mellowed seaweed, gambol above me on a transparent plane, sticking to each other in the emptiness of space.

This is the only time I wish I were a frog.

✦

My aunt is busy tidying her new room. It's a small space, more the size of a closet than a room, lying between the kitchen and the bathroom. In the Days of Plenty, it was used for food storage and was called "the weighing room." Today she calls it "House of Buttons." She removes some drawing materials and places them underneath the bed on Abu Ghayeb's side. The wardrobe has now become hers alone, and the boxes filled with buttons colonize the shelves.

She was upset yesterday when she heard about the attempted robbery at our neighbors' house. She went over to visit them. I accompanied her to see if it was true what the other children in our vicinity were saying, that all the freckles on the woman's face had disappeared completely. Her husband was still in prison, and her son had been buried with the chewing gum stuck in his windpipe. We found out later on that the thief had been after a Persian carpet he'd spotted when it was left out on their rooftop. He hadn't known that it had just been washed and was waterlogged, making it too heavy for him to carry.

My aunt ended her visit rapidly. On the way out, we came face-to-face with a young policeman who'd come to take the woman's statement about the details of the attempted robbery. My aunt stood in the young man's way. He was wearing a grim blue uniform, with a row of silver buttons running down its middle. The insignia of his police station was embossed on the buttons. My aunt gazed at the sight of the buttons like a drug addict. The stunned policeman couldn't understand why she was staring at him. I could imagine her reaching out to his chest, plucking the buttons from his uniform and running back to the flat with them. She would place them in a see-through container, and stick a label on it that said POLICE.

She asks me to help her clean her most prized possession, the sewing machine. I glimpse the word Singer as she wheels it past. We will polish it together. As she hands me the tin of polish, a tiny bead of oil drips from a small perforation in its eroded under-surface. I think it lands on a spider's back as it makes a rapid escape from underneath the sewing machine.

I say to her, "We've oiled that spider."

"Block off that small hole in the bottom of the tin with your finger. We don't want to lose any more oil; it's the last tin I have left. Are you sure it was a spider?"

"I thought it was."

"I wonder what it is with spiders this week?"

"What do you mean?"

"I went to Umm Mazin's flat two days ago, and a woman with an unnatural fear of spiders came to her seeking treatment. We were unaware that some of the other women there had a grudge against her because she was the second wife of their friend's husband. They took it upon themselves to harass her. One of them quipped, 'My dear, I don't know what's wrong with me today. I'm in a spidery mood.' Her friend then replied, 'Don't worry, Umm Mazin will give you a magical potion; fear, fear go away, this can't be the spider's day.' Then a third woman joined the conversation saying, 'I bought a bag of flour yesterday, and we were almost poisoned. It was past its expiry date and was full of spiders' webs. In other words, the flour had ex-spi-dered!'"

"What did Umm Mazin do?"

"Nothing. She disregarded her coffee cup reading charge, as the woman then ran away crying."

I say to my aunt, "The sewing machine has some rust here and there."

She answers as if scolding me, "What do you expect? Where could I possibly get any spare parts for it? Everything around us is slowly disintegrating."

She then adds, "We're living in an age where everything, even glass, gets rusty."

❈

Neighing. Abu Ghayeb repositions a painting of horses. They react to the Allied attack, lining up behind each other with their backs to the east. Their bodies are striped barrels. It looks as if they've been saddled with a traditional local rug. They watch fearfully as shells tipped with depleted uranium are fired from American tanks. Their necks are sometimes blue, sometimes red; fresh blood and stale blood.

The horses gallop in stillness; the beat of their hooves emerges from mouths aimlessly crying out in anger.

❈

Outside the painting, anger is forbidden. It is something I have never been entitled to. A minor deviation of the mouth inflicted by God is trivial in comparison to the fatal diseases inflicted by human beings. I must minimize my misfortune amidst the calamities surrounding us. The doctors explain that when the blood fails to reach a certain area of the brain, the result is a stroke. I was small at the time. I had a fever and then the stroke; a mini stroke. The blood failed to reach the left side of my brain, making my mouth deviate to the right.

❈

Suddenly the din of drumbeats and coarse singing descends upon the balcony. I look down onto the courtyard to find its source. A scruffy pickup truck has pulled up outside the building. The local folk musicians are crammed together in the back, their hands beating out a rhythm on their soiled tambourines. They chant a refrain, "Magical snake with two heads, crawl into their pot . . . poison everyone in the house, but their son harm not. . . ." A man hugs a bucket and dances around in the courtyard. He is calling out at the top of his voice, "Umm Mazin, how can we thank you, Umm Mazin?"

I can't believe it when I realize what is in the bucket. Worms!

The musicians are relatives of the bewitched and poisoned man. Umm Mazin has treated him from afar—by correspondence. She advised them to take the ripened fruits from the mountain flowers, dry them, and then remove the seeds. The remains had to be ground up, mixed with honey, and then molded into circular pellets, the size of fava beans. The dose was two pellets for children and small adults, and four pellets for well-built adults. These had to be swallowed, not chewed, first thing in the morning. The result was a bucketful of diarrhea, complete with worms. This confirmed the efficacy of her potion, and satisfied the sufferer's family.

I imagine Umm Mazin on the floor above us, waving to them from her balcony; her image resembles Boris Yeltsin dipped in cocoa powder.

❋

During the week, my aunt observes progress in the tennis court. The earth is ploughed, flattened, and divided into rows. The hives are placed along the rows. Flowers favored by the bees, mainly sunflowers, are planted in beds alongside them. The road leading to the apiary is paved and extended to the storage area and the separation room. The equipment, the boxes, and the honey extraction implements needed can now be brought in on a wheelbarrow.

To protect the bees from strong gusts, windbreakers are put up along the northern and western borders. It is for this reason that the tamarisk trees were planted. The next step is to provide water. Several small pools are constructed. They connect to each other by a network of pipes, and are furnished with wood and styrofoam floaters for the bees to settle on while they drink from the water.

My aunt's husband is a novice beekeeper; he has bought only thirty colonies, to try them out. He asks his wife to sew him a beekeeper's outfit. He emphasizes that it has to be secure so that the bees can't penetrate it. It has to allow him to work freely, and must consist of one lightly-colored unit. He then adds, "Without shoulder pads please."

After many days of preparation for the apiary, I sit down with Abu Ghayeb for an evening of relaxation. He has hurt his leg during the work. The wound has started healing, and itches intensely. He can't touch it, but he proceeds to scratch the skin all around it with his expert scratcher's hand that doesn't let any of his fingers slip onto the gash. He says, "Keeping bees is going to help. Moderate exposure to sunlight is a form of therapy."

"While avoiding sunstroke."

"Yes, and bee stings."

He asks me, "Has your aunt finished sewing the protective outfit?"

"Almost."

He sighs as he scratches himself. "I wish we could make protective outfits for the army. The Allies are using napalm to burn the soldiers."

"Is there no protection against it?"

"How is that possible, Dalal? Modern napalm has been developed further and is now even more lethal. The material spreads over wide areas by using balls of flame. Temperatures can reach eight hundred degrees centigrade. The fires are almost impossible to put out, and the substance can't be removed from human flesh."

The information congeals in my head. I make my way to my room. I lie back on my bed, with my socks on, thinking. My bedcover loses its softness and starts to feel like the dry hairy surface of a coconut shell. The electricity is cut off. I imagine the darkness filling the void inside my shoes.

I must sleep. Tomorrow I have an appointment with Uncle Sami.

❁

I ask him, "Who's Umm Raid?"

"She was my late wife."

"My condolences for your loss."

"Thank you for your sympathy."

"Where's Raid?"

"He's joined his mother."

"I'm sorry. I offer you my condolences once again."

"Thank you."

He doesn't appear troubled by my questioning.

"Is this her diary?"

"Yes. I determined that I would continue writing in her diaries and document all the events of the economic blockade the way she did. She used to while away her time writing down the day's events, and would conclude with her favorite refrain, 'Holy Virgin, you know these truths.'"

"What happened?"

"When they bombed the headquarters of the secret police, one of the missiles landed on the artist Layla's house and she was killed. They found the bodies of my wife and our son under the debris from their walls. She'd gone to visit someone in that area; it was as simple as that."

The words "as simple as that" ring in my ears. I ask him, "Is it true that her house was targeted intentionally?"

"Why?"

"We heard she was the one who made the mosaic of President Bush that was laid down at the entrance to the Rasheed Hotel which is used by a large number of foreign delegations, so they all tread on his face whenever they go in or out of the building."

"I don't know how much truth there is in those tales."

He then continues, "My wife documented the daily events of her life in her own words; I do it using images."

"Was she a journalist?"

He answers in a cynical tone, "No. She was an ordinary housewife. She spent her days raising her son, documenting her fears on paper, and attending to the needs of her husband, the renowned photographer."

He gazes for a while. "Dalal, I used to regard myself as such an important person."

"How's that?"

"I considered myself the master of the universe through my art. I truly believed that I was 'special' because of my camera, the tool that never lies. That was until I started reading my wife's diaries."

I notice how big his ears are. They quiver as he speaks, "Isn't it strange, dear neighbor? When I still had my sight, I used to think that my eyes could see what the others failed to perceive."

He shakes his head, "It was my arrogance that was my downfall. I thought I was the only one who possessed the truth, in my little box that recorded the moment without any falsity."

He wipes his short white beard. "My problem was that, as the saying goes, I used to carry the ladder sideways. I was mistaken when I thought I'd achieved perfection through my art. I became pretentious and considered myself superior to the rest of humanity, and in particular, to my wife. I didn't realize that until it was too late."

"You mean, when she died, God rest her soul?"

"And after I lost my sight."

Then he adds, "I was a photographer for many years, yet I was unable to see what I can see today!"

I don't wish to interrupt him as he continues, "The vision is converted from the outside to the inside."

"What do you mean?"

"I used to see what was happening around me, and I'd rush to record it with my camera. Now, I only see what's happening inside me. I'm now closer to myself, and I've come to understand it. In the past, I'd gauge myself by the level of my professional success, but it's only when I looked inside that I realized that people have colors. These colors are like a magnetic halo. They appear around the person's body, and envelop us wherever we go. Some people can sense them and see them, whereas others are oblivious to their presence."

"Why did you ask me to come and visit you, Uncle?"

He disappears for a few moments into the room next door. He returns with a small tape recorder.

"Because you're a sensitive individual. A deprived individual possesses this sensitivity."

He gave me the tape recorder and asks me to press the button. His voice emanates from the small loudspeaker, "How can people die smiling? Cluster bombs have rained down on the soldiers. They endured hours in a human meat grinder. In the morning, large areas in the south became giant scrap yards containing the remains of military and civilian vehicles. They were destroyed, blown up, and reduced to tangled masses of metal fibers. Some of the drivers were burned where they sat. One of them was turned into charcoal in an instant. All that remained were his teeth that smiled out to the camera."

He asks me to switch off the tape, his true voice blending with its recorded version. "This is how I write. I record what I wish to say, then I ask someone to transcribe it for me from the tape into the notebook. I usually contact the teacher who lives on the first floor. He helps me out in exchange for a small fee."

He goes out to the room next door once again and comes back with a small cloth bag.

"Are you willing to become my scribe?"

"You mean, will I be your hand-writer?"

His beard laughs with him. I ask, "In exchange for a small fee?"

He replies as he opens the bag, "No. In exchange for this."

He takes an old black camera out of the bag and caresses it like a lover.

"I can't take it from you, Uncle."

"You wouldn't be taking it away. You'd be using it to learn."

Before I can object, he sits me down in front of him, "You'll capture life as you see it; not the way other people see it, or would wish you to see it."

He raises his arm. "Your first lesson: never take a picture unless you're satisfied with the view. With one press of the button, you'll freeze a moment of life forever. You must be completely satisfied with it before you freeze it for eternity."

"I'm not sure that there's anything I wish to freeze for all eternity."

He ignores my objections and continues, "It depends on where you've positioned yourself. You'll come to appreciate in your second lesson that photography is not merely a technical skill. You also need a little luck. You have to be in the right place at the right time. Capture the dove before it flies away, or all you'll get will be the image of an empty nest."

I stand up. He follows my movements with his eyes, as if he can see me. "Uncle, why are you so insistent? I'll write down for you what you want, and I won't ask you for a fee; but I don't want to become a photographer."

"So what will you do with your life then? Will you become a seamstress? Or a beekeeper?"

"I'll complete my education."

"A convenient escape."

"Getting an education isn't an escape."

"Well said, but it won't help you earn a living in these times. Do you really want to become a schoolteacher who takes home a salary that's the equivalent of four U.S. dollars a month, like everybody else?"

I gaze at the two mice rolling over each other. He says, "Your monthly salary won't be enough to buy a tray of eggs."

He makes his way toward me; his gaze pierces through me. He places the camera in my hands. I can feel its weight.

"Here now is the third lesson. Technical expertise and luck aren't enough. The photographer must make his or her own decisions. You have to go out into the world and seek out that moment."

I touch the lens, and the other parts that bulge out from the camera. "Must, must, must. Uncle Sami, I'm weary of everyone in this building trying to teach me his or her profession. I'll end up having learned several trades, but still no prospects."

"Dalal, my dear. Don't be so pessimistic. Our entire life is but one brief moment. Enjoy it."

I walk down the stairs.

I didn't expect that very soon someone else would also be offering to teach me his profession. It was the new owner of the ground floor flat. His name was Saad.

CHAPTER SEVEN

We have devastated this country, so its level of childhood mortality is now worse than that of Sudan.
—*Iraq Under Siege: The Deadly Impact of Sanctions and War,*
Anthony Arnove, ed., 36

ILHAM'S ERECT POSTURE is molded onto her chair. She sighs. "I wish I could escape from the hospital, to get away from the image of the little ones when they die."

I hand her a lighter for her cigarette. She gazes at its glowing ember and says, "The children in the south play with leftover shrapnel from the bombing. They're the victims of depleted uranium from the air raids over the areas extending from Basra to Kerbala, and as far as Baghdad."

She slips her hand into a paper bag and brings out the toy I have given her for the children's ward, "You can have it back. He died. I'd become so attached to him. He didn't even make it to his eighth birthday. He bled to death. I realized that was going to happen when the red spots started to appear on his cheeks. He bled into his gut. Other children sometimes bleed from their mouths, their ears, or their bottoms."

She clutches the rag doll in one hand and the cigarette in the other. My aunt's husband had brought it back as a present for me from one of his trips abroad, long ago. She was called Raggedy Ann. She had a face made of cloth, her eyes were embroidered with a black thread: my aunt had plucked out the originals for her collection. She made them into buttons and sewed them onto an evening dress for one of her clients.

Ilham appears exhausted. She fondles the toy. She chats to me and tugs at the black embroidered eyes making them smaller without realizing what she's doing. Her voice is weary. "The work I did at the hospital in Basra two years ago has now started to bear fruit."

"What are you talking about?"

"The unexpected 'surprise fruit.'"

She hands me the doll as she stands up. She lifts up her dress, exposing her chest. There is a red swelling on her right breast. She squeezes it. I move toward her with a handkerchief in my hand. I cry out, "My God, Ilham, what's this?"

She takes the handkerchief and wipes the red lump with it. Her tears roll down her cheeks. I move closer to her. "What are you doing?"

"They told me at the hospital that it's a boil."

"How did you get it?"

She ignores me.

"Did they think they could fool me by saying it was a boil?"

"How can it be treated?"

"There's no treatment for it, Dalal; it's cancer. I've seen it often enough to be able to tell the difference. It seems that it's my turn now."

She puts her bra back on, and curses her mother. "I bet you, she's sitting in a Parisian café right now sipping a hot chocolate."

I couldn't make the association between what I was witnessing and a woman I didn't know in France. I could only say, "Forget about her, come on, let's go out for a little while."

Her tears don't cease while she adjusts her dress. I suggest that we go for a walk. She follows me, not voicing any objections.

We leave behind us a toy made of cloth, without a face.

Our footsteps lead to Abu Nuwas Street, which runs alongside the riverfront by the Tigris. The muscles of Ilham's lips contract and relax as she smokes in an angry rhythm: nightmare, reality, nightmare, reality. She inhales her diagnosis into her lungs as if trying to sieve out her predicament. We stop by the statue of Shahrazad just before sunset. The disk of the setting sun is melting into the palm of her extended hand. A copper hue is draped over the reclining body of Shahrayar who dozes off while listening to the tales recounted by his concubine. We sit on a wooden bench and gaze at the two statues glowing gently with a sleepy thyme-colored light.

Ilham is quiet for a long time, then says, "I wish I was like her."

She points to the statue. "Actually, I'm like her in some ways: the hard solid exterior. Bronze on the outside, hollow on the inside." She then adds, "Can you imagine how strange it feels to be a structure filled with emptiness? Just air going in, and air coming out."

I sit parallel to Shahrayar's giant thigh. I don't turn my head around to look, not wishing to interrupt her thoughts.

"Yet at the same time, she's lucky. If I had a man, maybe what has happened wouldn't have happened."

"I don't understand."

"I didn't feel the lump while it was growing. It continued to enlarge while I was preoccupied with my work. It never occurred to me to examine my body looking for a tumor. I just didn't have the time to prod myself."

She laughs in a sarcastic tone. "That's the benefit of having a man."

She lifts up her arm, raising her shoulder, "Even when I bathed, I used a thick loofa. It obviously prevented any contact between my hand and the rest of my body."

She throws her head back, saying, "I'm sorry, Dalal, maybe you're too young to be listening to this kind of talk. I'm aware that you haven't started university yet, but I may not be around when you graduate."

"Don't exaggerate now; and don't worry."

She interrupts her contemplation of the sunset to look at me. "A tumor that's four centimeters long and three centimeters wide is no exaggeration."

She puts her arm around my shoulder. A thin red smile finds its way to her pale face. "The main cause for my anxiety, my dear innocent neighbor, is the anticipation of the letter from the hospital administration. They'll terminate my contract when the nature of my illness is revealed."

"Why would you get fired from your job?"

"Because the disease will wear me out."

The sentence itself appears to be wearing her out.

"The first step will be an operation."

"An operation?"

"Of course. I know about the treatment of these illnesses in explicit detail. That will have to be followed by chemotherapy."

"Will you have to undergo that horrible treatment?"

"It's not a question of whether I have to take it or not. The question is where will I find the money for the operation and the medication?"

She twists her long black curls with her fingers.

"Anyway, how could I possibly go to work with no hair and no eyelashes?"

I don't have any answers to her questions.

A fresh darkness starts to mingle with the leaves in the trees of the public gardens where we now sit. Ilham asks me, "As we're talking about work, what plans have you made for your future?"

"I'll invent a talking garbage can."

She explodes into unexpected laughter. Her lips form a quivering circle made of stretched elastic, "What did you say?"

I take out an article clipping of the magazine *Worker's Weekly* from my pocket and read it to her: "A City Council in Northern England has announced plans to install a number of talking litter bins in various parts of the city which say 'thank you' every five minutes. Their aim is to encourage members of the public, especially children, to dispose of their litter in these bins. The tape recorders inside the bins are operated by a battery placed underneath them."

She takes the article from my hand; her mouth becomes more rubbery. I say, "I liked the idea."

"You're an errant child."

"And what do you think of the equipment that's being installed in some government offices in Europe that emits negative charges into the atmosphere to dispel any lassitude amongst their employees?"

She looks across at me as she lights another cigarette. I say, "My favorite innovation though, is what I've called a 'route finder.' They're computers that have been set up on the pavements in a number of large cities that tell you how to get to where you want to go. An illuminated map appears on the screen; the instructions are accompanied by a beautiful voice giving directions."

Ilham points toward a traffic light over the road that leans forward at a precarious angle. It casts its tricolored shadows onto a pavement that has disappeared under a pool of stagnant water. Three flavors of displaced sweets floated on the water: pomegranate, amber, and mint. She says, "Since you appear to be concerned with the city and its state, wouldn't it be better if you could come up with solutions for sights like these first? Anyway, I know that you're only joking, and you've succeeded in distracting my thoughts from my predicament. Thank you."

I repeat after her, "Thank you, and five minutes later, thank you, and five minutes later, thank you, then—"

She interrupts me, "Dalal, the time has come for you to start taking things seriously. Enough of these magazines and articles about life in Europe."

"What? Don't tell me that you too are going to suggest that I start learning how to do your job. Everybody else has already suggested that I learn theirs. Nursing?"

"No."

The hard wood of the bench is starting to feel uncomfortable. She adjusts the way she is sitting. "I was going to suggest that you should learn French."

"Why? To go looking for your lost mother?"

She laughs.

"No you evil child. Listen to me. The time will come when the Western nations will return to our country to reconstruct it. In the near future, we'll need a lot of interpreters and translators. You can prepare yourself for the task of translating the contracts that will be signed with foreign companies to rebuild our country's infrastructure."

"And why does it have to specifically be French that I should be learning?"

"Because it'll be the electric grid that will take first priority. I've heard that there are several companies moving in that direction. Besides, tuition is still free in our government-run universities, in spite of the current circumstances; you must make good use of this opportunity. It's also because you love to read, and because I can teach you the basics of that language, and help you in your studies."

She adds, "Pay attention to the team of United Nations inspectors looking for what they call 'weapons of mass destruction.' The United Nations Special Commission are the first group of foreigners who are going to need interpreters. The Security Police will not allow them to wander around on their own without an authorized local interpreter. You must learn all the scientific terms that are used in the fields of nuclear, chemical, and biological weapons."

"My aunt would be most upset; and her husband expects me to help him raise his bees; but I'll give your suggestion some thought."

We stand up to leave. When we reach the leaning traffic light, I turn around and look back at the spot where we'd been sitting. The park gradually fades into dusk as day fizzles out along the waterfront where the fishermen used to gather in the Days of Plenty. A man was standing beside a row of fish being grilled around an open fire. The fish have been slit open at the back. Their insides are the color of strawberries. The fisherman looks back at me with eyes of deepest blue that have no pupils. His feet protrude from underneath his dishdasha. He has a right foot on the right side, and another right foot on the left! It seems to me that he will be stumbling forever.

A few days later, Ilham asks me to accompany her on a visit to see Umm Mazin. She says, "She might have some natural calming remedies for me. My sleep has become very troubled."

In the waiting room, a woman sits, tightly clinging on to a bag; almost hugging it. A hyperactive child buzzes around her. The child takes pink chewing gum out of her mouth. She molds it into the shape of a flat square. She then smiles as she puts her finger into her mouth and pushes the chewing gum into a small gap over her gums to make it look like a pink tooth. The child stays in the room outside when we go in to see Umm Mazin.

It isn't a session with the coffee cups this time. The woman from the waiting room takes a white sheet out of her bag and spreads it out onto her lap. She says, "My daughter found this sheet hidden underneath my father's bedspread."

"Where's your mother?"

"She's separated from him and lives in another house."

"And who does he live with now?"

"He lives with his new wife. I sent my daughter to visit them at his request. She is, after all, his only grandchild; and she came back with this sheet."

Umm Mazin starts to mutter as she examines the sheet, "When the reason is known, the mystery is solved."

A yellow donkey has been drawn on the sheet. It has a human head, with long droopy ears, and a mournful look. A beautiful woman sits on its back, her legs dangle down. Umm Mazim asks, "Excuse me for this, but I must ask, does this face resemble your father's?"

The woman lowers her eyes. "It's an exact replica."

"And the woman?"

"His new wife."

"A great booby trapper!"

The sheet woman watches Umm Mazin analyzing.

"It appears that she's a malicious woman in control, or that she wants to become a woman who's in control financially in order to dictate her husband's destiny."

"What do you mean?"

"This is a domination spell. It's been painted with saffron water. An ounce of saffron costs four thousand dinars these days. Your father's new wife knows her position well. This means that she controls your father the way a human being controls an animal; no offense intended."

"So that's how she made him leave my mother in order to marry her?"

"That's quite likely. Anyway, I'll provide you with a counter-spell made from the essential oils of flowers. It can't be seen, and I'll attach it to the back of this sheet. You must ask your daughter to return it to where she found it next time she goes to visit her grandfather. Light a candle for him one hour before dawn, then recite all the verses of Surat al-Baqara from the Qur'an seven times. After that, I want you to burn a handful of iodized salt over a low flame until it evaporates. You must then take the residue, and sprinkle it outside his house."

Umm Mazin raises her hand. "The most important thing is that his wife doesn't find out what we've done, because she's knowledgeable. Women like that can turn a handful of wheat grains into Persian ants, just by reciting a few lines in reverse order."

The woman appears terrified. Umm Mazin stands up with the sheet in her hand and heads toward the kitchen saying, "Excuse me, but I have to prepare some spells myself. Badriya can't read or write. It took me a long time to teach her how to differentiate between the different herbs on the basis of their colors, their smells, and their texture."

She gathers her belly in her dishdasha as she goes on, "Her understanding is limited, she can't even tell the time. She divides the day into five parts according to the five calls for prayer from the nearby mosque. But she's an honest woman. I'll be back in a moment."

While we wait, Badriya comes in with cardamom tea.

Umm Mazin comes back. Before requesting some sedative herbs, Ilham asks her, "Umm Mazin, how did you learn all these things?"

"Out of necessity."

She hands over the sheet to the other woman, receiving the money for the spell she had prepared. She then tells her, "Please take an ablution jug from Badriya in the kitchen. It's a free gift from us, as the Holy Month of Ramadan is approaching. May God accept your fast."

The woman leaves with her sheet, the blue plastic water jug, and the child with the pink tooth.

Umm Mazin turns toward us. We are now the only ones left in the room.

"I was fifteen years old when my parents died. I had my younger brothers and sisters to look after, but I was fragile and inexperienced. My late mother used to work as a cook in one of the restaurants on Rasheed Street. One of the local traders who was a frequent customer there offered me a job. I told him, 'I could never sell goods in the street'; but he said, 'This is trade. God's Prophet (Peace be upon him) blessed this profession.' That was how he was able to convince me; and so I joined his profession."

She sips her tea as she speaks, making a distinctive slurping sound, "We dealt with imports and exports to Kuwait. We traded in clothes, car spare parts, okra, soap, sesame seeds, wool. After that we bought a shop together in the Women's Market; there I met an Indian trader called Mirjan. He taught me how to revoke certain spells, and in return, I read him his fortune in his coffee cup."

She takes a black handkerchief out of her pocket and blows her nose into it with all her might. "Aah, this cold is killing me!"

She calls out to Badriya to get her an antibiotic capsule. She swallows it quickly without any water. The capsule sticks to her palate. Umm Mazin becomes agitated. She burps, and a fine mist, the size of her mouth, emerges from within the white capsule. Ilham and I are taken aback by her appearance. The dust from the medication flutters around her as she gasps. Badriya brings her a glass of water. She closes her mouth like a heavy trapdoor, attempting to swallow as much water as possible in one go. A moment later she spits out the shell of the capsule that has opened up in her throat; the green half emerges first, then the white half. She constantly repeats her prayer to God asking for protection from the evils of the devil, while cursing the pharmaceutical factory in Samarra that manufactured the capsule.

Ilham says to her, "Thank God you're all right, Umm Mazin. I'll get you some tablets from the hospital that are a little easier to swallow."

When she has calmed down a bit, Umm Mazin says to her, "Well, since you're a nurse; how can I be of help to you?"

"In my profession, we're fed up with drugs and medication. I need a natural remedy. I always feel exhausted, and I'm having difficulty sleeping."

"For your troubles, I suggest that you take one kilo of sugar, and half a kilo of yeast. Dissolve them both in two liters of cool water, and place this mixture in a glass jar that you must seal firmly. You must wait for one week to allow it to ferment. On the seventh day, open the jar and add to it two handfuls of the flowering tips of dried rosemary. You must then seal the container once again, and leave it to brew for a whole month. After that, filter it and store it in ordinary bottles, and take a dose whenever you need it. It should last you for a whole year. The dose you need to take is a small cupful, three times a day before meals."

She calls out to her maid, "Bring me the dried rosemary and a bag of yeast."

Ilham takes the items. "Thank you, Hijjia."

Umm Mazin glances at me. Ilham asks her, "And what happened to the Indian trader, Mirjan?"

"May God bestow His blessings upon him. He simply disappeared. I think he went back to India. In 1990, when things got bad over here, we abandoned our shops as they were. We had bought a lot of goods from Kuwait and were liable for substantial amounts in taxes that were imposed on everyone who'd traded with Kuwait. My partner fled during that time, and I took up this line of work."

She turns around and looks at me. "You don't say very much."

"You have no cures for me."

"Your visit here doesn't have to be for treatment. We can chat about other things."

An energy emanates from Umm Mazin. I feel it go through my left shoulder. She asks me to sit in front of her so she can look me in the eye. I do not feel comfortable.

"Like what?"

"Like your honey. I hear that you're about to start harvesting it."

"You mean collecting it."

"Yes, yes, that's what I meant. You wouldn't believe me if I told you that I use more than twenty kilos of honey each month. It's an essential component in so many of the charms, and it's also an ingredient in most of the remedies that I dispense."

I don't like the way she strikes up a conversation with me. Her tone is dry, and her pupils are cloudy. "My clients, sorry, I meant my friends, trust me because I'll only use pure honey. I know my honey. No one can deceive me on that account."

Ilham is settling her bill with the maid. Umm Mazin carries on, *"And thy Lord taught the bee to build its cells in hills, on trees, and in men's habitations; then to eat of all the produce of the earth, and find with skill the spacious paths of its Lord: there issues from within their bodies a drink of varying colors, wherein is healing for men: verily in this is a sign for those who give thought."*

Her servant, in the corridor murmurs, "Verily spoke God Almighty."

I reflect on what the people in the building say about her. When she gets bored in the evenings, she asks Badriya to get her the castanets made of four small brass discs, which she wears in each hand by fitting them on her thumb and index finger with elastic bands. She then starts to play a tune: *chum chum cha cha chum chum cha.* Badriya provides the background beat with regular taps on a metal mortar.

She adds, "Even the Bedouins have appreciated the importance of the bee for over fourteen centuries."

I say to myself, "I must introduce her to Abu Ghayeb." As though she has read my thoughts, she says, "Give my regards to your aunt's husband, and your aunt of course, and tell him that I'm interested in buying the first batch of honey he produces."

After a short while she calls out to Badriya, "Is lunch ready?"

"Yes, Hijjia."

She invites Ilham and me, "Stay for a meal. We have cooked first-grade Basmati rice. The grain is big and whole, so the rice will sit on the plate like rows of baby geese's eyes."

We excuse ourselves and decline the invitation. We leave the flat just as she is saying to her maid, *"There is no moving creature on earth but its sustenance dependeth on God."* I visualize Badriya behind the door nodding her head in assent.

❂

Abu Ghayeb impersonates the role of a farmer. He wears a yashmak and has his photograph taken in order to obtain a farmer's identity card. He tells his wife, "The damages that have resulted from the blockade are estimated at billions of dollars. We've returned to the pre-industrial age, so the government is encouraging farming to support the economy."

"What I can't understand is why they bombed the mosques, the schools, the homes for the disabled and the civilian shelters. What have they got to do with the military targets?"

He replies with a shrug, "Who can afford to buy food from the markets at the present prices?"

He then adds, "We used to import seventy percent of our food requirements. Now they have deprived us of the seeds. The stranglehold on the animal products became complete when they bombed the only lab that produced vaccines against animal diseases. That came after they ruined the irrigation canals, and we can't obtain fertilizers or pesticides."

He raises his eyebrows and continues, "And I'll tell you something else, the committee from the UN supervising this blockade has prevented us from importing the fibers and threads used to produce children's clothing on the pretext that they'd be used in industry. They've also stopped us from buying the cloth used for shrouds. Can you imagine that! They prevent us from weaving cloth, as if that could threaten the security of the region!"

My aunt gets up from her seat, "It's a catastrophe!"

"Of course it's a catastrophe."

"I mean with no threads and no cloth, how will I be able to work?"

The next day, my aunt decides to go to the Arabic souk very early in the morning. She wants to buy the largest possible amounts of colored threads and a wide variety of different types of cloth. She gathers together all the cash that is available in the flat, and leaves her husband

90

sleeping late. She knows that he has taken medication for his psoriasis. It contains a hefty dose of sedative, and waking him would not be easy.

The water is running again. I decide to take a long shower. I allow the clear drops to slide down over my hair and my face. I am afflicted by a delightful dizziness when a drop strays from its path and enters my ear. I stand aside to allow Umm Mazin's suggestions to flow down into the drain with the water. The rough surface of the wheatgerm soap from Nablus rubs against my skin and invigorates me. I don't use the loofa, instead; I cautiously prod my body checking for lumps.

I have to save the rest of the water for washing our dirty clothes this afternoon. Though I long for more, I turn off the tap. My ears are assaulted by the sound of Abu Ghayeb's infuriating snores. I head toward my aunt's bedroom. I want to shut the door, to entrap the cacophony of his sleep behind it.

I place my hand on the door's handle. Abu Ghayeb is submerged by his snores and the heat. The corner of the bedsheet covers part of his naked body. He lies flat on his back. I insinuate a third of my body into the room to stealthily cast an eye on the scene, and linger for a while. His 'thing' resembles a little mouse, blind, scalded, creased, and crumpled together at the base of his groin. Suddenly his right foot moves. In a split second I find myself in the sitting room, by the big window.

I will store that image in my mind for two years, at a temperature of 10° C, the same way I will soon learn how to store honey.

CHAPTER EIGHT

HARD, HARD.

I don't like the sound of his voice in the beginning. His tone dribbles, like melting Dutch butter. "We need hard currency."

The man carries on explaining to the teacher from the first floor, "And even with that, we won't emerge from this crisis easily."

The teacher answers him, "That's right, but at least you have your own independent business."

"But it's not covered in the 'Oil for Food' program."

They're unaware of my presence. I cross the road, heading toward them. I watch their backs strain to hang up a decorated sign announcing "Saad's Hairdressing for Ladies."

After we have been introduced, he says, "So you're Dalal. I've had a brief resumé about the inhabitants of the building from our esteemed teacher."

"Are you a hairdresser then, Saad?"

He adjusts his collar pouting out his lips as he says, "I'm a 'coiffeur.'"

"Congratulations on your new salon."

"It's only one half of the premises actually. I'll be living in the back half of the flat."

The teacher said, "It's strategically positioned. You'll get lots of customers here."

A small child crosses the road behind me. He resembles the teacher in his thinness. He wears a torn pair of trousers and carries a bundle of newspapers under his arm. The teacher takes one of his papers, gives him some change from his pocket and says, "Give my best regards to your mother, Hamada."

I ask, "Do you know him?"

He shakes his head. "I used to know his father. He was the chief editor of a cultural magazine. For one of his assignments he visited the village of Halabja, the site where our brothers, the Kurds, suffered from chemical bombardment. He was struck down by a yellow haze. He vomited repeatedly for three days, then died. Now his son sells newspapers to support his mother."

Hamada stares at my mouth. He kisses the coin from the teacher, and takes it away with him, heading back in the direction he'd come from. He disappears into an alleyway, beside the "Wahbi" restaurant that used to be a Wimpy's until the government issued an order that no shops or restaurants were permitted to have foreign names. All commercial ventures had to acquire Arabic names.

❋

Saad looks at me. The center of his eyes is like the transverse section of an oily black olive. He asks, "Did you know that deaths of children under the age of five have increased five-fold since the Gulf War."

He lifts his hand up to wipe away a black cluster of hair on his forehead. "Before these times, had you ever, in your entire life, heard of depression in children? It now affects most of those who lost relatives or friends as a result of the explosions, and those who were rescued from underneath the rubble of collapsed buildings."

At that moment, Umm Mazin comes down the stairs panting. She is followed by Badriya, who rushes up behind her, almost colliding with her. Umm Mazin stops close to where we stand; she starts to analyze Saad.

"Welcome."

He replies, "And you are doubly welcomed."

"Are you the new neighbor?"

"I am."

"We heard that you're a barber."

He replies in French, "A coiffeur."

"Have you got any real henna. . . ." Then she adds in a southern accent, "Mr. 'Kafoor,' did you say?"

I exchange giggles with the teacher from the first floor over the rural manner in which she pronounces "camphor." This herb is boiled with tea in the army to minimize the soldiers' desire for sex, or so they say.

He caresses his forelock with delicate fingers, smiling. "The henna I have has been mixed with Turkish coffee."

"I want a kilo."

"Kindly come back for it next week."

"Thank you, I'll send you my assistant. We're going to the auction."

"Which auction, may I ask?"

"May God protect you from such situations; there are some families who have resorted to selling their possessions outside their homes before they too are sold. They say that the pavements are covered with jewels, cooking utensils, carpets, and clothes." She sighs. "Everything's for sale."

Badriya butts in from behind her saying, "Even the wooden doors, Umm Mazin."

Her mistress agrees with her. "Yes, even the wooden doors that have been pulled from their hinges. Prosperity brings choices, but poverty brings changes."

She adjusts her abaya before she crosses the road toward the bus stop in the direction of Kifah Street. As they recede in the distance, the arched shadow of the Monument of the Unknown Soldier would have enveloped them, but it is no longer there. It has been pulled down and rebuilt in a non-residential area. Instead, they are enveloped by the shadow of the mosque's minaret.

❁

I meet my aunt as she is leaving the flat. She says, "You've come just at the right time."

She places a copy of the magazine *Burda* in my hands as she locks the door behind her. I ask her, "Where to?"

"Come with me to the dentist. One of my teeth is inflamed, I can no longer bear the pain."

The nearest dental clinic is next to the French Institute, a twenty-minute walk away. I remember what Ilham said, that I was wasting my time reading magazines. She explained to me that the pastries called *mille feuilles* which we used to eat in the Days of Plenty meant "a thousand leaves" in French. She was proud of this discovery.

We cross the road that separates the Sheraton Hotel from the Meridien Hotel. We walk past the house that burned down because its owners had been hoarding petrol. They were afraid it would get stolen, so they stored it under the ground; but it had leaked, and their garden exploded. Ten minutes later we turn by the stairs leading to the institute, which is now closed down because of the blockade. The young dentist opens the door; a fresh graduate, the cheapest available at the moment.

The waiting room is also the treatment room. A girl waits while the dentist works on her mother's teeth. My aunt is trying to show me how to trace out the pattern for a summer dress from the intersecting green lines on the patterns page that is folded in the middle of her precious magazine. I don't concentrate on her anxiety as she tries to ignore her toothache.

I watch the girl as she tries to fasten a huge hair clip. She perseveres, but it's futile. Her slack, slippery hair slips out of the clip's teeth. A fly annoys her, and instead of dropping what's in her hand to shoo away the fly, she blows on it to send it away while she continues to struggle with her hair. Her head spins in all directions, then she lifts up her arms and wipes the thick ball of hair underneath her armpits with a sheet of toilet roll that she has taken out of her handbag.

The electric disc that lights up the patient's mouth contains three bulbs. Two of them are out of order, and the third one emits a dim light. The dentist's younger brother comes in with a flashlight. He stands behind his brother, the graduate, and points his light in the direction it is needed.

The dentist's couch is a leather seat that has been removed from an old car. It has been converted by an ingenious mechanic into a dentist's chair. It doesn't go up or down, but can be moved forward and backward with assistance from the patient who has to extend her trunk this way or that.

A short while later we find out that the instruments are being sterilized in a small oven that, in the Days of Plenty, would have been used to roast chickens. The dentist uses a plastic syringe filled with a solution of tap water and Dettol. It floats in a small glass that had once been a container of "Heros," an imported brand of cream cheese. He squirts the solution into the patient's mouth. He asks the patient to rinse and then spit into a dented bucket to get rid of the germs.

The lady looks like she was nailed to the chair. Something is hurting her. Suddenly, the dentist's younger brother comes in and calls out to him, "There's a phone call for you."

The doctor asks, "Soft or coarse?"

"It's the soft sex."

He leaves his patient with her mouth open, and disappears.

We make our escape before he returns.

❦

The next day, Abu Ghayeb comes back to the apartment at three o'clock in the afternoon wearing his protective suit. He has spent the morning examining his bees. He sits down on the couch and starts removing the stingers that have become embedded in his soft leather gloves. My aunt hurries toward him and places an ashtray on the coffee table in front of him. She says, "Put all the bees' tails in there, and don't let any of them fall on the floor."

He becomes more engrossed in what he is doing, and says, "I have to get rid of them all. If a few of them remain, their scent will enrage the bees. Then I have to wash these gloves well, and rub them down with vegetable oil to keep them soft and supple."

It's not only the bees that are enraged by this sight.

The spaceman looks at her through his mask. It is cylindrical in shape, made of wooden strips connected to each other by leather ribbons so that it can be folded when not being used. He says, "The bees become enraged because they're sensitive creatures!"

I can't see his expression behind the dark wooden grid covering his face. He has chosen the mask as instructed, because it must also be rustproof.

He unfastens the suit's collar releasing the laces at the base of the mask. She says to him, "And what's the news of your beloved ones?"

"Everything is as it should be."

She lifts up her eyebrows as he removes his headgear. She places a bundle of cash in front of him and says, "I suggest that you close down this apiary before we lose even more in expenses."

"Have you gone mad, woman?"

"No, but it seems as though you're going to be boiled alive by your psoriasis in the hot sun; and we still won't have achieved anything."

"Time alone will tell."

"We haven't got the time. Our situation gets worse every day."

"We're not the only ones in this crisis."

He starts to fold the mask and places it on the couch beside him. He asks her, "Where did you get this money?"

"From my work, of course." She then adds, "My work, which generates a speedy income."

"From sewing shrouds?"

"If you'd listened to me, we could have opened a shop that sold cloth, and we could've fought off this poverty. If you'd heeded my advice, and become a used car dealer, or traded in cigarettes many years ago, we wouldn't be in the state we're in now."

He shakes his limp glove in her face. "If, if, if . . . IF is a plant that doesn't sprout."

"My profession will be the winner in the end, you'll see."

Her husband picks up the bundle of cash from the table and tosses it into her lap saying sarcastically, "You nectar-provider."

He walks past her as she follows him with her eyes. "You'll fail."

When he reaches the kitchen door, he turns around and says to me, "As I explained to you this morning, Dalal, the bee uses its tongue to suck up the nectar. Bees with a longer tongue can penetrate more deeply into the flowers to reach the nectar."

He gestures to me with his hand, indicating that I should come closer. He then says, "Your aunt thinks that she'll be able to gather more nectar if her tongue is longer and her voice is raised."

I say to myself, "Heaven help me. So today she's the queen, he's the male, that leaves me the role of the worker."

Two hours later, the flat has calmed down. My aunt has gone out to find an experienced dentist, while her husband returns to the back of the club. I stand at my bedroom window for a few moments. On my bed I have left a magazine article translated from Hebrew, "How to Raise a Laughing Hyena in Your Home." I observe Abu Ghayeb's movements in the rectangular area surrounded by wire fences. It occurs to me that one day he'll be able to write an article entitled "How to Raise Bees in a Tennis Court."

The apiary is taking shape. The storage room and the honey filtration room have been fitted out and prepared for the arrival of the frames that the bees will need to build their hexagonal cells. Space has been set aside for the tools, the containers used as travel boxes for the bees, the wax discs, the fumigation boxes, and the incubators.

I search for my homework in a green booklet with a little bee printed on it. My aunt's husband knows very well that I would rather chase after his insects than trace out the patterns from women's magazines. My aunt informs me with relish, "You lay out the tracing paper on this page. You then trace out the printed lines following the numbers and the letters, and then draw out the lines you need using a pencil. This way you can obtain the patterns for a beautiful dress or a skirt." I don't tell her that I can't differentiate between the pattern for the shoulders and those for the hips.

I read, "The worker bees are considered the working class within the colony. The role of the queen bee is that of mother to all the bees. The males have one duty only, and that is to fertilize the virgin queens."

I close my eyes to imagine myself as a worker bee. When my glands start to develop, I start to secrete royal jelly, and I must feed the young larvae, and the queen. I put my hand on my neck to feel for them, then I remember that they're located in the lower abdomen. I lie back on the bed for further reading. The nectar is a sugary liquid that contains disaccharides, glucose, and—

The phone beside me rings. I pick up the receiver as I'm saying "fructose."

Ilham's voice at the other end draws me into her world. There's a tremor in her voice. "My fears have been confirmed. It's a malignant growth."

"How do you feel?"

"Lost."

"Where are you?"

"At the hospital."

"Are they going to fire you?"

"Not yet. I'll try to keep it a secret, and arrange for the operation at another hospital."

"When?"

"As soon as possible, so that I can start the treatment after that."

"Are you afraid?"

"I don't fear the operation, but I'm worried about how I'm going to get the money, and how I'm going to look after myself when that's over."

"I'll help you."

"Thank you, Dalal. Help yourself and your family first."

"I meant, I'll look after you."

"Damn, I don't need pity."

She is quiet for a few moments as if inhaling on her cigarette. She then says, "I'm sorry, I didn't mean to rage at you. What I need is cash; I don't need to trouble other people with my condition."

"Should I ask my aunt's husband? He might have a suggestion."

"No, no. I don't want you to do that."

"We could start raising some money as a charity in your name."

"I certainly don't want that."

"What will you do?"

"God will provide." She adds, "Anyway, what're you doing?"

"I'm trying to understand the world of the bees."

"So have you decided to help him out?"

"No, but if I have to choose a profession, I wouldn't become a seamstress. I'd rather water the vegetables, protect them from the perils of the wild parasitic eggplant, and exterminate the German cockroaches."

"You learn fast. What about your studies?"

"I don't know."

"The day will come when you'll know what you want to do."

The connection starts to fade; her sentences start breaking up. I take a small piece of tracing paper that my aunt uses for her dress patterns. I use it to wipe the wall by my bed. I crumple up the paper and mold it into the shape of a fist. I try to obliterate a small splash of brown that two nights ago had been a fat annoying mosquito. She asks me, "Are you still there?"

"Yes."

"I'll speak to you when I get back."

I continue reading the green booklet. "Bees are exceptionally clean insects. They will not die inside the hive. When they become aware that their death is imminent, they will leave the hive to avoid leaving their carcass inside it. We can see a number of bees accompanying the dying one to the outside in a dance of death to honor the bee that is about to die."

As evening descends, my aunt returns to the flat. It is obvious that she has spent her money on some anesthetic. Her mouth is numb and drawn to one side of her face. At last, if we walked down the street together, people might think I was her daughter. And who knows, perhaps she'd experience a motherly feeling!

She has a hot story from the dental clinic about a burglary based on a bet. She attempts to straighten her mouth as she tells the tale of a man who boasted to some people that he could burgle their house while they were in it. They accepted his challenge, and waited for him in their house at the time they'd agreed upon. He went to the police and informed them that illegal sexual acts were being committed at that address. The police went around and immediately arrested everyone in the house. They took them away for interrogation; and the man was then able to enter their house and burgle it as he'd said he would.

On the shelf in front of me, the sculptures move like my aunt's story. Primitive shapes of men and women seem to be embracing. The sand sculptures love each other; the stone sculptures sow distrust.

CHAPTER NINE

OUR DAYS REVOLVE around themselves like a cylindrical Sumerian seal. A deer, followed by another deer, followed by another deer, followed by another deer.

People living in the provinces have started calling Baghdad "Paris, the city of lights." We hear reports from the major cities in the north that Sulaimaniya and Arbil have been affected by daily power cuts. The drainage of the sewage and the city's drinking water supply are affected. Duhok has no electricity at all except for a single generator that supplies the hospital. From the south, we hear that ten thousand inhabitants from the city of Basra lost their homes as a result of the bombing. They are now living in buildings still under construction without running water or any other services. Their children play in the pools of stagnant water covering the streets.

Ilham and her smoke are inseparable. She says, "He seems nice."

"Yes, he does."

"So you met him as well?"

"Yes. I think he'll attract a lot of clients. He loves gossiping."

"What has gossiping got to do with the price of meat?"

"Meat? What're you talking about?"

"The butcher who's opened a small shop at the bottom of the road."

"You're interested in a butcher?"

"No, I'm interested in his shop. He's called it 'Gilgamish's Butchery.'"

Our laughter pierces through the haze of her smoke. I say to her, "I was talking about Saad."

"Who?"

"The hairdresser, I mean the 'coiffeur,' on the ground floor."

"So do you think he's nice too?"

"We'll see."

The lift only started working again a few hours ago. We decided to take a risk and use it. She says, "He used to be a civil engineer, but couldn't find any work, so he decided to sell meat instead."

"Umm Mazin says everything is for sale."

"He told me that most of the major engineering projects have been put on hold because there are no maintenance services. He also mentioned that large areas of the green belt around the cities have started to disappear. This is because people have been cutting down the trees in order to use the wood as fuel."

"How's Saad going to keep his shop going?"

He is standing outside his shop saying goodbye to a very short woman whose hair looks like a starched bird's nest. She waves to him with her little hand. Five circles of black nail varnish flash from the tips of her fingernails. She trills out as she leaves, "Bye-bye from Bonsai."

He turns to us saying, "Do come in."

He explains as we enter, "That's the name that this crazy woman has called herself since the Days of Plenty. She thinks that her hair is a bonsai tree that needs to be cut, pruned, and trimmed every month."

"Let me introduce you to Ilham who lives on the second floor."

"I'm honored."

He gestures, indicating that we should sit down.

"We don't see you very often."

"Yes, my job involves long working hours."

"We're all having to work extra hours these days."

His premises reflect his style: modest, but elegant.

There are two revolving chairs. In front of the first chair is a large mirror and the second chair has a smaller mirror in front of it. There's a two-seater couch for the customers who are waiting their turn, and beside it is a wide seat with a white ceramic bowl fitted on top of it. A segment has been nibbled away smoothly from its side so that it can support the customer's neck. We later find out that because of the small size of the salon, the lady waiting on the couch would have a few drops of water splattering her left cheek from the woman having her hair washed next to her. She would either have to put up with it, pretending to find it refreshing, or pull up one of the small wooden chairs and sit by the entrance. The spray comes from a crack in the plastic handle of the hose that lies coiled up inside the basin.

I point to the hairdryers hanging from the wall between the mirrors. "What are you going to do about the electricity?"

He's folding a pile of clean towels, laying them out neatly one on top of the other.

"I've reached an agreement with the Alwiya Club. They'll provide me with a few amperes from their generator for a price."

"And the water?"

"I've installed an extra tank in the garage and linked it to my flat. I don't have a car, so I don't really need the garage."

The shop front's aluminum door still has its maker's sticker on it— AL-SUMOUD FACTORY, THE MANUFACTURERS OF STEADFASTNESS. The window frame is made from the same aluminum, but somebody has scratched out the label with their fingernails. Below the window is a pot containing a green feathery plant that will grow into a mulberry bush, the type that silkworms feed on. Beside the inner door, which leads to the second half of his shop, or rather his flat, is a row of crooked metal shelves. Bottles of hair coloring, chemicals, and cans of hair spray are stacked there. There are straw baskets filled to the brim with traditional wooden and modern plastic hairbrushes of every size and model. They're so numerous, they appear to be pricking each other intentionally. Some of them are about to fall off the shelves.

Saad hands Ilham an ashtray, and hands me a magazine. She offers him a cigarette, while I give her a cushion to support her back. We're getting on well together.

Ilham says, "Prepare yourself."

"Whatever for?"

She picks up a box of twelve hair rollers, each the size of a finger. Printed on the box, in golden letters, are the words "Hair Rollers," "Made in Germany." "Umm Mazin has a client who has a phobia of these things."

"Is there anyone in the world who's afraid of hair rollers?"

"Her sister died of a stroke while she was wearing them in her hair. The poor woman is now in shock. She needs therapy because she firmly believes that her sister died of electrocution as a result of using electric hair rollers."

The word stroke divides my thoughts in two. Before the sanctions started, I used to feel that my life was divided into two halves, the time before the stroke and what came after it. Nowadays, everyone talks about the Days of Plenty, and the times that followed; the days before the war, and those that followed; life before the crisis, and after it. I, too, find myself, reluctantly, thinking like everyone else.

Saad is amazed. "Don't tell me that that's the type of customer I can look forward to!"

I join their conversation. "At least you call them customers, and the relationship is clear-cut. Umm Mazin treats them in these weird and wonderful ways, yet refuses to call them patients. She insists on referring to them as 'my friends,' 'my dear ones,' or 'my neighbors.' Even Badriya is called her assistant rather than her servant."

"So she must be a civilized woman who's considerate of their feelings."

"And would you call this tale civilized? A woman who'd become unable to walk went to see her. The doctors had been unable to diagnose her condition, so she headed off to consult Umm Mazin to see

105

if she could find out the cause of her paralysis. Our friend, 'the healer,' convinced her that the Blue Jinni had entered her spinal column and was refusing to leave. Umm Mazin spoke to the jinni through the woman's foot, and he answered her by writing out various words on the sole of this woman's foot. Apparently, the jinni once wrote the word 'scorpion.'"

Saad recoils in disgust. "And what happened to the patient?"

"She's still continuing with her treatment. We call her 'the woman with the blue spinal column.' When we see her driver carrying her up to the top floor, we know that Umm Mazin won't be seeing anyone else that day. They say that Badriya lights incense to clear the air after a lengthy session. That's when the loud, frightening shrieks are heard."

"You intrigue me. I think I'd like her to foretell my future by reading the signs in my coffee cup."

"Not possible, unless it's through an intermediary. She doesn't accept visits from men."

Ilham turns her head toward me. "You could take Saad's coffee cup with you for her to read it, couldn't you?"

"I'll ask my aunt to do that."

Ilham smiles, and says to Saad, "Dalal has her doubts about Umm Mazin's abilities."

"Of course I do. She once told me that a woman with a red flame in her belly button stole away my smile during my childhood. She told me that this woman seeks out children when they're asleep, and takes from them parts of their bodies so that she can make herself a child of her own. Can you believe that she offered me a magical counter-spell that would restore the shape of my mouth? She then said the treatment could take several years."

Saad stands up and places his arms around my shoulders. "Dalool, don't become fixated on this issue. There's a defect in each one of us." He adds, "Come."

He drags me by the hand, and sits me down on the revolving chair in front of the big mirror. He takes out a bag of paints and powders that looked like stage makeup. He says, "Close your eyes and don't move."

He thrusts his hand into the bag, and starts tickling my face as he applies the powders. A soft brush caresses my eyelids, and with another, he thickens my eyelashes. I find it difficult to keep my eyes closed as his fingers caress my mouth. A greasy feeling overwhelms me. He says, "You can open them now."

He has drawn on my face a continuation of my mouth in a smoky fleshy color that matches the original color of my lips. "What do you see?"

"My dream coming true."

"And what else?"

"That you're mocking me."

"Be serious. What's this face in front of you trying to say?"

"That it's been painted on, that it's a fake."

He takes a handkerchief and wipes away the artificial half of my mouth. "The person sitting in front of me is still the same person, before and after." He squeezes my shoulders. "Dalool, don't follow an illusion."

Suddenly, the small boy selling newspapers sticks his head through the door without any forewarning. He says, "Susu, have you got any old stuff for me?"

"Not today, come back at the end of the month."

"Do you want a newspaper?"

"No."

Hamada stares at my face. "Are you sure you don't want a newspaper?"

"I'm sure, and close the door when you leave."

Saad starts to prepare some coffee for us all. He tops up the coffee with some more water, so that we can have more cups of diluted coffee. The black hairs of his forelock tickle his left eyebrow. "Hamada is fascinated by old shoes."

I remember, "The teacher on the first floor often sells his old shoes."

He glances at me with a wicked smile. "So you know the story."

Ilham intervenes, "What story?"

"Hamada is the teacher's son, by the elderly widow."

I say to him, "We never knew that."

"That's the back street gossip. Have you never noticed how much he resembles him?"

I pause for a moment to compare their appearance in my mind, "Was he her lover before her husband died, or afterward?"

"It doesn't matter."

The coffee doesn't taste as bland as I thought it would.

"My compliments on the way you made this cup."

He says in a Lebanese accent, "In good health, multiplied by two."

Ilham asks him, "Why does he call you Susu?"

"It's my nickname."

"Would you like us to call you that?"

"Some people call me Saaoudy. You can call me whatever you like. All names are blessed and honorable."

The coffee has moistened his voice. He says to her, "Did you know, I was the one who named that child Hamada?"

Ilham starts on her second cup as he begins to tell the tale. "His father, I mean the teacher and not his deceased father, wanted to call him Hamid, but because I had helped his wife, well, his lover in this case, when she was having the baby, he asked me to name the boy."

"You attended the birth? He allowed you to do that?"

"He had no choice. My previous salon was right next to her house. The phone lines were down, and he came running to me saying the woman was about to give birth at home. I grabbed the rubber gloves that I use when I'm dyeing customers' hair and ran out after him. When we got there, we had to make do ourselves and pray for help from God."

"And how did things go?"

"I caught the child's head first, as they do in the movies, then cut the umbilical cord using a sterile shaving razor. I had no idea what to do after that. In the films, they never show you anything about delivering the placenta."

A moment later he adds, "I love children. I hope that I might be able to have a child someday."

I look at Ilham, who starts to react. "Whatever for? To add another individual to this tragedy?"

"I'm not responsible for this tragedy. We must try to live in as normal a fashion as possible. We have to dream of the things that we're entitled to hope for."

She puts out her cigarette to light up another one. "That only applies if you're able to live in a dream."

"It seems to me that I've annoyed you. Was it something I said?"

Ilham starts to grind her teeth. "Look at what's happening outside your shop Saad—or Saaoudy. Those children aren't going to school. Only one percent of the oil revenue now is allocated to education."

"I have no say in laying down those resolutions, Ilham."

Ilham is no longer enjoying her coffee. "What's worse is that out of those who are lucky enough to be offered an education, seven children at least pass out every day because of hunger or lack of medication. If they have a stomach upset, they have to go home because school toilets don't work."

He shrugs his shoulders. "I refuse to give up my dreams just because the toilets don't work."

She becomes more animated. "And the less fortunate ones end up in my department."

I don't know why, but he lowered his gaze. It may be because he is aware of how upset she is, or it may be simply that he wants to place the coffee cup on the tray. "I said what I said because I feel lonely. I was an only child."

I give him back the magazine, hoping to interrupt this flow between them, but Ilham persists, "Loneliness is spending your last days in a hospital where there's no heating or cooling. Loneliness is biting your lip when you see the nurse forcing a used urine bag into you because there are no new ones; or staring at a dialysis machine that doesn't work."

He has stopped arguing with her as her tone becomes more high-pitched. "Loneliness is putting up with the pain while you wait for your turn on the operating list. In the past we used to perform thirty operations a week. Nowadays, the most that we can manage is six."

She strikes the table with her fist. "That's loneliness."

She stands up, full of emotion, but ends up throwing herself onto the couch and then bursts into tears. Saad runs toward her, unsure of what to do. He decides to go and get her a glass of water.

When he returns she has left, leaving me behind to offer her apologies.

I stand outside the salon for a few moments trying to decide where to go. Somebody behind me says, "Excuse us, Miss." It is some laborers who are removing a number of boxes from outside the Alwiya Club. They place them in an open-topped vehicle. The club is selling the equipment that it no longer has any use for; the fax, telex, switchboard, and film projectors. I watch as they move past me soundlessly. They remove the memories of my childhood in big wooden boxes that contain metal chairs and loudspeakers. They are getting rid of the spools of film. They take away with them *Hans Christian Andersen*, Norman Wisdom, and the Arabic romance *Amira My Love*.

❋

I find her at Uncle Sami's flat. She opens the door to let me in. "Did you apologize?"

"And I drank the glass of water on your behalf."

Uncle Sami joins us. She says, "I'll go over and apologize in person tomorrow."

"I don't think you need to. He seems to be a sensitive and understanding person."

"Then I'll get my hair done at his place." She then adds, "Before I lose it."

Uncle Sami intervenes. "You won't lose him just because of that. We all have the right to express ourselves in front of others."

"I meant, losing my hair, Uncle."

I love the way he embraces us. Today, he's wearing an old pair of jeans, and a white shirt that has a few spots of dried blood on it from his last hospital visit. He must have had the misfortune of encountering a male nurse who wasn't very skilled at taking blood. He smiles at me.

"I know what you're thinking."

"What?"

"Santa Claus is on holiday."

I turn around to face Ilham. "You cruel tale-teller!"

He says, "And why not, I like to be called Santa Claus. After all, he does bring happiness to children."

Ilham gives him a hug. "May God never deprive us of you."

I say, "Actually, I was thinking of Umm Mazin. If you went to see her dressed like that, she'd throw you out of her flat."

He picks up a ceramic crucifix that lies on the table beside the photograph of his wife. He lifts it up in front of his face and says, "She'd never receive me in the first place."

"Besides that, she'd throw you out because you're wearing jeans."

"Why? Is it because they're made in America?"

"No, it's because she calls them 'tanned dog's skin' and considers them unclean. She says they spoil her spells."

Ilham makes her comments as she leafs through Umm Raid's diary. "I see you're biased against Umm Mazin."

"I can't understand how she manages to mislead those foolish women with her hocus-pocus!"

"Have mercy on her. She does know a lot about herbal remedies. At least her mixes are effective."

"But it's the illiterate Badriya who makes up the concoctions. I've seen her place the herbs in at least fifty different containers that vary in shape, size, and seal, so that she can tell them apart. Some are marked with a color or a symbol so that she can recognize them."

"So what. At the end of the day, Umm Mazin dispenses some fabulous remedies."

"I have to disagree with you. She uses verses from the Qur'an to deceive people, and makes use of honey and herbs to convince them of the effectiveness of her spells. She also encourages women to wear the hijab, and insists that a woman's religious duty is to stay at home. She says that a woman's task is to serve her husband and devote herself to prayer."

"Are you implying that wearing the hijab is a sign of being backward?"

"No, but if we stayed at home, how would we be able to earn a living?"

I take Saad's cup out of the plastic bag in my handbag and hand it over to her, "Since you, the nurse, are such a fan of her knowledge, you can take his cup for her to read."

"What's wrong with you, Dalal? Don't you remember how she dealt with that woman who thought she was sexually frigid?"

"On the contrary, I remember it well. She told her, 'Your problem my dear, is that since you were a child, you've been so used to hugging a pillow when you sleep at night. You must abandon this habit, the pillow has been your substitute, and you hug it instead of hugging your man. That's why you think you're frigid.'"

Uncle Sami calmly adds his voice to the debate, "Excellent. This means that the woman has accepted Umm Mazin's suggestion."

He senses I am staring at him, so he continues, "Dalal, a treatment is more likely to be successful if we believe in it. If we're convinced that we've been cured, then the treatment has worked, regardless of whether or not other people believe in it."

"But this is trickery, Uncle!"

"Every person needs to believe in something. Believing in trickery willingly is another form of faith."

He wipes his beard as he watches me. "Let's change the subject. How are your aunt and her husband?"

"When he starts selling his honey, he'll regain the upper hand in the household. At the moment, she holds the balance, as it's she who's providing for our daily expenses."

Ilham comments, "So they're still having problems."

"Their dispute still rumbles on. She has a strange philosophy: spend what you have in your pocket and the unknown will compensate you. She's started stockpiling cloth and thread in every corner of the house. He insists that she's an unenlightened consumer since the Days of Plenty. Then Abu Ghayeb comes up and says to her, 'Don't overextend yourself.' He reminded her that there are no pesticides in the shops. She now lives in fear of a moth epidemic. All the cloth she's bought could be ruined, and she worries about it constantly."

"A successful marriage has gone out of fashion."

I say, "The magazines say that the ratio is one divorce to every three marriages."

Uncle Sami says to her, "It's marriage itself that has gone out of fashion."

She smiles. "Anyway, I bet you Umm Mazin has a remedy for moths."

She picks up her cigarettes. "What I don't understand is why she charges more for revoking spells for residents abroad than for spells cast locally?"

He explains, "Because the jinni needs a travel permit." He then adds with a roar, "He'd have to be frisked and searched at the Rweishid Border checkpoint."

A moment later she adds, "Did you know that she's now asking to be paid in dollars for reading her clients' coffee cups?"

CHAPTER TEN

I WONDER WHAT the teacher from the first floor told Saad when he gave him a brief description of the people who lived in our building!

Did he tell him that it was the building of self-sufficiency? Ilham provides us with the medicines that we can no longer get in the pharmacies. Uncle Sami provides us with Arabic and Western magazines through his acquaintances in Damascus. Umm Ghayeb refers clients she sews for to Umm Mazin, and in return, Umm Mazin sends her clients whose coffee cups she has read. Umm Mazin will send her patients to Saad, and he will generate publicity for her. Abu Ghayeb will sell his honey to everyone. As for me, I've decided that I will learn French.

Ilham comes to return Saad's cup to me. The coffee has dried up inside it. "Please return the cup to him."

"Why hasn't it been washed?"

"Umm Mazin refused to wash it in her house after she read it."

"What did she say?"

"She described the owner of the cup by saying, 'He cowardly threatens, like a woman, with a dagger like a cow's tail.'"

"And how am I supposed to understand that?"

"I don't know. She said she could see a man in the cup, not a woman."

"Did you tell her it was Saad's cup?"

"She knew that from the smell of the coffee dregs."

"So what should I tell him?"

She thinks for a moment, then says, "Tell him that Ilham dropped the cup by mistake, and that it got broken."

❋

Indeed, Umm Mazin does end up becoming the first buyer of Abu Ghayeb's honey. She asks me to accompany her to the apiary so that she can see the site for herself. She gives me a preamble as she waddles beside me like a soft ball. As we go through the gate in the court's fence, she says, "In my entire life, only one person has been able to fool me with impure honey. He only succeeded because he used an old dried out segment of wax. He moistened it, placed inside his fake honey, and sold it to me as the real thing."

Umm Mazin doesn't shake hands with men because she says that would invalidate her cleanliness after her daily ritual washing, and it is almost time for her to perform her midday prayers. That would mean having to repeat the washing ritual. When my aunt's husband presents her with the sample, she gingerly inserts her brown finger into the container, and then licks it slowly. She tastes it without closing her lips. She moves the mouthful of honey to the left and to the right before swallowing it. It is as if she is tasting a fine French wine. She gazes at Abu Ghayeb intently as she tries to read his thoughts. She attempts to determine his integrity, as she looks for evidence of dishonesty in his eyes. Suddenly, it seems like she has witnessed a miracle as she says, "First class."

In spite of his dislike for her, Abu Ghayeb plays the role of the amiable salesman. He says, "Your approval is an honor, Umm Mazin." She doesn't need to smile in return, her mouth has been set in smile mode since the day she was born. Her teeth have become more yellow in color since she has licked the honey. A moment later, she notes that one of the workmen's sandals has been left upturned beside one of the honey vats. She nudges me with her elbow saying, "My dearest, turn over that sandal to its correct position. The sole of a sandal pointing upwards is an insult to the heavens. That would bring bad fortune." I turn the sandal over and we leave. She takes away with her the first kilo of pure honey. As we walk back, she sings to herself, "My darling, how sweet the pomegranates are, when gathered in a cool breeze."

We leave the club behind us. Abu Ghayeb's tennis court is gradually becoming a productive apiary. The second court remains as it is: abandoned.

At the entrance to our building, I offer to carry the honey for her. The lift is still not working, and she is barely able to lift herself up the stairs. When we reach her flat, we find the door open, and we can hear the sound of women's shrieks coming from inside the flat. Umm Mazin hurries in to find out what is going on. She is so shocked by the scene, her eyes shift with horror from horizontal to vertical slits, as in the folklore saying. Two women are engaged in a cockfight, or rather a hen fight. Badriya is in there, attempting to break up the conflict. She looks like a boxing referee wearing a nightdress. Her head shawl has come off. Streaks of gray are woven into her hennaed hair, which is coiled around itself like a smooth droopy serpent. The woman above is bearing down, and the woman below is pushing up.

The woman on top shouts out, "You took him from me!"

The woman below her shouts back, "You mean I got him back from you!"

"But he loves me, and that's why he left you."

"He used to love me before you cast the spell of blind obedience upon him."

They shake each other vigorously, "So what're you going to do now? Cast a returning spell to get him back?"

The situation reverses itself: the chicken on the top ends up at the mercy of the chicken who was underneath and who now clucks, "I'll get my revenge, you shameless thing."

"He'll never divorce me, in spite of your efforts, you fool."

Umm Mazin realizes that Hen A is the wife of the same man that Hen B was trying to seduce, with her help. She provided both of them with concoctions for those purposes recently. She quickly puts an end to their confrontation by pouring a bucket of cold water, conveniently sitting just by the kitchen door, over both of them. Petrified, Badriya screams at her, "Umm Mazin what have you done, that was a bucket of worms someone delivered while you were out!"

After the storm, Umm Mazin refunds both women with the payment they'd given her in advance for her services, with an additional amount that she calls compensation for the damage that has been done. She curses the devil for the way he brought those two together to see her!

A week later, Umm Mazin puts up a sign inside her flat that says in big bold letters FIGHTING AND HAIR-PULLING ARE FORBIDDEN.

❊

I submit my application forms to the university. At the registration department, where we go to hand in our applications, a colored poster pinned to the wall catches my attention. It reads, OUR ACHIEVEMENTS INCLUDE: NATIONALIZING OUR OIL, FREE EDUCATION, AND THE ERADICATION OF ILLITERACY. As I leave the office, I read another sign that has been stuck to the window where payments are made: ALL IRAQIS ARE BAATHISTS, EVEN THOSE WHO HAVE NOT JOINED THE PARTY.

I spend my time with my aunt's husband or with Saad while I wait for the results. Abu Ghayeb asks me to work for a few hours with him in the morning, helping him out in the apiary. He doesn't object when Saad also asks me to help out in the evening at the salon. In return for my services, Saad promises that he will pay me a modest wage. He suggests that I save up what I earn to cover the expenses I will incur in my studies. This way I will be able to avoid further sewing lessons from my aunt. Yesterday, she added another box to her collection. She collected some date seeds, dried them, and then painted them using Abu Ghayeb's paints. She then placed them on the shelf with a label that said FRUITS.

As soon as the women enter Saad's salon, their names change immediately. Haifa becomes Madame Falafel and Miss Uhud becomes Dudu. What I can't understand is how the aged Mrs. Dhia has become Shushu! Saad calls them what he likes, and the women don't seem to object.

I ask him in a whisper, "Why would such an old lady want to restyle her hair?"

"Some women need to have their hair played with by a man's hand."

Falafel is engrossed in her discussion with Dudu. "The competition is getting worse, my friend. I've started to lose my grip on my husband. There are pretty women at every corner. What should I do?"

The boiler isn't working, and Saad is washing Dudu's hair in cold water. Underneath her revealing blouse is the silhouette of two breasts responding to the cold.

They pursue their conversation, like two actresses in a play who have learned their lines, and are reciting them fluently. "In the beginning, a woman longs for the man of her dreams."

"Then she longs for a brave knight."

"Then the ideal man."

"Then a suitable man."

"Then a man."

"Specifically, a married man."

"Whereas nowadays, a woman just looks for a man."

"Any man."

The scene ends.

A little later, they embark on an unrehearsed discussion. Falafel's ruddy complexion and red hair remind me of a Swedish milkmaid. Dudu says, "You wouldn't believe what happened to my neighbor."

"What?"

"Her husband has started drinking heavily since he received a warning telling him to cease his trading in cigarettes. He was told that this trade had now been restricted exclusively to the sons of eminent politicians. He had to quickly dispose of the stock he held and look for another source of income. He came home drunk two nights ago, and in a moment of anger, he opened their large freezer cabinet. It was empty of course, power cuts and all that; so he pushed his wife into it. Then he sat down on top of the lid, and started singing. If it hadn't been for the neighbors, the poor thing would've suffocated."

Falafel replies, "So, thank God, I suppose, for my minor problem with my husband. I shouldn't complain."

What a large woman! She walks past me. I can feel the impact of her high heels striking the ground. They shake the fillings in my back teeth.

In the first week that I worked for Saad, I learned how to direct the hot air from the dryers onto the ladies' heads without singeing their hair. I learned how to make dilute coffee, and how to gather up the shorn locks while he prepared the hot oil therapy for those with damaged hair.

As for my aunt's husband, he teaches me how to smoke.

I find him waiting for me by the fumigation unit. It is a metal cylinder with a cover that resembles an upside-down funnel, like a chimney. Beneath it is its fuel container. The cylinder is connected at its lower end to a leather pump. When it's lit, the smoke emerges from the opening at the top of the chimney.

He says to me, "The best fuel to generate smoke is cloth, thick paper, or cardboard."

He then takes out a bag of cloth. I recognize it immediately. It is from Umm Ghayeb's moth-damaged collection. He stuffs it into the incinerator with a cunning smile. "Some benefit from others' dilemmas."

In order to get rid of his previous label, "the seamstress's husband," he has started calling himself "The King of the Bees"; as for my aunt, behind his back she calls him "The Furry One." She says that his chest and his shoulders are where his body hair is most dense. In the past, she used to evade his advances in the summer, and snuggle up to him in the winter. Nowadays he only comes back to the flat for a few hours. His scales are the only sign that he's been home, unless, to avoid my aunt's complaints at sweeping them, he gathers his flakes swiftly and hides them around the roots of the vine before he leaves.

He lights the cloth and places it inside the cylinder. He activates the pump a few times, and soon the smoke starts emerging from the funnel, but without any flame. "Some beekeepers use coarse wood chippings or dried sheep droppings."

In spite of his new interest in bees, Abu Ghayeb hasn't turned his back on his love of tourism. He tells me with sorrow, "Some of the retired employees from the Department of Archaeology tell me that the bombing has affected the city of Babylon. The excavation had been concentrated around Nebuchadnezzar's Southern Palace, to reveal all its features that'd been buried underneath the rubble. But now, everything has come down once again, including the Eastern Gate of Keshno. All that remains are the city walls."

I move a glass container away from his foot, fearing that he will knock it over as he works. I ask him, "Do you still see your friends from the Ministry of Tourism?"

"No, except on rare occasions, when we meet by chance as we go to pick up our pensions. We then go over for a cup of tea at the ministry cafeteria. By the way, the fumigator mustn't be used excessively, as it might release hot smoke, and that could harm the bees."

He points to the aluminum lever, indicating to me that I should pass it over to him. His tone is serious. "This is how the fumigator should be emptied and cleaned. All the remnants of the burnt material and the ash must be removed after it's been used."

He asks me, to see if I have learnt what he has been teaching me, "So tell me, why do we have to fumigate?"

"To calm the bees. When they're exposed to the smoke, they'll head toward the hexagonal cells that are full of honey and gorge on it. That calms them down, and makes them less likely to sting."

He says exuberantly, *"Tesekkür ederim."*

"'Thank you' in Farsi?"

"No, Turkish. You mustn't forget that we were ruled by the Ottomans for four hundred years."

"I know. Then the British ruled us since 1917. They lost their power after the 1958 revolution and the fall of the monarchy. Right?"

"Right. We must know our history well."

So I say, "And also our bees."

❁

Ilham somehow manages her affairs when she says, "God will provide." She went into hospital and emerged five days later without voicing her concerns. The surgeons removed lymph nodes from the armpit affected by the disease. She took time off work, and my aunt helped her take a bath while attempting to keep the wound dry. A line of pink embroidery lay where her breast had been.

Umm Mazin sent her a "shepherd's bag" mix, to heal the wound and regulate her periods. She also provided her with a treatment made from the leaves and branches of a flowering Melissa plant with lemon peels and coriander seeds. She battered the seeds and powdered them. She then asked one of her Christian acquaintances to soak them in pure 45 percent proof alcohol, as she wouldn't allow her hand to touch the white cognac. The mixture was shaken in its container from time to time, and then filtered. Ilham didn't like its taste, but adhered to the recommended doses.

Everyone, except Uncle Sami who didn't leave his flat during her absence, enquired about her condition. Abu Ghayeb donated some money to buy her some painkillers. The teacher on the first floor kept sending her fresh flowers that he'd picked from the public gardens on Abu Nuwas Street. He'd ask me to give her the bouquets saying they were "To lighten her heart a little." Saad, whom we later found out had many other nicknames, sent a wig that was a replica of her own hair, and a set of false eyelashes. He almost cried when he gave them to me saying, "Tell Lulu this is a gift from Aboul Su'ud." Even her friend, the engineer who worked as a butcher, sent her a slice of liver twice a week to provide her with the proteins she needed. In spite of all that, she still refused to see any visitors in her flat. She flicked through Uncle Sami's magazines without uttering a single word.

But Ilham is puzzled: how is she going to acquire a false breast? She can't tell her colleagues at work that she's had it removed as she might lose her job. My aunt does the thinking for her, and says to her, "Take your top off."

Ilham stands up. My aunt places a measuring tape around her chest and notes the measurements on a small piece of paper: the circumference of the breast that remains, and its height. She leaves, saying, "Don't worry, leave it all to me."

My aunt spends the whole night making a breast. She prepares a mixture of beeswax, sawdust, and tiny off-cuts of nylon. She molds the mixture into a moderate sized dome. She then sews a bra with double lining. She places the lump of wax between the two layers of the cotton lining and lifts up her handiwork to reassure herself of its quality. She looks like she is examining a pair of cloth spectacles that dangle down on the right side.

❈

It's another morning and Abu Ghayeb doesn't need me today. He has a meeting of the Amateur Farmers' Association. I will join Saad. He is going to show me how to mix a dull blond hair dye with a grape red color. He will get a bordeaux with a greenish hue that should satisfy the client with the ten o'clock appointment. He is showing me how much peroxide to add to the mixture when we hear angry knocks on the shop's front door. Ilham sticks her head in: "Good morning."

She doesn't allow the rest of her body to come in. "Thank you for the present, Saad."

She nods in my direction. "Dalal, I want to talk to you now, please."

We stand outside. She takes a medium-sized gelatinized blob out of her bag and places it in my hand. Her thin lips twitch as she says, "What about the nipple?"

"What?"

"Ask your aunt to add on a nipple for me. She shouldn't need any measurements for that."

She disappears from sight, with her smoke wafting behind her.

❈

My aunt is rearranging her hair. She uses her reflection in the glass that covers the photo of her father that hangs on the wall. I give her the false breast. Its texture reminds me of the white jellyfish that I caught on the seafront in Copenhagen. How small I was then. I stuck my finger into each hole in its back, then ran all the way up to the thirteenth floor with the dead fish quivering in my hands. I threw it out of the window, watched it leave my hands, and eventually splatter on the pavement. I watched it change as it fell past the floors from a fist-sized shivery fish into a distant ball of spit.

My aunt rummages through her old belongings looking for a solution. She takes out a piece of old wrapping paper made of a thick plastic. Small air-filled bubbles protruded from its surface. It was usually used to wrap fragile things. She takes her nail scissors and carefully cuts a circle around one of the bubbles without piercing it. She then places it over the center of the breast and carefully melts the plastic edges using a lit matchstick, making the bubble stick securely.

My aunt is pleased with the result, but her features change the next moment. Her face takes on a combative appearance that I have not seen there before, as if she has suddenly put on a warrior's mask. This is because of what I said, "By the way, Abu Ghayeb has suggested that I call him Khalo—maternal uncle."

"What?"

I am taken aback by her reaction. "He said that the time had come for us to leave formalities aside. He says that Khalo is more appropriate than Abu Ghayeb or 'my aunt's husband.'"

She cries out, "How could he dare?"

I grow more concerned. "Why don't you want that, my aunt?"

Her response is not directed at me. "Has he decided that he and I have become siblings, or what?"

She drops herself into her chair, and starts bursting the bubbles from the wrapping paper between her fingers, one after the other.

❁

Two nights go by. I head toward the fridge—the heat keeps me awake. I open the door and stick my head into it, seeking a whiff of chilled air. I don't mean to eavesdrop, but my footsteps draw me toward their bedroom. My aunt and her husband are reminiscing about their wish from the Days of Plenty when they hoped they could have a girl of their own. They planned to call her Zahraa, in memory of Abu Ghayeb's mother. Her nickname would have been Zuzu.

After a few *aahs* from her, and an *oof*, and another *oof* from him, I hear him whisper to her in a low voice that sounds like an inhalation of smoke from a hookah, "Give me something to wipe Zuzu with."

The next day, I clean their room, the way I always do, and change Abu Ghayeb's pillowcases. I pick up a few sheets of pink tissue paper from the floor. They are stained with white splotches, like the flowers we used to make in kindergarten. They accidentally fall off the bed. The Zuzus have dried onto them. In the past they were my aunt's dream for a daughter; last night, they were just viscous *aahs*.

After that, the fridge becomes my excuse to eavesdrop.

❁

So, we achieve what the papers call "economic equilibrium." Both my aunt and her husband are now providing for the household equally.

I manage to get a suitable grade in my exams. I am therefore accepted as a first year student at the College of Art at Mustansiriya University, in the Department of French Literature. I take the small minibus that is licensed to carry eighteen passengers. We complete our journey together at a reasonable pace. There is an unpleasant whoosh-ing sound coming from a car beside us; a nylon carrier bag is caught underneath it. The car moves away from us, diminishing in size. An artistic thought goes through my mind. I want to stretch my arm out of the bus to remove the bag and stop the noise. I remember what Abu

Ghayeb said to me when I was a child, about the importance of dividing the ratios in a painting. He started by talking about what he called 'The Art of Arranging the Fridge.' He said, "We have to place the tall, large items at the back. The items that are less tall and large go into the middle row, and then the short and small items are placed at the front."

I lose track of time. The young man sitting next to me spits out of the window. He has a bundle of papers in his lap, and I catch sight of the title, Machiavelli's *The Prince*. He quickly covers the title with his hand when he realizes I am looking at it. I think he might be a student of psychology. I must not forget, Umm Mazin has asked me to photocopy some papers for her. She wants me to use the machine at the university library to make photocopies of the ingredients list for her mixtures. I try to relax in my seat. My head is full of rows of thoughts, like hanging gardens that have not been watered well.

Ilham refused to give me any proper lessons. She just taught me a few basic principles, and how to pronounce words like "camion" and "citron." She's been refusing to speak to anyone, and has recently started saying, "I'm no use anymore." I am forced to depend on myself. My need to spend money forces me to continue juggling my time between my studies and working for both Saad and my aunt's husband. The sanctions choke us like a woolen blanket in the heat of summer.

I wait for Saad under the shade of a palm tree. I remember that Abu Ghayeb told me palm trees had been around for more than eighty million years. I also recalled what Umm Mazin quoted to me from the sayings of the Prophet Muhammad, "If the end of the world is nigh, and one of you has a palm sapling in their hand, then they should plant it in the ground, if they are able to, before the end comes."

A quarter of an hour later, Saad comes back from the baker's shop and unlocks the door to the hair salon. Slung across his shoulder is an old carrier bag with a black-and-white photo of John Travolta and Olivia Newton John on it. The steam emerging from the hot bread inside the bag has distorted her smile. He says in a Lebanese accent, "Hello and twice hello!"

He's barely set foot in the place before he runs out again, almost knocking me over in his haste. He shrieks as he goes by, "Oh Mummy, they're back!"

He stops by the palm tree, panting. He is gesturing at me to go back into the shop, so I do. The hysteria that has struck him is due to five silk worms crawling across the glass window like beautiful finger-length green accordions. I gather them up. I take the bread out of its bag and put them inside it. I then hand him the bag that has the word "Grease" on it, with the insects squirming inside it.

He laughs, "You're my friend, Dalal."

"And you're a coward."

"I admit it."

We go back into the shop together. It is as though he is afraid he might have to face some more. "Talking about friends, you don't seem to have any."

"Ilham is my friend, even though she's a few years older than me. Unfortunately, she no longer seems to be interested in our relationship."

"Poor thing, she's going through a difficult phase. She didn't even ask me to attach those false eyelashes for her."

"Yes, she wears her wig, and then disappears from early in the morning, till the sun goes down."

He hands me a piece of bread with some cheese. That is our breakfast. He then says to me, "I once had a friend. Then I found out that he was picking flowers from my garden. He'd then ring the doorbell and offer them to me."

We are refreshed by the taste of the tea. It has a few mint leaves floating in it. He adds, "If a person is nice, Dalal, then let them bloom in your garden, but if they're evil, then turn them into manure."

"At least my aunt and her husband have embarked on a new phase of friendship."

"So they're now like cream and honey?"

"Not to that extent."

"Is there hope to save the marriage?"

"I don't know about that, but at least he no longer sleeps on the sofa the way he's been doing recently."

"Dalool, when will you realize that the pillow is always the best solution?"

We mix the sugar paste that will be used to remove clients' unwanted body hair. Saad advises me that it is not a good idea to start calling my aunt's husband Khalo. Two cups of sugar, half a cup of cold water, a sprinkling of lemon salts; and it would be better with a spoonful of Abu Ghayeb's honey to make it more malleable. We bring it to a boil briefly, then let it cool while we wait for the next customer.

Saad has allocated the back half of his shop for these hair removal procedures. His flat is just one very clean bedroom, with one very tidy bed. The walls have been painted black and decorated with exceedingly unusual silver stars. Suddenly, there's a flurry of activity amongst the three customers in the shop. The first one says, "Hurry up, Umm Hassan is on her way here."

I watch her gather up all the ashtrays and place them in a corner. She then covers them with a towel and says to Saad, "This is one of Umm Mazin's patients. She'll steal any ashtray she comes across."

The second woman adds, "She'll tuck it away in her handbag and add it to her collection at home."

The third woman puts in her contribution, "They say she has the most beautiful collection of stolen ashtrays. And she doesn't even smoke."

I am at the back when I hear one of the women ask for the services of "the little sugar wax girl." I get so annoyed when I'm called that. I'm no longer a child. I've started to study French literature, yet I still can't get rid of this silly description. But, as Saad says, we have no choice sometimes in the way we earn a living. I open the bedroom door. It is one of my aunt's customers, who has also become one of Umm Mazin's. I remember her; she is the woman who complained that her breasts produced a lot of milk even though she was still a virgin. She lies down on the bed and lifts up her legs. She starts telling me about the premature hormonal imbalance that afflicts her. I curse the times, while I clean up her ugly triangle for her. These are the moments when I hate myself.

By the time I have finished with the lactating virgin, Umm Hassan's face and neck are covered in a paste of honey, ground chickpeas, and blue flower extract. Saad caresses her mask delicately as he says, "Remember my dear, happiness has no wrinkles."

Her blue mask is cracking. He blows gently onto her eyelids. "Happiness doesn't argue with time. Moments of joy don't age."

She checks her wrinkles and leaves. When Saad removes the towel that covers the ashtrays, he cries out, "Oh no, there are two missing!"

CHAPTER ELEVEN

IT'S NOVEMBER. I stick my foot out from underneath the covers to check the warmth of my room, the way cartoon characters would dip their toe in the ocean to check how cold the water was before they leapt in.

The television is showing archive images of war donations. During the conflict with Iran the government insinuated to the people of Baghdad that they should donate their gold. Queues of men and women line up in the large hallways at one of the presidential palaces. They smile to the camera when their names are read out. Unbelievable amounts of women's jewelry are taken out of large carrier bags. Words of gratitude are measured in kilos. The names of those who donate their gold are registered and printed in the next day's newspapers. The hall erupts with applause. The program is followed by a commercial break, and then an announcement about the opening of the Baghdad International Fair.

Abu Ghayeb now attends the inaugural sessions of the fair to discuss the scientific papers that deal with crop yields, pest prevention, and agricultural education. He disappears for ten whole days while he is displaying his product at the honey exhibitions. Umm Mazin is unable to pay my aunt's husband for her quota of honey this month. Instead, as a substitute for the cash, she sends him the only painting from her flat. She has obviously heard from Badriya what our flat looks like. Abu Ghayeb is delighted with the painting of the field that Umm Mazin had acquired from a family fallen on hard times. She accepted the painting as payment in exchange for reading their coffee cups for a whole year.

The war, sanctions, and the Varroa mites have led to the annihilation of ninety percent of the bee colonies, reducing the country's honey production. However, the fruit trees that were planted in the 1980s compensate for some of the destruction that befell the orchard groves in the Gulf War. On the other hand, the creation of a lake in the Shatt al-Arab area using heavy machinery has resulted in large numbers of palm trees being uprooted. This is what I learn on my first visit to the fair with Abu Ghayeb. I am hoping that our visit will end soon as I have an exam the next day. The subject is French theater. My lover will drink the poison: diluted ink in a mouthwash bottle. I'll call out to him, "Chatterton, Je t'aime, mon Chatterton."

My aunt does not accompany us to the fair. She is busy sewing a number of winter coats. I tell her that there are thirty-seven participating nations from Europe and the Arab world. She asks, "So why is Vietnam attending?" I explain to her that the national strategy to promote the cultivation of rice is being developed in collaboration with the Vietnamese. I also tell her that there is an open invitation to market the honey in other cities to coincide with various other agricultural fairs due to be announced soon.

What I do not mention to her are Abu Ghayeb's frequent visits to the Jordanian pavilion after he meets the lady in charge of Dead Sea Products. As she puts her hand out to shake his, she can't conceal the skin condition that affects them both.

"I'm honored. My name is Randa."

He replies with a smile, "Maybe psoriasis is better than a thousand introductions."

They exchange soft chuckles. After that, their meetings become an addiction.

❖

Two months after her operation, Ilham disappears. It isn't because she has died of her cancer, but because she has been imprisoned. The mood of the people living in the building has been shattered by this news, which is conveyed by Hamada, the newspaper boy. We find out that she was arrested along with her boyfriend, the engineer-cum-butcher, in his shop. We were told that Ilham had been selling human organs to him that she stole from the operating theater at the hospital where she worked. He would mince them and sell them with his beef or lamb.

I stay in the salon with Saad. I don't feel like going to the fair with my aunt's husband. I clean the floor, return the brushes to their place, and start washing the dirty towels. Saad has sunk into the chair by the washbasin. He's flung his head backward; he's thinking. We don't say much. His forelock appears mournful as it dangles down to one side. Abu Ghayeb knocks on the door and walks in. "Saad, I want to ask you a favor."

"Please do."

"Can you lend me a bottle of white nail polish? I'll return it to you this evening."

He doesn't mention Ilham. No doubt he has decided that life must go on. Saad hands him the bottle of nail polish. He thanks him and leaves. Saad asks me, "What's he going to do with it?"

"He's going to change the queen."

He returns to his seat. "I don't understand."

"He'll color her back with a spot of white nail polish. That'll expose her wherever she goes." I then add, "The queen bee must be changed every year or two because the Varroa parasites suck her blood around the clock. That weakens her, and she may no longer be alive by the autumn."

As he talks, his neck settles in the washbasin, which takes on the look of a white ceramic collar. "So what will he do with the old queen?"

"The warrior bees will instinctively kill her when the new queen enters the hive."

Saad freezes in his seat. As though posing as a model for a still life painting, he listens to me. "There are many things you don't know about these insects. Can you imagine, in order for Abu Ghayeb to gain one gram of honey, the worker bee must collect three grams of nectar, which means it has to visit more than one thousand apple blossoms, for example?"

He extracts his head from the washbasin. "You've enlightened me. Now I want you to wash my hair."

I am learning by practicing on his scalp. First the avocado shampoo, the scalp must be massaged thoroughly; then the peach-scented conditioner. Then repeat two more times. He says, "Poor Ilham. We won't be seeing her for quite a while."

He then adds, "We may never see her again."

"Maybe."

I say, "It's quite likely that there will be another group of women that we won't be hearing of from now on."

"What do you mean?"

"Some women have disappeared from the streets, accused of prostitution."

"This might just be a rumor."

"How can you tell what's a rumor and what's the truth, Saad?"

He reflects for a moment, "The same way you can differentiate between pure honey, and honey that's been tampered with. You put it underneath your tongue; then you swallow it."

He adds, "Do you remember how she kept saying she was no longer of any use?"

"Now we know why."

"I wonder why Umm Mazin didn't predict this and try to stop her."

I say to him, "In these situations, Umm Mazin merely says, 'People follow their destinies, they have no choice.'"

He gets up from the washbasin. One black hair clings to the white porcelain. I rinse the basin and start drying the boss's hair.

"Mouth, nose, and eye . . . he who talks will die." That was the way that Umm Mazin has abbreviated her new spell to protect those living in our building from all harm. She warns her clients that magic spells can be renewed each year by the one who's cast them. If the person whom the spell was cast upon becomes aware that they have been enchanted, then the spellbinder must rapidly renew the spell and bind them in a more powerful way. That way, it will be more difficult to break the spell. Umm Mazin insists that Ilham's scandalous downfall was caused by a spell, and that it was cast by someone who envied her. She then asks Badriya to purify all the floors using a mixture of Indian incense and moon disc herbs. She calls the concoction, "the termination of all sorrows."

Abu Ghayeb doubles his efforts at the apiary. He is expecting a visit from a number of delegations that had attended the fair. They are coming to view what some of the younger members in the Beekeepers Association are calling "Cells under Sanctions." In these hard times, producing honey has become a source of nutrients and a cure.

I find him in the separation room. He is measuring the viscosity of the honey. To assess its consistency, he places it in a glass container. He fills it, almost to the top, covers it, then turns it upside down to watch the air bubble rise to the surface. His little notebook is filled with memos. Lemon honey, to calm the nerves. Mint honey, to relieve pain. Clover honey, a diuretic. Acacia honey, a cough suppressant.

He turns around when he becomes aware of my presence. "Dalal, how can you differentiate between pure and adulterated honey?"

"If I buy it from you, it's pure; if I get it from somebody else, then it's been tampered with."

He laughs out loud. No one has laughed since Ilham's affair. He says, "Take a spoonful of this. It'll give you heartburn within a few minutes. That's because it's been tampered with."

I don't experience the acid heartburn. Maybe he is testing me by giving me pure honey. He adds, "Pure honey is gelatinous and rubbery in consistency when it's eaten with a spoon; look. Impure honey doesn't have this form."

A short while later, I eat an unripe date. Its unpleasant taste numbs my mouth. "I heard that the owners of the date grove are going to use half of their crop to make arak; and they're going to make vinegar out of the other half."

"Yes, they're planning to launch their produce at the fair next year."

A heavily laden shelf by the window catches my eye. The sun's orange rays traverse the glass jars filled with honey of varying hues. Watery white, brilliant white, white, very pale amber, pale amber, deep amber. I ask him, "How's honey tampered with?"

"Some beekeepers tamper with their honey before it's even taken from the cells. They provide the bees with a sugary solution."

He replaces the top back onto the uncovered honey jar and says, "That type of trickery can be detected by analyzing samples of the honey in a lab."

"So how does Umm Mazin detect evidence of tampering?"

"Umm Mazin analyzes the salesman, not the honey."

He then asks me, "How are your studies coming along?"

"Third year is no joke. And what's happening in the corridors at the university is no joke either."

"You sound exceptionally serious."

"The brother of one of our lecturers has been executed because he was a communist. The lecturer has now been reassigned to the library archives, and is no longer allowed to teach. We're forbidden from having any contact with him. His wife is American. She has taken their daughter and left the country."

"Stay away from politics, Dalal."

"This isn't politics, husband of my aunt; he was my favorite teacher."

"Do you want a break from work at the apiary so that you can concentrate on your studies?"

"No."

"Then prepare yourself for the first delegation that'll be visiting us this week."

I leave, and in my head I can hear Umm Mazin's voice saying, "From the fruits of the date palm and the vine, ye get out wholesome drink, and food: behold, in this also is a sign for those who are wise." And of course, the conclusion comes from Badriya, "Verily spoke God Almighty."

❖

My first meeting with Adel coincides with studying Flaubert.

I come down the stairway, heading toward the apiary. I feel a hair tickling my mouth. Like a child who doesn't know how to deal with a situation like this, I fidget angrily. The hair sticks to the roof of my mouth, half swallowed. Before I reach the ground floor, I put my finger in my mouth to try and get it out, but I am overcome by a choking feeling and the urge to vomit. I decide to pop into Saad's salon for a drink of water, and maybe even a crust of bread to slide the hair down and get some relief.

The door is open. Before I can call out "Saaoudi," I hear voices from the back half of the shop, the part he considers to be his flat. I am intrigued by sounds that pitch like a whale's moaning. I go closer; the voices are speeding up. Saad is ordering, "Put your tongue out."

The second voice obeys, "Please don't overdo it."

"Is it sweet?"

"It is sweet."

The other voice suggests, "Let's try this one, Saad, you bird of happiness. What do you think?"

"I like it soft."

The second voice replies, "Well, I like it grainy."

Saad, the bird of happiness, flings open the door to his room. I try to conceal my eavesdropping by rummaging through the items on the sloping shelf. He does not appear at all surprised. In his hands is a glass container. He is followed by a man carrying another jar. Saad says, "You're just the right person. We have a question."

I say to the other man, "Good morning."

Saad then introduces us, "Adel, meet my friend, Dalal."

He puts his hand out to shake mine. Saad says, "This is smooth honey, and that's grainy honey. Which one is healthier, Dalal?"

"Graininess in the honey indicates that it's been exposed to low temperatures. The sugars inside it have crystallized."

The voice repeats, "I like it grainy."

I answer him, "That means it's pure. Honey that's been tampered with doesn't crystallize in the winter."

I can no longer bear it. I ask Saad, "Have you got some bread?"

"Yes, take what you want from the back."

I go into his flat. The whale song is coming from the television. It is *Calypso*, the program about oceans that is on every Friday morning. His home is always the same, one very clean bedroom, with one very tidy bed. I finally swallow the hair.

Saad insists that I spend the day of rest with him, but Abu Ghayeb is waiting for me. The man with the voice glances briefly at my mouth. His eyes are the color of nutmeg whip. He is taller than me, and taller than Saad. His neck is slender and strong. His facial bones stand out to the side like the muscles of a horse's jaw. The way he stands is so rigid; he reminds me of Ilham. His temples have streaks of gray like strands of castor sugar. We sit down, and then Saad says, "Dalal is a beekeeper."

"I don't intend to become one; I do, however, help out my aunt's husband in his work."

Saad says, "She also helps me out in here, and in addition to all that she's a student of languages." He adds, "How clever!"

Adel acknowledges with a nod while Saad steers the introductions, "You too are very clever!"

"I'm only doing my duty."

I ask him, "So what is it you do?"

"I work in the field of social education."

Saad cries out, "Gosh, how modest you are!"

"Don't get yourself worked up, Aboul Su'ud; that's the truth."

Saad interrupts our concentration on each other. He leaps into our midst offering us cigarettes. "Adel is a physiotherapist. He fits false limbs."

I don't smoke. He doesn't smoke either. "No thank you, Saad. You know that smoking kills the salary."

"Then go out and become self-employed."

"Where do you work?"

"In a specialized clinic. We look after those who have been injured in the war and as a result of the bombing. We try to provide false limbs made of wood or plastic for those patients who've had one of their limbs amputated. One of my responsibilities is to paint those limbs to match the patient's complexion."

Saad interrupts once again, "You provide the suitable limb for the individual patient."

"Once the limb has been manufactured, the wood or plastic must be covered with the appropriate color. What I mean is, if the patient has a dark complexion, I can't provide them with a white hand."

"A spare parts engineer."

"Orthopedic surgeons are in great demand these days. I wish I'd studied medicine."

"As the proverb goes, 'When his youth was gone, he went to the scribe.'"

"The problem we have is that we're beginning to run out of the dyes we need. We no longer have the suitable ones. The only colors you can get these days in the markets are blues and greens. Can you imagine amputees walking around with multi-colored limbs?"

I ask him, "What did you study?"

"Nursing, and then physiotherapy. You can't imagine how difficult it is when you have to deal with children who've lost a limb. How can you convince a nine year old to wear a blue hand made of wood, and go to school with it?"

Saad brings in the coffee. "My God, how can you deal with things like that?"

"By accepting my mission."

His mustache has no shades of gray in it. It's neatly kempt and trembles as he sips his coffee. "I came to ask you for a favor."

"Ask away, Addoula."

"You know how I hate nicknames."

"Of course, Addoula."

His voice reaches me like a wave of warm olive oil.

"I need hues that are close to the color of human flesh. Fair, dark-skinned, or pink. I want you to sell me hair dyes. I'll mix them with other agents and use them to paint the artificial limbs."

Saad heads toward the shelf and starts handing him some boxes. "This one I've used. Try it; if it works, I'll order another batch from the salesman."

"Thank you. You're contributing to a good deed."

I close the door on my way out. Inside, Saad's merriment alternates with Adel's seriousness.

✻

My aunt's husband is optimistic about the opportunities that the fair will bring him. The laws now allow Iraqis to sign contracts with individuals and Arab companies who wish to invest in livestock and agricultural projects. In his case, he embarks on his private trading on the third day of the fair. Abu Ghayeb invites Miss Randa to join him at a meeting attended by scientists and researchers from the Ministry of Higher Education and Scientific Research and the Atomic Energy Commission. She attends as an elegant listener, then expresses her admiration for the meeting's emphasis on palm trees, dates, and sugar beet production. In return, she invites us to attend an exhibition of her country's products.

It is a five-minute walk to the Jordanian pavilion. She takes out some packaged products. The covers have beautiful images of sea waves underneath red and green suns. Her presentation is as smooth as her hair. "These are tonics, refreshing liquids, invigorating agents, and also pain killers. These are antibiotics that must be given directly into a vein for serious illnesses. Less serious cases are dealt with in the patient's home."

Abu Ghayeb says, "With phototherapy, soaks, and wearing cotton clothes."

"Precisely."

They speak the same language, but his questions overpower her delicate accent, "Have you got anything that controls the dandruff?"

"This is a shampoo that contains coal tar extracts."

She then suggests, "Why don't you try them, sir?"

I can visualize his joints relaxing as he listens to the way she talks to him. She continues, "I have an oily ointment that relieves itching."

He sits down on a chair. In his lap rests a large map of the fair that he picked up at the north gate. She says, "We also have treatments for mildew, should you need them."

In the end, they perform an exchange. He gives her a jar of honey, and she gives him special tablets to make his skin more sensitive to sunlight. She warns him to expose himself to no more than a moderate amount of sunlight so that the treatment will be effective. She adds, "Eating a small piece of bread before this treatment would make it easier on the stomach."

She lifts a blotchy finger and points at him, "As you are a beekeeper . . ."

His eyes shine as she says the word "keeper." "You must avoid getting sunburned. It would make your condition worse."

He knows that information well, but still he says, "Is that so?"

"We also suggest that those who develop the illness mix with other patients in order to exchange opinions, complaints, and experiences."

Abu Ghayeb is keen to exchange information with her. He takes down her work address: The Health Spa at the Dead Sea Hotel, Aghwar Road, Jordan. He also writes down his details for her on a small piece of paper: Tennis Court No. 1, the Alwiya Club, near the Teachers' Building, Baghdad.

He then adds, "By the way, the roundabout that our building looks out onto—it used to be known as the Square of the Unknown Soldier. It's now going to be officially renamed Firdaws Square; and they're going to put up a statue of the president in it . . . another one."

CHAPTER TWELVE

WE WAIT FOR Miss Randa in the reception area at the club. It is his turn to display his local produce on-site at the tennis court. Before going to bed, Abu Ghayeb applied her ointment to his skin, and wrapped up the badly affected areas. When he woke up, he noted that the color of his skin had started to change. The Sudanese delegation is late, so we spend half an hour in the lounge drinking tea. She asks for coffee. She says to him, "Don't worry. Psoriasis always gets worse in the winter."

"I ache in my joints."

"That too is part of the illness."

She takes something out of her handbag. It is a gift; a bottle of phenol. "Try this and see if it helps you."

"I'm going to develop premature skin damage with all these treatments I'm trying!"

"We have no choice. Your affliction is much less severe than some of the foreigners who come to our health spa. They spend weeks in the salty water before they see a result."

"It's a curse, Miss Randa."

"Or merely our fate."

She inserts the tip of her blotchy finger into the cup's handle. "In any case, we have to maintain our general health. We have to exercise, eat well and in moderation."

She adds, "And avoid stress, of course."

She can't understand why my aunt's husband and I exchange glances. He says, "Your psoriasis is painful, is that right?"

"You can't imagine."

"Have you tried soaking in marigold?"

"Yes, for six months, but it didn't do me any good."

"Then try soaking in almond oil."

"I'll try."

"The general advice is to keep the skin clean by showering daily, and avoiding contact with all chemical agents that are used in domestic cleaning solutions."

"I see that you're well-informed regarding this condition."

"I had no choice."

Her gentle smile does not befit the topic of conversation she is about to embark on. She adjusts the way she is sitting. He does not avert his admiring gaze from her matching elegant black trousers and orange top made of soft wool. She lowers her voice and says, "I'll tell you another secret if you promise not to embarrass me."

"I promise."

"Urine treatment; an accepted method in France."

"Topically?"

"Unfortunately not, and that makes it even more difficult. Some health institutes recommend drinking—I'm sorry to use the word 'pee'—as a treatment for psoriasis. But most people are reluctant to partake of this treatment and prefer to take vitamin pills instead."

I join their discussions involuntarily. "That's disgusting!"

"I know, but the patients don't have to drink other peoples' fluids, just their own. They also have to be vegetarians, as meat eaters produce high levels of urea."

My aunt's husband says, as his face wrinkles, "In other words, the treatment for the disease is based on the illness itself."

"Exactly. Some experts suggest that since the urine contributes to the illness, it can therefore be used as a treatment."

Miss Randa is once again totally relaxed as she continues, "The doctor sends the sample to the pharmacy with the prescription. The usual dose is fifteen drops of urine diluted in water, to be taken half an hour before breakfast."

He says, "But if the body is excreting these substances, then why are we putting them back in again?"

Randa laughs. "In any case, it doesn't matter. We're not vegetarians."

I say to her, "But this is vile."

"Not as vile as the miserable existence of some patients."

❊

The circle of visitors is now complete. The group comprises the delegate from the Agricultural Reform Society in the Sudan, the representative of the Modern Irrigation Projects in Algeria, and Randa. They all sit down in the warm sunshine. The chairs form a half circle in the middle of the apiary. Abu Ghayeb stands in their midst, surrounded by his teaching materials. Their first enquiries concern the effects of the no-fly-zone regulations that prevent all flights between a latitude of thirty-two and thirty-six degrees. This means that no crop-spraying airplanes are allowed to fly; and the fields cannot be protected from disease. However, once they have tasted the honey, they become engrossed in the delivery my aunt's husband is making. He enthusiastically explains to the delegate from the Sudan who has asked, "How is the honey ripened?"

"A number of worker bees stand at an angle to each other. They flap their wings, creating an air current that promotes the evaporation of water from the solution. That results in ripening of the honey."

"What about this heating and cooling of the hives that I've heard about?"

"Yes, bees are cold-blooded insects so they adjust the temperature of the air inside the hive."

Abu Ghayeb points to the basin with the floaters on its surface and adds, "That's where the bees get their water. They store it in the discs while another group of bees stand on the cells and aerate the water to cool the hive."

"And when it's cold?"

"The bees congregate in the form of an intermingling mass. They consume honey and metabolize it as they breathe. That generates heat and provides warmth for the colony.

Randa asks the next question. She hides her stained hand underneath her woolen blouse in the presence of the others. "Excuse me, what's swarming?"

"It's a natural instinct that the bees inherit from one generation to the next. The queen bee leaves with a significant number of worker bees in order to set up a new home, away from the hive they've lived in."

"Why do they do that?"

"The benefits of swarming are to multiply and increase the number of colonies. For some beekeepers however, swarming is a financial loss as the bees may leave the area and their keeper is unable to retain them."

We feel a cool breeze. My job is to serve hot lemon tea to those attending. The Algerian delegate is aware that I am studying French. He says to me, "Merci," then asks a question in his North African accent: "Mr. Abu Ghayeb, do these apiaries provide you with a good profit?"

"Let's say that we're now able to eat more than just potatoes on their own, with dates for dessert."

As he talks, I sit down in a corner that has a variety of wild plant life. I test myself to see if I can identify them: wild mustard, dog's tongue, and stork's beak.

Suddenly, Randa indicates with her orange arm to where I was sitting and asks me, "What are those?"

"Liquorice roots."

"And that?"

"A small radish."

"And that one?"

"The plant we call 'the beads of the farmer's daughter.'"

"Your world is fascinating."

I think to myself that I doubt my aunt would share this opinion. I catch a glimpse of her every now and then peeping out at us from my bedroom window. Abu Ghayeb is answering a question I missed: "Of course, there are those who guard the hive. Each colony of bees has their own distinctive scent. They'll prevent any enemy or unknown bees from entering their hive."

I watch my aunt from my position by the grassy area. Abu Ghayeb carries on, "If an enemy approaches, the defending bees will stand on their hind legs, lifting their front legs into the air. Their feelers stand up, and they fold their wings. They stand ready to defend their colony."

My aunt has disappeared for a few moments. She soon returns, with the phone in her hand. She speaks on the phone as she observes our gathering.

Randa asks with emotion, "Do the bees learn to fly like birds?"

"Each bee has to practice flying with the larger bees to identify the landmarks that surround their colony."

Adel, Saad's friend, was right about the lack of dyes in the market-place. It seems that the local producers have started mixing whatever dyes remain with any other product. I offer the guests a sweet snack, dates stuffed with nuts and sesame seeds. They are placed inside small napkins of a shocking red color. Abu Ghayeb then offers each one of them a small jar of honey. He has placed them in carrier bags that are a bright, screaming purple. They say that the only toilet paper available in the shops these days has a silvery hue, and that it leaves its glittery mark when it's used.

The meeting is over, and Randa is given a bouquet of flowers. It is made up of wolf grape stalks decorated with bride's arm flowers. As the sun inclines in farewell, she says to my aunt's husband, "We'll soon be organizing a brief presentation about the benefits of the Dead Sea Products. I'll provide you with the details."

"I'll most certainly be attending."

They all leave via the club parking lot. Their drivers are waiting for them. One is black, and the other is white.

I can't believe that my aunt has acted so promptly! It didn't occur to me that she was talking to Umm Mazin on the phone. She had asked her for a charm while observing our movements in the apiary that day. I found out later on that the spell they'd agreed upon consisted of the words "Flee and die cursed bee . . . Get away, shoo . . . Let God preserve this nest." Badriya told me that Umm Mazin had acquired a dove and cut off its head. She assumed that I was aware of their plans. Her mistress had then stuffed the bird's head along with the potion into its abdomen. She had then sewn up the bird's neck with a black thread she asked my aunt to provide. It didn't end there. She'd then asked our neighbor, the woman with the freckleless face, to take the dead bird wrapped in cellophane, and leave its body in the Jordanian pavilion at the fair. Our neighbor was going to use the pretext of showing Randa some beautiful textiles. She was going to pretend that she was an agent for the weaving factories in the Indian pavilion.

So what should I do now? Should I warn Abu Ghayeb, or ask my aunt to desist, or attend the lecture with him and look for the bird wrapped in cellophane during the intermission?

Her lipgloss shines when she notes his presence beside me in the middle of the lecture hall. We were a little late. Randa had already started. "The beneficial minerals in the water include the chlorides of calcium, potassium, sodium, and magnesium."

They exchange glances from afar.

"There's a high level of evaporation from the waters of the Dead Sea. This layer of water vapor creates a mist of gases that acts as a natural filter for the atmosphere."

She continues, "This mist filters out the harmful ultraviolet rays, thus preventing these rays from causing sunburn."

Half an hour later, Randa concludes her talk by explaining the benefits of dissolved bromide. Her young assistant starts handing out little booklets about the health spa to those attending. She says, "You'll feel completely relaxed during an experience such as this. You'll not feel any embarrassment as you lie in the sun with the others."

She concludes, "I thank you all for attending."

So far, Umm Mazin's dove hasn't prevented Randa from accompanying Abu Ghayeb as he makes his preparations to exhibit his honey during the Spring Fair in Mosul. Nor does it prevent them on the seventh day of the fair from traveling to Dyala, to the Citrus Fair where he will meet the delegates from the Arab Association of Beekeepers.

At the fridge door I hear, or rather, I decided to listen in on my aunt's argument with her husband. She says to him, "You don't love me anymore."

"It's no longer an issue of love between us."

"Is that so? Have our feelings for each other gone?"

"Love at our age is a question of understanding."

"And do we no longer understand each other?"

"After all these years together, you can still surprise me with a question like that!"

"I want to be sure."

"Love is the ability to converse, and we've lost that interaction."

"You mean we no longer have a relationship."

"We've lived our lives together. What more do you want?"

"I feel that we're growing apart."

"Don't you think that we've outgrown romantic scenarios?"

"No."

"What? Do you no longer consider me to be a fungal swampland, an arrogant art aficionado? Not even a failed trader?"

"Maybe I've wronged you."

"Don't retreat."

"Things have just started to brighten up. We were exhausted in the past."

"Do you associate our success at work with our relationship?"

"Not entirely, but at least the financial pressures we were under have now been resolved."

"I therefore wish you an even larger income."

"Don't say that; 'People can decimate their wealth by afflicting themselves with their own evil eye.'"

"It seems that Umm Mazin is still providing you with her wisdom."

My aunt's voice becomes slightly uneasy. "What does that poor woman have to do with our situation?"

"Poor woman? In any case, it doesn't matter. We've had our share of genuine drama."

"What do you mean?"

"I mean that life will go on, and I'll continue to treat her courteously."

"And will you treat me courteously as well?"

He doesn't answer her. It seems that he is trying to go to sleep. She insists, "The same way you're courteous to that fresh creature from Amman?"

"Now I begin to understand your anxieties."

"I have every right."

"What's wrong with you? All we're doing is discussing the problems we have in common."

"Don't you have enough problems in common with me?"

"I meant our illness."

"I don't want to hear that you're spending most of your time with her."

When Abu Ghayeb starts growling at her, I hurry back to my room. "You can hear whatever you want."

A few moments later, he ends up on the sofa.

✳

The next day, my aunt expresses an unexpected interest in the experiment that is due to be undertaken in the storeroom, under the supervision of an expert Tunisian apiarist. She hears her husband discussing it on the phone. The plan is to extract the venom from the bees for medicinal purposes. He is due to arrive at one o'clock. She turns up at five minutes to one.

They set up the necessary equipment. The expert places the worker bees in a clean glass container, and covers it with a sheet of filter paper soaked in ether. The bees are soon anaesthetized, and their venom flows out along the walls of the container and onto its base. He then washes the beaker and lightly heats the resulting cloudy solution. The water evaporates and what is left behind is the venom extract.

He says, "The next step is to dry out the bees in a warm room, or in the sunshine, and then return them to their hive."

He wraps up a rubber hose and returns it to its box. He adds, "The benefit of this method is that it can provide reasonable amounts of venom from a thousand bees, without killing them. This, however, isn't the total amount of venom since a large number of bees may die during the extraction process."

Abu Ghayeb then asks him, "What about the use of bee stings as a form of treatment?"

"This form of treatment is practiced in Japan. The stinger is removed from the bee using a fine pair of forceps. It's then inserted into the patient's skin. It causes a minimal amount of pain, and the venom is absorbed into the body to exert its effect."

My aunt interrupts, "Excuse me sir, what illnesses are treated with this venom?"

He answers her while drying a long-necked vial, "Ringing in the ears and blockage of the nasal septum."

I return to the fair with Abu Ghayeb and the Tunisian expert. In the taxi, I wonder what was going through her mind.

❈

When my aunt learned that bees could be affected by disease, like any other insects, but that, unlike any other domesticated creature, they didn't transmit these diseases to human beings, and when Abu Ghayeb informed her that he was considering the official invitation he'd received to visit the Dead Sea, she retreated to her room for two whole days. Her Singer sewing machine hummed continuously throughout that time.

Baghdad International Fair closed its doors, and Abu Ghayeb packed his suitcase. He said he'd only be away for a few days. That week, my aunt produced the most beautiful coat I'd ever seen. It conformed to the contours of her body. The shoulders were padded, it had a narrow waist, and a wide train. Its beauty, however, resided in the excellent quality of the mustard-colored wool she used. She acquired it from our neighbor, who had bought it from the Afghan pavilion. My aunt then proceeded to embroider its broad collar with some unusual cord that resembled fur. She used alternating shades of mustard and black. She wore her high heels, and put up her blond hair with the bronze-colored streaks that Saad had applied for her. I was laughing inside as she paraded herself in front of me haughtily. Is this what jealousy does to women?

I was mistaken. Her interest was no longer in the bees' venom. It was the appearance of Randa on the scene that had released her creativity. It was jealousy that had driven her to the apiary without her husband's knowledge. She collected the dead bees that dried out in the sun after they had been anaesthetized. She pulled off their heads and their stingers, and submerged the rest in a preservative mixed with a clear glue. She left the bees' wings attached to their bodies before she mummified them. This gave them an extra sheen. That was how she obtained round balls of synthetic fur that she used to embroider the coats this season!

❖

Saad opens the door. I feel the need for a change, so I adopt his style: "Hi."

He adjusts his forelock: "Hi. . . ."

His smile widens as he continues to stand in the doorway: "Along with God's blessing and his mercy."

I go in, and he shuts the door behind me, "What's new?"

"'Buzzy Bee' has gone, and 'Fashion Chick' is at home."

"What about you?"

"I'll do my studying at the apiary till he gets back."

We sit down and Saad says, "I presume Umm Mazin felt dejected when she found out that her spell had no effect."

"In spite of that, she didn't give up or desist. She's preparing another concoction to recapture my aunt's husband."

"Will you tell him?"

"I don't think so."

"How innocent you are, Dalal."

"There's a difference between innocence and being fed up with paranoia."

I take my shoes off to rest my feet. "I don't know how things ended up like this. Did Abu Ghayeb reject his wife before or after he met Randa? Was my aunt attached to him before another woman appeared in his life, or did she start rushing about trying to hang onto him after that, because she was afraid that she might lose him? And what does marriage have to do with success at work, outside the home? How can the situation be salvaged with mixtures of herbs and spells?"

Saad replies, "Do you think that Randa seduced him intentionally?"

"It didn't seem that way to me. All they talked about was their psoriasis."

"Maybe their relationship is a clean one."

"How could my aunt be jealous of an afflicted woman?"

"Because she's a woman."

"Jealousy and envy are for beautiful women only."

"Do you really think that it's only beautiful women who attract men?"

"Of course."

"I disagree with you."

"Disagree as you wish."

"And I'm not the only one who thinks like that."

"Sometimes, I can't understand the way you think, Saad. Tell me, why would a man be attracted to a woman with a problem like mine?"

"I told you that I wasn't the only one who thought like that. I'll answer your naïve question by telling you that my friend was fascinated by you."

"Adel?"

"Yes."

"Don't tease me."

"I swear to you. He said that your eyes were beautiful."

"Then, he must be attracted to faces drawn in cubism style."

Saad is unable to control himself. He bursts out laughing vigorously. "So you insist that you're not attractive?"

"An attractive personality is one thing, a beautiful appearance is something totally different."

"And his visit to me asking for dyes was one thing, and his enquiries about you were also totally different."

"He came to see you a second time?"

"This morning."

"All right, for your sake, I'll translate his attraction based on the fact that he's so used to dealing with people who have a disfigurement."

"You're belittling the issue."

"What issue?"

"Give him a chance."

"You look so serious, Saad. Don't frighten me."

"It's he who's serious."

"How strange."

Saad leaps up from his seat, "That's it! You've just described him. He loves things that are strange: foods, faces, places. He always says that each person looks at life through his own eyes, and not through anyone else's."

"Saad, I'm warning you. Don't entangle me in things I can do without."

"Do you mean that you're afraid that you might do wrong?"

"Brother, don't force thoughts into my head."

"Dalool, are the memories of our mistakes not the most beautiful things we possess?"

"Our mistakes make us more cowardly."

"I'm the one who commits the right error at the right time."

"Rubbish!"

"Believe me. I classify errors into two types: mistakes and delightful mistakes."

"And do you also classify the price we pay into two types?"

"What's wrong with you? Even clouds will eventually become water and end up coming down as rain. The clouds themselves are merely water from this earth that has grabbed its chance to fly."

"In other words, it's a closed circle."

"You stubborn girl, it means that life is a natural cycle!"

<hr>

My head is filled with half-formed thoughts. I have to find a way to pass my exams in the compulsory civic education lessons. I can't understand the assigned text: Theoretical Applications in the Context of Applied Theories. The teacher of this subject offered to exempt me from the exam if I'd translate his thesis for him about the life of the Khedive Ismail in Egypt. I also have to write an essay about a poem of the Middle Ages. I sit down in the apiary analyzing verses by Guillaume de Lorris in the sunshine. On the floor beside me is an empty bottle of water that Randa drank during the meeting. I gaze at the label. It has the word "Rivulet" in big blue letters. Below that, it says, "A ton of water passes through our bodies each year, be aware of the water that you drink."

After an hour, I am bored. I pick up a scientific journal and read about a means of eradicating the Varroa insects. I love the words "Ant's Acid," a translation of "Formic Acid." Apparently mixing it with their nutrients protects the honeybees from the parasitic mites that live in their respiratory system. The parasites reproduce there, preventing the bees from getting enough oxygen. This eventually results in the bees' death.

My aunt calls out for me to join her in Umm Mazin's flat; she has new potions for sale. A lack of marriage proposals can be dealt with by giving a girl cedar leaves after verses from the Qur'an, from Surat al-Baqara, have been recited over them. The girl must bathe in water that the leaves have been soaked in. The water must not be allowed to drain into the sewers; it has to be thrown outside the house. She refers to a woman who remains unmarried as having her tail knotted.

For infertility, she recommends a candle and honey. The verses from the Qur'an that have to be recited are from Surat Maryam, to reaffirm that nothing is impossible. The infertile woman is then given the oil of the seed of blessing. In order to cast a love spell, Surat Yusuf must be recited over the loved one's name and the name of his mother to make him come back.

They are muttering up there on the top floor. Umm Mazin smears the green grease that has been extracted from wind grass onto a small sheet of paper. She hums to herself, "She saw his mustache and fantasized about him. . . . Were it not for the mustache, she would never have wanted him." She then writes on a sheet of paper that has a triangle drawn on it, inside a circle, inside a square. She writes the letters of Abu Ghayeb's name, son of Zahraa; and Randa's name. She wraps the paper around something she claims is the protuberant part of a hoopoe bird's ribcage. Then I follow my aunt as she goes downstairs to the apiary and sews this charmed bundle into the lining of Abu Ghayeb's protective suit, which hangs behind the door.

After she is done, I ask her, "My aunt, are you that jealous of her?"

"I'm jealous over him."

"What if Abu Ghayeb were to find out?"

"He won't."

"Didn't I find out about the secret of the dove from Badriya?"

"That stupid servant has no social contact with any men."

"But Aunt, you're burdening me with weighty secrets."

"Maybe you bear secrets for him too!"

I hadn't expected that reply. "Why do you have no doubts about Umm Mazin and the truths she offers you?"

She kicks the plastic water bottle with her foot. "Because I have no choice."

At that time, we had no idea that that green bundle would be one of the last concoctions prepared by that woman on the fifth floor.

CHAPTER THIRTEEN

WHAT UMM MAZIN hadn't predicted was the missile that ripped through the air just after midnight. Its blast took out the left wing of her flat. Like a razor blade, it cut through the tops of the trees in the orchard behind the club. It embedded itself at an angle, on the riverbank, but it failed to explode.

It shook our beds. Within minutes we'd gathered in the corridors of the building and started checking on each other. I knocked on Uncle Sami's door, who called out from inside, "I'm alright, don't worry." The knock on Umm Mazin's door, however, wasn't answered. In the end the teacher from the first floor and Saad broke it down by force. They stood aside to allow my aunt and I to rush in and find out what was going on.

The missile had broken all the windows. The curtains were torn to shreds, and some of the chairs had been knocked over by the force of the missile's trajectory. The bedrooms were empty. We found the two women on the floor in the kitchen. The lady of the house was sprawled out on the floor. Her dress was lifted up revealing cuts and bruises all over her body. Her servant was hunched up with a big cooking pot over her head. The pot covered her head and shoulders. Below it, the rest of her body was shaking uncontrollably. It looked as though she was sitting underneath a church bell made of tarnished brass. It seemed that they'd been in the middle of preparing some potion or other.

Hundreds of small fragments from the wreckage of the windows, the glass containers and the porcelain cups were scattered everywhere. Chickpeas and lupine had been thrown up into the air. The damaged plastic ablution jugs were stacked in a corner. Colored fluids oozed out from bottles mingling with each other: vinegar, milk, and beetroot juice. The table was covered with aniseed. Several cloves of garlic hanging on the wall had burst open from the effect of the pressure. A cup full of cumin and a container full of chicken claw plant had fallen into a vat of emulsified lamb's tail plant. The borage plant had mingled with the sweet marjoram. Half made-up bags of goat's beard and Venus's eyelashes that had been requested by her clients lay to one side.

As I made my way forward, I stepped on some hawthorn berries, while my aunt inadvertently crushed some of the lawyer's ear plant beneath her feet. Tongues of regular honey and tongues of enchanted honey were crawling across the floor in every direction. Badriya's quaking voice could be heard from underneath the pot that still protected her head. She was repeating a phrase form the Qur'an incessantly, "Say: I seek refuge with the Lord of the Dawn." The echo of her words reverberated from underneath the copper pot that looked like a skirt. They sounded like the chimes from a bell, "Dawn . . . dawn . . . dawn."

Saad and the teacher dragged Umm Mazin out by her abaya. She was still as unconscious as a punching bag sliding on its back, with two fat, dark feet capped with bluish toes protruding from the rim. As for Badriya, we were able to remove her with some difficulty from inside her hideaway. We placed the servant on my bed, and sat Umm Mazin down in the big armchair in the sitting room. We washed her face with cold water, and my aunt removed the top of a bottle of strong perfume underneath her nostrils to try and rouse her. When she opened her eyes, the first thing she saw was the scene on the wall in front of her, an oil painting. Everything in it had a black tinge mixed with a reddish, purple hue. From the bottom corner, two skeletons and two skulls leapt out. Through their eye sockets, one could see a darker background. There were no openings for their mouths; but they did however have hair. Coils of barbed wire hung down like tresses from either side of their heads. I tried to imagine what was going through Umm Mazin's mind. She might have imagined them to be two women attempting to straighten out their barbed wire hair. The first skeleton might have been telling the second, "Skully, darling, I feel like a braid today." Umm Mazin's eyes rolled upwards flipping into slots of white as she looked at the painting, and she passed out again muttering, "Death has caught up with the one who has neglected her prayers."

❁

The next day, Umm Mazin asks my aunt for the keys to Ilham's empty flat. Nobody has come forward to claim it, so she suggests that she can live there with her maid until she is able to sort out her affairs. Ilham's things are just as she left them, everything is still in its place. Her cotton nursing uniform hangs in the cupboard, the white rubber shoes are under the bed, and the stethoscope hangs behind the door. We hadn't attempted to aerate the flat since she'd gone. The odor of her cigarette smoke still lingers in the curtains. It feels strange moving Umm Mazin in there. She has developed problems with her blood pressure, and hardly moves at all for two weeks.

The date palms have lost their heads. The orchard has become an area of upright trunks with no palm fronds above them. My aunt gazes out onto those silent columns. She hardly ever leaves her position by my bedroom window. She narrows her eyes as if she's trying to concentrate angrily on a pressing matter. She curses Abu Ghayeb because he didn't leave her a contact telephone number. She was unable to join her husband. The travel restrictions forbid a woman to travel without a male member of her family to escort her. She needs a father or a brother or an uncle to accompany her; and where would she be able to generate such a relative for this purpose? She sits down beside the phone, hoping he will ring, but the phone remains quiet for several days. She eventually gives up and decides to spend the night on the second floor to look after Umm Mazin whose condition has worsened. She will check her blood pressure and temperature using Ilham's equipment.

My aunt and I won't be missing each other tonight.

❀

I go down to the ground floor to spend some time with Saad. He has just been to visit the owners of the orchard to console them about their impending bankruptcy. He is a slick communicator, and he ends up buying a large container of date arak from them, to try it out.

It is an onerous sundown. The fears of a further bombardment of the city are renewed. The activities quiet down as everyone questions the shape of the morrow. Saad is playing a tape of soothing Chinese music. The soft tone of the singer reaches our ears like the mewing of a cat. "Has Umm Mazin settled in?"

"Not yet, her low blood pressure is stopping her from getting about."

"Maybe she needs a curative potion!"

Badriya has taken over looking after her affairs that have been put on hold. She spends hours on the fifth floor trying to clean up their flat, then returns to the second floor to look after her mistress.

"And your aunt?" he asks.

"She spends most of her time sitting beside the telephone. She distracts herself by sewing, then goes down and joins Umm Mazin."

"Your aunt is loyal; always waiting."

"Does she love him that much, Saad?"

"Perhaps she hates him."

"How, after all these years of being together?"

"This is a case that builds itself with time, it's called the relationship of 'I love you because I hate you, and I hate you because I love you.'"

He walks past me adding, "Mind you, this applies to both parties."

He pauses a little to think. "Either she hates him, or she feels it's too late to change him."

"Why would she want to change him?"

"Have you ever heard of a woman who doesn't want to change her husband?"

He stands in front of the mirror to cut some hairs that aren't in line with the rest of his forelock. "What about the teacher?"

"He's volunteered to replace the broken glass in Umm Mazin's apartment."

"The residents of the building are now just like the value of the U.S. dollar—up and down all the time!"

A short while later he sighs. "What shall I do? Women won't go to their 'coiffeur' in times like these."

"Do you want to help me out in the apiary until my aunt's husband comes back? Maybe by then, things will have returned to normal."

His face curls up in horror at the suggestion, "Ew! Certainly not! Thank you, anyway. Bees? Me? That's impossible."

A voice lands on us from the front entrance: "What's impossible?"

Saad runs to welcome him. As they hug, I compare Adel to all the students in my class. He turns toward me: "Thank God you're unharmed."

"Likewise."

"Dalal is suggesting that I might spend some time with her amidst the bees. Imagine!"

"Why not? You could do with a sting or two."

We sit down in a triangular layout, with Saad at the tip, sitting on the sofa. Adel and I sit on the revolving chairs. We draw them forward to the edge of the table that stands in our midst. Adel says, "The missile has been examined. It was faulty, that's why it failed to explode when it struck the riverbank."

"Wow! Can you imagine a missile being faulty; like children's fireworks that sometimes don't go off."

"You should be saying, 'Thank God for that.'"

"I'm beginning to get depressed with this destruction all around us."

"Sometimes, Saad, we have to experience destruction in order to concentrate on building ourselves up."

Saad lifts up his hand annoyed. "Where do you come up with these silly philosophical concepts from?"

Adel hesitates slightly before answering him. "From that little caterpillar crawling up the back of the sofa behind you. Don't move."

Saad freezes in his spot. His neck contracts as he starts screaming, "No, no, I beg you, save me!"

We both burst out laughing. Saad is still suffering seriously. "What are you waiting for?"

Adel leaves him in torture. "And what would my reward be?"

He squeals at him, "Adel, quickly, remove the beast from my back."

"Not before you tell me what I deserve in return."

"A bottle of arak."

"And what about Dalal?"

He starts to shake as he imagines the green creature coming closer to him. "Oh my God, Dalal, do something."

I get up from my chair, but Adel's hand stops me, "What's the hurry? What did you say, Saad? What's Dalal's reward going to be?"

"A box of Kit Kats."

"Where from?"

"I bought them yesterday."

"How can you afford to buy sweets in times like these?"

"I didn't buy them, brother. I had a craving for them, so I arranged a small exchange."

"What did you trade them for?"

"Are you interrogating me?"

"And I'll enjoy doing that."

"I can't move."

"The creature is very close to your neck."

Saad's eyes are about to burst out of their sockets. "Stop it!"

"Now tell me, what did you trade them for, Saad?"

"Electric hair rollers."

His forelock turns solid in front of his head. "Dalal, save me!"

We only rescue him from the silkworm after he has reassured us that the chocolates are imported, and haven't been looted from Kuwait, what is known as 'the spoils of war.' Like many people, we had sworn never to lay hands on items that were brought back from the crisis.

Saad shouts, "Anyway, many years have passed since that war, what kind of chocolate would stay fresh all that time?"

Adel then places the bottle of arak on the table. Inside the three glasses, the arak turns from a clear colorless liquid into a thick milky one. We start dipping the delicious Kit Kat fingers in it. We extinguish the bitterness of the alcohol with the sweet, then extinguish the sweet with the alcohol, and so on. We have no idea what we are celebrating.

We divide the night among ourselves until the objects around me begin to dance. Saad gets up and changes the tape to Arabic songs. Suddenly he takes his shirt off. He takes a wide eyeliner pen and starts to draw several slanting lines across his abdomen. He says they are the chords of a guitar. He takes another sip of arak, and then starts tickling his tummy in a comical, theatrical way. He is pretending to play his guitar. He then starts singing, "You with the burning eyes . . . tell me when will we meet."

A short while later, he gets hold of a black scarf and starts dancing around me. He covers my face with the scarf, except for my eyes. His hips don't stop wiggling to the rhythm. He says to Adel, "Are you still afraid of beautiful women?"

I feel safe behind the scarf. Adel answers him as he toys with his glass, "A beautiful woman smells of danger. I don't like it when someone tosses me a piece of creamy cake. I could slip, or it might be a trap."

The waves of his voice reach me across the table; but Adel isn't looking in our direction. Saad continues, "You claim that you've been with a thousand women, but still you hesitate!"

"And I helped more than thirty of my friends get married."

"Your experiences when you're sober aren't those you experience when you're drunk."

"Sometimes generosity justifies flitting between women."

I have started to enjoy this session, listening to men talking. I am bored with women's gatherings and their problems. Adel says, "Calm down, Saad. You're annoying Dalal with your excessive dancing."

Saad laughs out loud, "Movement is a blessing, isn't that what they say?"

Adel smiles as he watches him, while Saad carries on, "We must continue to move. Movement is important. There's salvation in movement; ceasing to move implies dying."

He then adds, "People must continue to move, the economy must move, and our weapons must continue to move."

Adel asks him, "What are you blathering on about, Saad?"

"Haven't you seen what's been on television today? The teams of inspectors looking for weapons of mass destruction? They've changed their name. They're now called UNMOVIC. Did you see the way they combed the area with their equipment?"

Adel interrupts him, "Calm down, Saad."

Saad pays no attention to him whatsoever, and carries on, "We're all starving to death. Where would we get the money from to make these weapons that would cost a fortune?"

Adel gets up from his seat. "I told you to calm down, Saad."

"Ha, ha. Doesn't the West know that the people responsible for hiding those alleged weapons watch a lot of Road Runner cartoons?"

Adel hands him an ashtray. "Let's change the subject."

He asks me, "Is he bothering you?"

"Not at all."

Saad sticks his tongue out at him. "You see."

Saad draws on his cigarette. The room has filled with smoke. "From my point of view, an intelligent woman is more frightening than a beautiful woman."

I join their conversation. "An intelligent woman?"

Saad smiles cruelly saying, "The one that overcomes her embarrassment?"

He grabs the eyeliner pen and, heading to Adel, he says, "Put your head back."

Adel does as he is told and Saad starts drawing a tattoo on his face. When he is done, an eye settles between his brows. Adel doesn't move and starts to smile. I ask him, "Don't you want to know what he drew for you?"

"Another eye, right?"

"Yes, how did you know?"

"It's his favorite game."

I turn around to Saad, who is drinking his arak like gulps of water. "So explain to me then."

"There's nothing to explain. All I did was darken with the kohl something that was already there."

Adel says to him, "The alcohol is going up to your head."

Saad cheers him with his glass: "Here's to your third eye."

Saad burps as loud as he can then starts to talk seriously, "This man here showed me how to see things through this 'eye' and not with our regular eyes. It's the center of the unconscious in human beings. From it we feel, follow our instincts, and our spirits meet."

Adel says as if he was correcting him, "It's not physical eyesight, it's a type of vision."

I tell them, "Even you, Adel?"

They stare at me and I say, "What's wrong with the people in this building! Everybody thinks they have super powers in understanding life in their own way. First Umm Mazin claims that she sees in the coffee cup what others can't, therefore she can read the future. Then Uncle Sami believes that he sees the truth through his camera only, but after he lost his sight, he started seeing what he never experienced in his life before. And now, you tell me that you have an invisible third eye, one that feels rather than sees! Has everybody gone mad?"

Saad drags me by the hand, so that he can sit in my place on the revolving chair. He pushes the ground with his feet to spin around. He starts going round and round. Suddenly, his broadcast stops.

Adel gets up to make sure he is all right. He lifts him up from the chair and drags him over to the sofa where he sets him down saying, "You're going to sleep deeply."

162

I watch him leading Saad to the sofa. I say, "He's passed out."

"He'll rest. His thoughts have exhausted him."

My body starts to sway. "Adel, I feel like a woolen blouse that's just been taken out of a hot washing machine."

He bursts out laughing and leans over toward me. The next moment, I am lifted into the air. "You're still too young to be drinking."

"What are you saying! I'm about to graduate from university."

"Yes, and I'll get you a present."

"Another box of Kit Kats!"

He holds me against his chest and leads me toward the bedroom.

It is a darkened space. The only light comes from a small gap in the curtain. The light from the backstreet lights up the stars that hang on the black wall. A stranger's two arms lie me down on the bed. His fingers reach out to remove the scarf from my face. I stop him. "There isn't anything attractive underneath here."

The smell of his breath is like fermented dates. "It attracted me before today."

"Don't be considerate of my feelings."

"Take my eyes and look through them."

"Which one?"

He laughs, and starts wiping the third one. "Without the extras."

"I wish I could stay like this, forever the image of a Bedouin woman."

"Don't be shy with me."

I point to my mouth. "But it's distorted."

"Don't say that. Imagine your mouth being caressed by the wind; you'll feel the difference."

He starts to pull the scarf away gently. "I'll light a candle. Will you let me do that?"

"Please don't embarrass me."

"Trust me."

I feel more numb as he lights it. He then says to me, "Look."

I gaze into the small mirror that he holds up in front of my face while I remain lying on my back. "Imagine that your lips are about to take flight."

His voice flows into my ears like misty olive oil: "And now, give me your feet."

He starts kneading them with an expert touch. His fingers play with the sole of my foot. I lose track of time when his voice reaches me: "Concentrate on the silver stars. You're just like them; you have to be rubbed so that you may shine."

The room melts away around me; I leave the rest to the candle.

❖

When I wake up, Saad is standing by my side gazing down at me. "Good morning, flower bud."

The darkness and Adel have evaporated. "What happened?"

"I don't know, you tell me."

"We left you on the sofa."

"And then?"

"Adel laid me out on your bed."

"That's obvious."

"Where's the scarf?"

"Beside you. It seems to be the only thing that you've taken off."

"Shut up. I can't remember what happened."

"What a pity."

He starts gathering the congealed candle wax from the table, "The important thing is, Adel dropped by an hour ago to make sure everything was all right."

"Did he ask about me?"

"Yes, and he also asked me for color fixers. I gave him a can of hairspray to try out. It might fix the dye onto the wooden limbs."

I can taste hairspray drizzle in my mouth. "Has my aunt been in touch?"

"No."

I fix my hair. Saad says, "Stay and have breakfast with me."

"Thank you Saaoudy, I'll go."

I manage to balance my head on my shoulders, with difficulty. I then make my way up to the third floor.

My aunt's husband hasn't returned; but I find traces of him in the buttons cupboard. My aunt has added two new boxes there. One is a large one that contains the mummified bees. It is labeled "Husband 1." The second is a smaller container. It has silvery scales inside it. The label says "Husband 2." I am shocked when I open it. It is a collection of psoriasis scales.

I throw myself down into her chair in the living room. She is still on the second floor. I open my handbag and am assailed by the smells of last night. I take out my timetable and try to concentrate in spite of my overpowering headache. I have to study a text by Proust. The lecturer is going to discuss the association between memories and the taste of madeleine cakes. I put my notes away and head toward Ilham's flat. I hope I can find a painkiller in the medicine cabinet in her bathroom; or maybe Umm Mazin will have something.

I say to the maid, "How are things, Bidour?"

Umm Mazin called out from inside, "You mean 'Saucepan Girl.'"

Badriya lowers her eyes, shuts the door and follows me in.

We enter the room. The floor is covered with dozens of different types of herbs scattered all over a nylon sheet. My aunt sits in a chair, knitting. Umm Mazin is lying down on a mattress on the ground. Behind her are a large number of plump cushions.

"Good morning, you appear to be in better health, Umm Mazin."

"You're wrong. It's merely my anger that's keeping me alert."

"What's happened?"

"You mean on top of everything else that has happened!"

I exchange glances with my aunt, but she is unable to help. Umm Mazin calls out to Badriya to sit down beside her. "We'll start again. The herbs on this side are to deal with water magic and those on that side are for wind magic. Do you understand?"

The servant answers her in a low and hesitant voice, "I understand, Hijjia."

"Now give me the pumpkin seeds."

"There you are."

"No, this is birdseed. Didn't I show you the difference between them yesterday?"

I sit down to watch. "And what do we do with these leaves, Badriya?"

"We use them to treat indigestion."

"No, we give them to patients who have lost their appetite. What about this leek?"

"That's for anemia."

"No, it's for infirmity. Take this; you know this one."

"These are dried grilled apples. We use them in the mixture for the feeble-minded."

"Eat a lot of it then, before I become even more ill because of you."

My aunt is trying to hide her chuckles. The two women are gathering together all the herbs after the incident. They want to place them in nylon sacks so that Umm Mazin will be able to resume her work sometime in the near future. Umm Mazin holds up a white grainy substance in front of her maid. "Do you remember how we use these clusters of cats' eyes?"

Clumsy Badriya is scratching her head. Suddenly, she stops as though the movement of her fingers is annoying her, forcing her to think. She says, "For migraine."

Umm Mazin tugs on her assistant's headscarf. The rage is now obvious on her face, "Even a donkey would learn by repetition. This is for dried skin and corns. What have you been doing with me all these years?"

Badriya starts crying. "Baji, I was able to recognize these various items from the shape of their containers. Now that all the jars and bottles have been broken, I'm finding it difficult to differentiate between one herb and another, and one powder and the next."

Umm Mazin strikes the back of her hand with the palm of her other hand in exasperation. She turns to us in supplication:

"Always bear tall and dignified
And ask for what you need
But only from those,
Who are wise and specialized"

A short while later she says, "Go and make some coffee for Dalal."

I sit up and say, "I don't want any coffee, thank you; but have you got anything for a headache?"

Umm Mazin points to a clay-colored substance in a small cup. She asks her servant to boil it for five minutes, add some honey, and then serve it to me. I agree, but I want to supervise the preparations in the kitchen. I notice Badriya is trembling. I ask her, "What's wrong?"

"I'm afraid."

"Of being tested on the different herbs?"

"No, Miss Dalal. Much worse."

Badriya stands on an iron box with a sticker on it: WARNING: NON-FLAMMABLE STARCH. She stretches up to get the coffee pot from the high cupboard. I ask her, "Are you afraid of the bombardment?"

"Worse, worse."

"What?"

After adding two spoons of honey to the mix, she passes the cup to me with shaking hands. "When Umm Mazin was ill this past week, I sold several mixtures to a lot of women without her knowledge. I told myself I would make her happy with the cash when her health improves. But now I realize I've made a lot of mistakes in the herbs and items that I used."

"How did you dare do something like that?"

She strikes her cheek in distress. "May God protect us from her curse."

I drink the hot liquid as I watch her wailing, "My God, what have I done? I sold the remedy for memory loss to the young girl with a sore throat. I gave the powder for heartache to the woman whose son has acne."

She uncovers a plastic container; its contents have gone moldy. It is full of a smelly gas that emanates from the stale substance. As she removes the rubber lid the container releases a choked noise: *hufff*. She is repelled by the stench. She continues, "Another potion has failed."

She gets rid of it, saying, "Then I gave the woman complaining of persistent constipation the treatment for a hoarse voice. And the woman with insomnia ended up with the remedy for hemorrhoids."

She strikes her cheek a second time. I ask her, "You did all this in one week?"

"Worse, worse. I gave the woman with asthma the treatment to bring down a fever, and mixed it with ground pebbles that break the curse that brings bad fortune."

Umm Mazin calls out, "Where are you? Come back and let's finish what we have to do."

Her servant grabs my hand; for a moment I thought she was going to kiss it. "I beg you, please don't tell her about this."

"I promise."

She returns to her lesson, striking her cheek one last time before she enters the room. Umm Mazin lifts up a dried fistful, and holds it out to her. "We'll start again from the beginning. This is mountain chamomile. You can't prepare it in a steel pot because it'll react with the iron just like acid reacts with copper, and in both instances, a poisonous agent is released."

Badriya looks at me with two droopy eyes. Her mistress continues, "And for the millionth time, this is the sacred herb that is given to dry up a wet chest."

Umm Mazin glares at Badriya. "Is that understood?"

Badriya swallows. "Yes, ahem, yes Hijjia."

Their appearance reminds me of the illiteracy eradication programs that were shown on our television screens in the seventies. "Rashid plants. Zainab works."

I miss Ilham.

CHAPTER FOURTEEN

FOUR DAYS LATER Abu Ghayeb returned from the Dead Sea. That was when my aunt put plan "Husband 3" into action. It appeared that she intended to rely on herself this time, as Umm Mazin was still unwell. The box contained nothing more than a number of rusty pins. His skin had gained a tanned look from his exposure to the sun and salty water. He went about showing us how some of his spots had disappeared here and there. He reiterated, however, that psoriasis could only be eradicated after numerous courses of treatment. My aunt noted that he asked how the bees were before he asked her how she was; and when she realized he hadn't brought her back a present, she put her plan into action.

She scattered the pins around the sofa. She knew that he always took his shoes off and walked around there barefoot. One of them clung to his socks, but didn't prick him. That was when it flared up between them. "So you're determined to hurt me?"

"Why didn't you even remember me?"

"Do you blame me?"

He placed the pin on the table. "Explain to me the meaning of all this."

"No. I won't explain."

"Why not?"

"Because it'll make me look small."

"You can rest assured that you've already mastered the art of shrinking, if that's the case."

He set about looking for more pins. "Do you hate me that much?"

"I hate her."

"Your jealousy is unjustified."

"She took you away from me for ten days. And that came on top of the torture during the fair."

"Nobody took me away from you, so please don't push me in that direction."

"We almost died, and you weren't here."

"I don't think so. I checked, and everyone seems fine."

"Umm Mazin has been affected, and her flat has been badly damaged."

"Don't worry about her. She'll pull through; like a cat with nine lives."

She commented thoughtfully, "You've changed a lot since you met that woman from Amman."

"So what do you want to do now? Reform me?"

"I want you to go back to the way you were."

"The only thing that's changed in me is my psoriasis."

My aunt burst out crying. "I admit that I went through a phase of murderous jealousy. Maybe I wasn't jealous of her specifically, but I was jealous of the people and the reasons that made you become the person you are now."

"Am I that bad?"

"On the contrary, you've become someone else. You've adapted in your work. You've fought against adverse circumstances, and you're always optimistic. On top of that, you're able to get around without any hindrance. You represent to me everything that I'm unable to become."

He picked up another pin from the floor, and placed it beside the first one. "Nice recovery."

My aunt tried to control herself. "I started to ask myself, why wasn't it I who was the incentive for your transformation?"

He placed his hands behind his head as he relaxed. He watched her and said, "If it's a trip to Jordan that'll relieve your anxieties, then I'll take you with me next time I go."

She didn't believe him. She also couldn't believe that she'd ended up in this dilemma. Was she jealous of him, or over him? He said to her, "Do you have any other confessions?"

She wiped away her tears, not knowing how to answer him.

"For example, what did you put in my bed?"

My aunt became depressed and when my aunt becomes depressed, her shoulder pads shrivel.

❖

I take the bag full of beauty products Saad had asked Abu Ghayeb to get for him from Jordan. I open the door; Adel is waiting. "Hello."

"How are you?"

"I'm fine. Where's Saad?"

"He's gone to get some hot, freshly baked bread."

"Another late night, brothers?"

"If you like."

I place the bag on the table. "Adel, what happened that night?"

"You relaxed."

"And what about you?"

"I relaxed as well."

"What do you mean?"

"I mean that I relaxed because you were relaxed."

I start taking the contents out of the bag. I look up at him, wanting to know more. He says, "In other words, I like to see other people totally comfortable."

"Is that all?"

"That's all; no more."

He watches me placing the boxes on the shelf. "In any case, that arak was for beginners."

"That wasn't the first time that I tasted alcohol."

"What I meant was that the people who made it were beginners."

"Yes, it was somewhat bitter."

A short while later, I say, "Adel, what were you doing to my feet?"

His voice laughs, "I was checking the stability of your infrastructure."

He senses my irritation. "By the way, Dalal, I don't like what's given to me. I prefer what I manage to get for myself. You have no reason to be worried."

"The problem is that I can't remember what happened after that."

"What happened is that I turned a woman made of wood into dough."

"And how did you do that?"

"That'll remain my professional secret."

I feel like a cat circling around itself, trying to catch its tail. "Tell me, please, how?"

"By giving her what she's entitled to."

"So is it true what Saad said, that you've been with a thousand women?"

"What's said in the night is erased by the day."

"It's now nine o'clock in the evening."

In spite of his smile, I am afraid that he will be annoyed by my questions. "How can you justify flitting between women?"

"So you do recall several segments of that evening."

He gets up from the sofa, and asks me to sit down beside him, "Imagine that being with me is like your favorite childhood toy. Do you remember how you used to play with it all day long and not get bored with it? The toy hasn't changed; but your fantasies change from one day to the next, while you play. That's creativity."

A thought comes into my mind: "Why didn't Madame Bovary do that with her husband?"

Saad walks in, the bread swung over his shoulder as usual. He says excitedly, "Have you heard?"

I turn toward him as Adel asks, "What?"

"Umm Mazin is being investigated."

Adel asks him, "Is she that ill?"

"No, not medical investigations."

I exchange glances with Adel. Saad says, "She's being investigated by the Security Services."

I get up from the sofa. "How could that be? My aunt and I checked on her this morning. When did this happen?"

He hands me the bag of hot bread, "I've just found that out at the police station. It's next door to the bakery, and it's full to the brim with files of recent complaints against her."

Adel arches his eyebrows. "Where did you get this information?"

"I shared some hot bread with the policeman on duty outside the station. He told me that many women in the area had put in complaints, stating that she'd harmed them. Some had become ill as a result of her potions, while others had been scarred mentally. The officer is going to call her in for interrogation very soon."

Saad notices the new boxes on the shelf and heads toward them for a closer look. "Wonderful, this is exactly what I need."

He takes a few dollars out of his pocket and hands them to me. "Tell Abu Ghayeb that I'm very grateful."

I ask Adel, "What will her punishment be?"

"I don't know; but I presume that she'll be forced to give up her practice."

"And Badriya?"

"Her fate is most likely to be the same as the fate of her mistress."

❖

Umm Mazin had barely recovered her health and some of her herbs before they sent for her. Two policemen went up to the fifth floor to search the flat. She tried to convince them that the weird and wonderful recipes for potions and spells were merely a modern creative way of teaching the alphabet and the multiplication tables. She claimed that she was teaching her illiterate servant the basics of arithmetic and reading. Half the materials were still in Ilham's flat, but nobody mentioned anything to the police as we watched her leave with them. She went down the stairs sobbing. Badriya followed her, stumbling over her abaya. In spite of her emotional state, her mouth remained fixed in a smile. She pinched her servant's arm viciously. "You've ruined me."

She pinched her a second time. "You've destroyed the reputation of traditional healing."

Badriya moaned from the pain of the pinches, but submitted herself to her mistress's punishment. "Forgive me, Umm Mazin, forgive me."

We stood at the entrance of the building trying to console her. Saad said to her, "May God be with you."

The teacher expressed his sentiments: "Look after yourself."

My aunt patted her on the shoulder. "Umm Mazin, my dear sister, don't worry. I'll come to visit you and bring you whatever you need."

The afflicted one murmured, "May God preserve you all; may He grant you long lives."

When it was my turn, I found myself saying to her, "Umm Mazin, find strength in your heart."

She straightened her abaya. "God is my strength, and my best support."

That was how we all said goodbye to her, except Abu Ghayeb who was at the club.

❁

I join him there. He doesn't seem too troubled by the news. He carries on examining the bees. He picks up a soft brush, and starts gently moving the bees away from the discs. He says to me in a voice that is almost a whisper, "Examining the bees and dealing with them is easy. It's not at all dangerous if you take the proper precautions, and understand the bees' habits and behavior."

He moves extremely slowly from one honey disc to the other. "We must avoid any sudden movement."

He uses a metal implement to lift up the discs. He attaches it to the side of the box, and places the disc on it once he has examined it.

The bees are very sensitive to any unusual smells, especially animal scents. That's why the apiary's special clothing shouldn't be worn outside the apiary, and it must always be clean.

He then asks me to move back a little from where he is working. "Dalal, woolen clothing, materials that shed fibers, and dark colors are not appropriate for the apiary. They can enrage the bees."

I take a few steps back. He stands beside the hive with his back to the sun. The sunlight falls onto the hexagonal cells, showing the contents clearly; this enables him to estimate the age of the eggs and the larvae.

I observe him dissembling the frames and extracting them. He lifts the discs upward to check that the queen isn't on the frame, as she might then fall outside the hive. He locates her, and goes about examining her externally to make sure that she is undamaged. He points with his finger and says, "Look in here, these sluggish bees have got diarrhea."

He then adds with a smile, "It's a pity that Umm Mazin isn't around to heal them."

"Aren't you at all upset by what has happened to her?"

"From a salesman's point of view, yes."

"But they're likely to stop her from continuing to practice."

"If that were the case, then I'd offer her a job here."

"You're joking."

"She claims that she loves bees and understands honey, but she knows nothing. She'd have to learn from these insects the philosophy of life."

It is the first time I have heard my aunt's husband talk like this. "Dalal, if we could only learn from the bees!"

He checks that the bees have enough honey and pollen for the winter. He carries on, "Greed is the main problem. Look at the way the bee behaves when it goes out to collect the nectar. The first thing the bees do is check the amount of sugar in the flower. They suck from it what they need and won't exceed their limit."

I say to him, "And will you get Badriya to take down notes for Umm Mazin?"

He laughs. "By the way, on cold days, when it's rainy, and at the end of the season, the bees become aggressive, so do be careful."

He finally concludes his lecture, "We have to start preparing the hives for the winter. We'll cover the boxes with jute. We'll also need to put straw around the sides."

Two hours later I leave the tennis court. I can't imagine Umm Mazin in a protective suit.

❋

At the flat, my aunt is still tackling her jealousy. Whenever she is reminded that her husband is a beekeeper, she feels uncomfortable because of his paternal instincts toward the insects. She imagines the bees having cravings, and Abu Ghayeb rushing out to plant the flowers that they love. In return, I gave her a brief resumé about the role of the worker bees in exceptional circumstances. They lay the eggs instead of the queen bee and end up being called false mothers.

I ask her, "And do you know why that happens, my aunt?"

I feel as though she is humoring me. "Why?"

"That happens when the queen either dies or gets killed. The hive is thrown into chaos and the worker bees start laying their eggs in the royal cups in a random and irregular manner."

Her eyes become narrow as if she is trying to balance the equation in her head. She is busy attaching a length of lace onto an overcoat. She gazes at it, then says, "Do you know, Dalal, marriage is like lace. . . ."

She tries to cut a thread with small scissors while adding, "Beautiful, symmetrical, artistic, and when it's new, it's pure and white. It sits proudly on the shelf in the shop. . . ."

The small scissors are not sharp enough to cut the thread, so she cuts it using her teeth, carrying on with her conversation, "But after you buy it, and use it to garnish your clothes, you get used to its texture between your fingers. Then you realize the truth. . . ."

She looked at me intently. "You discover that it's just a boring pattern, made out of a strip of white threads. It soon becomes faded, and its edges turn yellow."

She checks with her fingertip every now and then that the beauty spot she has applied to her cheek with eyeliner is still there. She claims that she has a cold so that her clients don't kiss her. She doesn't want it to get smudged. Her heart fills up with joy when they tell her that she looks beautiful today. I watch the movement of her beauty spot, saying to myself, "Didn't her husband tell me in our first drawing class that everything starts with a dot?" Then I ask her, "What news of Umm Mazin?"

"She cries on her own. Everybody else has abandoned her."

"And Badriya?"

"It seems as though her mind was unable to cope with the shock. She sits in the police station all day singing 'I want baklava and sweets. . . . Where will I go, where will I sleep. . . . If I sleep in the alleyway, the cats will cry for me. . . . If I sleep in the station, then the ducks will cry for me.' And she strikes her cheeks between each verse."

"When will they be coming back to the building?"

"I don't know. They're still under arrest, accused of practicing witchcraft and sorcery."

CHAPTER FIFTEEN

AFTER THE PALM trees were bombed, the bees no longer had the dates to feed on. Instead, they fed on the fruits that fell from the citrus trees. Abu Ghayeb said that his bees were lucky to have this alternative. The residents of Fatima Khatoun Building, however, weren't so lucky. It was located a few streets away from our building. The second missile landed on it and exploded on impact. That happened two months after the first missile struck, and all of Karrada Dakhil was thrown into turmoil.

Hamada was our correspondent. He traveled with his newspapers and the latest news between the alleyways and the rubble. The explosion shook our block of flats. Women, children, and men, choked, burned, and were shredded underneath the collapsed building. We were told that dozens of families perished in the incident. The rescue teams joined the local people to pull out all the dead, whose names were added to the list of martyrs. No one slept a wink for many days.

The second night, at three o'clock in the morning, I heard men's voices, mixed with the sounds of hammering and banging. I got out of bed and tried to make out what was happening from my bedroom window. I could see a gathering of shadows in the distance. They moved about swiftly without any lights through the club's grounds. Something was going on, in the darkness.

The next day I accompanied Abu Ghayeb to work. We were surprised to find that the appearance of Court No. 2 had changed. The fencing around the court had been covered by khaki colored cloth. It was similar to the material that was used to make tents. The top of the rectangular court was also covered. It now looked like a room made out of thick cloth. A young soldier sat outside the entrance. A sign had been hung up on the outside, at the front of the khaki room. It said in clear letters, DO NOT APPROACH. We therefore complied, and kept away.

We head toward the apiary. My aunt's husband instructs me to behave as if nothing has happened. We walk across a patch of grass that is still coated by the morning dew. It looks like a lawn of emerald fuzz. He tries to concentrate on his explanation of the propolis. He says, "It's a sticky substance that the bees collect from tree bark. They use it to narrow the entrance to the cells in the winter."

He then adds in a distracted manner, "The word is derived from Greek, and made up of two segments. Pro meaning the beginning of. . . ."

Suddenly, the soldier moves from his position. Abu Ghayeb follows him with his eyes. I tug on his sleeve to regain his attention. "What about 'polis,' my aunt's husband?"

He replies, "It means town."

He readjusts his thoughts. "When we join the two together, the meaning of the word propolis becomes 'the beginning of the town.' That's the elementary construction material used by the bees."

He blows some smoke around the entrance of one of the hives. This is to encourage the bees to do something else instead of defending it. He blocks the opening with his hand and waits for two minutes to allow the bees to sip the honey and thus be less inclined to attack. He then starts removing the wax worms from the hives. He treats the affected frames by fumigating them using sulfur dioxide.

My aunt's husband is busy, but he is still watching the movements in the other court, out of the corner of his eye. An officer arrives and speaks to the soldier for a few minutes. He then goes around the rectangular tent. Finally, the young man executes a military salute, and the officer leaves through the club's front entrance.

He hands me the sticky, greenish brown substance. It has a relaxing smell like a mixture of buds, honey, wax, and vanilla. He says, "When it's burned, it releases a smell reminiscent of very old aromatic gum. It's a substance that stimulates the secretion of the female sex hormones."

❁

Saad asks me to look after the shop till he gets back in the evening. He fills his bag with his hairdressing tools and makeup kit. In spite of the sorrow that has enveloped our area, people are still getting married in other parts of the city. He has been called out to attend to two brides that evening in their homes before the start of their wedding party. He says to me as he leaves, "Please don't tell anyone that I'll be attending weddings."

I shut the door after he has gone and sit down to flick through a magazine. They have published an article in color about this amazing invention called the Internet. I let out a long sigh. Any information you might want can be obtained at the touch of a button, from whatever source you can think of. And what was this I was reading about electronic mail? You could actually communicate with another person at the other end of the world in a matter of minutes!

When Adel sticks his head in through the door, the chewing gum starts melting in my mouth. He says, "How are you, Dalal?"

"I'm fine, thank you. Come in."

"Where's Saad?"

"He's been called out to attend to two brides this evening. He doesn't think he'll be very late."

"Have you got any coffee?"

"I do."

He sits down on the sofa. "When will this all be over? I can't bear to go on making false limbs."

"You look exhausted."

"I haven't slept. This explosion has shaken us."

How can it be that I hear both the sound of the birds, and the rain at the same time? I head toward the window. The waters from the heavens are cascading violently down. It seems that the rain is beating itself against the pavement. Adel joins me. "What beauty!"

"Did you want anything from Saad?"

"Do you want me to leave? Is that it?"

The rain is tracing strange patterns on the windowpane. It trickles down on the outside dribbling into the pot that houses the mulberry bush. Adel's voice blurs into the hiss of the rain entering my head like the noise of a needle scratching on a surface of mercury. He walks to the door, but instead of leaving, I realize that he has locked it. Then he leads me, not unwillingly, to where the silver stars are.

We drift, young squirrels cleaning their fur under autumn shadows. I feel his hair, Gujarat blossom tendrils. He lays me on my back. He makes contact with me through the buttonhole in my shirt. He tastes my cherry stones. His fingers like softened okra find their way, slip down, lose their way. I look into his eyes. A lilac cover floats above him. We play, our hands are exploring silky corners. The olive oil voice asks me gently to hush. The legs of the bed quiver.

❋

Abu Ghayeb cannot understand why his docile bees have suddenly become fierce and aggressive!

It seems as though they are about to swarm. He rushes to check them one more time, to make sure everything is all right. The hives are not overcrowded with bees. The wax discs are not overfilled with honey and the queen has not run out of room to lay more eggs, nor has she reached the age when the amount of eggs she lays is insufficient. That would have driven the bees to leave their nesting grounds and exchange their queen.

In spite of all that, the bees start circling around the hives in a distinctly different manner from the way they usually fly—in a straight line. Some of the bees also appear very heavy, and unable to defend themselves. We then find unusually large groups of bees aggregating around the entrance to the hive. Suddenly Abu Ghayeb calls out, "Swarming normally takes place between ten o'clock and midday. Hurry up, Dalal, we have to stop them from leaving."

His shouting disconcerts me. "What should I do?"

"Spray them with water. When they get wet, they'll stop flying."

I approach them with the water hose and proceed to obey his instructions. I am worried that I will kill them by drowning them. He calls out from the separation room, "Have they calmed down?"

I spray the water in all directions. "A little."

"That's not enough."

Suddenly, my aunt's husband appears with an empty tin can. He starts to strike it with a wooden stick. He is hoping to irritate them with the noise and prevent them from flying. He asks me amidst the racket, "Are they still about to take off on your side?"

"I think so."

We notice that the soldier guarding the second tennis court has stood up and is observing our sudden flurry of activity.

We finally manage to control them when my aunt's husband brings out a medium-sized mirror and reflects the sun's rays onto the restless cells. For some reason, their agitation starts to subside when the reflected rays land among them.

Abu Ghayeb sighs with relief.

❧

In the afternoon, my aunt opens the door to the flat just as we are to go in. Abu Ghayeb asks her, "Where to?"

"I'm going to visit Umm Mazin."

As she leaves, she turns toward him, her cheeks reddening. "There was a phone call for you from Jordan."

"Who from?"

"Who do you think!"

She then slams the door.

He looks at his watch. It is not a good time to ring back. We relax briefly after the day's experience, then start making the sugar blocks. Abu Ghayeb thinks that one of the reasons the bees may have wanted to swarm was because they needed more nutrients. He thinks that might be due to the prolonged cold spell this winter. His fascination with the bees' behavior continues in the kitchen. "Bees have an exceptional ability to differentiate between a wide variety of smells. They can remember them even if they're kept away from them for up to five days."

I can't find my notebook, so I take down the information using my university notes. I write on the back of an article analyzing a novel by Balzac. He starts preparing a solution using four parts of sugar to one part of water. He heats it up on an open flame bringing it to the boil. That makes it thicker and stickier. I then help him to spread it out onto the trays that we have sprinkled with sugar dust. As we wait for it to cool down, I ask him, "Is it true that bees communicate by means of signals?"

He sits down on the chair, rolling up his sleeves, and starts to assess his psoriasis. He smiles. "Yes, just like your aunt and me; the way the deaf and dumb communicate. Bees' signals are transmitted through their movements that resemble a dance to show their wishes, directions, and distances. When they want to indicate the site of a food source, or a spot they've chosen to swarm to, they convey that information in relation to the position of the sun."

My head is weighed down with all this information. The sugar paste has finally solidified. We proceed to cut it up into pieces. We are going to offer it to the bees the next day by placing it above their frames.

❋

Either we are late, or the battle started very early in the morning. We arrive at the apiary carrying the sugar blocks in order to lay them out between the hives. We find the bees killing each other. A strong colony is stealing from a weaker one. We are able to identify the thieving bees; they fly with their feet pointing forward. They attack the hive in raids, while the normal bees are still flying in straight lines.

Abu Ghayeb drops the bag of sugar candy and runs toward the raided hive. Its entrance is a battlefield. We see the casualties dropping in mid-flight, and outside the hive. We also note that the thieving bees are now flying more heavily, and in curves. He points out to me that the thieving bees seem to be sticking to each other. They fly as a mass around the outside of the hive they are attempting to enter. He calls out, "This way."

He then orders, "Get me some grass."

I hand him a few clumps of grass. He starts blocking up all the openings that the thieving bees might attempt to use. He then says to me brusquely, "Dissolve some salt in a bucket of water, quickly."

I run into the separation room and make up the salt solution. He starts spraying it onto the thieving bees and their flight path. He tries to fool them into thinking there is nothing there to steal, hoping that will make them stop. However, our rapid movements between the boxes have agitated the rest of the bees. They all start to whiz about crazily, in every direction, all around us. *Bzzz, izzz, bzzz, izzz.* Two bees attack me, committing suicide in my neck. It feels like a hot knife has pierced my skin. I scream out in pain, and Abu Ghayeb comes running. He sits me down and extends my head backward as he tries to remove their stingers with his fingernails. He covers the wound with his other hand to try and stop the smell of the poison from spreading as that could enrage the other bees.

He smiles when he notices my tears, and says, "Immunity; this will give you immunity."

He can think of no other solution to try and calm things down. He therefore resorts to using the bellows. He sprays the bees, and they calm down after a while. The thieving bees, however, continue to assault the weaker hive. Abu Ghayeb eventually removes it to another part of the apiary and seals its entrance saying, "We'll reopen it in a few hours' time."

He finally sits down beside me. The soldier sits down too. He has spent his time watching us. We both glance at him. He leans his chair back against the cloth of the rectangular tent. He is wearing a khaki uniform, so he merges into the khaki background behind him. All we can see of him now is his face, his two hands and the reflection from the metal part of his weapon.

Abu Ghayeb opens the bag of sugar candy and offers me a piece. "Why not?"

We share it to distract ourselves with the sweet taste beneath our tongues. He strikes his forehead. "It's all my fault."

"How?"

"Last month, I didn't feed all the colonies at the same time. The other thing I didn't take into account was that I should have fed the strong colonies first, and then the weaker ones. Only now have I realized my mistake."

He helps himself to another piece of candy. "One of the factors that contribute to thieving is when the bees feel they've been cheated. I must have distributed the food unequally amongst the different colonies. Or, maybe I left one of the hives uncovered when I was examining it. That was when the thieving bees became aware of the amount of stored honey the other colony had."

An energetic bee starts circling around his face. It is trying to steal a lick of the candy he chews. We check on the hive that he has moved away before we leave the apiary. The battle has resulted in the decimation of the weaker colony and the death of most of its members.

My aunt's husband bows his head at this grievous loss.

❋

Umm Mazin has taken her nine lives and left us.

The same two policemen accompany her back to collect her affairs from the flat. She says her goodbyes to everyone with bitterness as she mutters, "Numerous were my friends when my days were treacle, now that my good fortune has dried up, away they trickle."

After she asks for my aunt's help in finding a buyer for her flat, the first policeman then takes her away. He gets her a taxi. She has to leave for good. The investigating officer had been prepared to let her stay. She, however, refused to sign any documents stating that she will renounce her practice. The police officer therefore ordered her to leave the city, and to refrain from harming anyone else. She decided to return to Hilla, the city of her birth. She felt obliged to drag her servant along. She was afraid that Badriya would starve if she abandoned her. The second policeman stayed behind. He gathered up all that had been left in the fifth floor flat. He collected the dried plants, the bottles of liquid, the potions, the jars of honey, and the talismans. Then he burned them inside a big barrel in the parking lot, next to Saad's salon.

❧

I decide to spend the evening cleaning Ilham's flat. It still contains a large amount of dried herbs, spread out on a plastic sheet on the floor. Handfuls of colored powders lie on one side, while dark-colored sticks and paler ones lie on the other side. In the center are collections of seeds, leaves, and hairy roots. Scattered around them are crystals and earthen lumps. Strips of acid are laid out in one spot, and a random arrangement of solid masses is laid out in another. A fistful of cactus needles is stacked in the corner. There are mounds of a yellow powder stacked in alternating waves of sulfur. I recognize the plant called "the Earth's bellybutton." It is a perennial shrub with fleshy, watery leaves. Its stems are long, with a constriction in the middle, giving it a trumpet-shaped appearance. Umm Mazin once told me that mixing it in a potion made from the skin of an old turtle would prolong youth. As for the clumps of carpenter grass, they have been compressed together into cubes. They are like tiny building bricks piled up on top of each other.

I settle into the chair to gaze at this scene for the last time. I am going to put it all in bin bags and send it to the incinerator. I open the window. The sound of the call to prayers from the Mosque of the Unknown Soldier intermingles with the multicolored compositions spread out in front of me. The dried plants respond to the sunset. The rays of light from the setting sun disperse themselves harmoniously amidst the herbs. I submerge myself in the scene to the point of stupor. I am aroused by the sound of a voice calling my name. It is as though I am in a large hotel where someone has walked past me, carrying a black notice board. It has my name written on it in white chalk, and a small brass bell dangles from its side. It is being rung to attract my attention by a young bellboy wearing a Syrian fez. Suddenly, I am awakened by a persistent knocking on the door. I get up to answer it. "Adel! What're you doing here?"

"Saad told me that I'd find you on the second floor."

"Yes, on a mission to clean."

"I'll help you."

He makes his way into the flat. He too is amazed by the pattern on the floor. "What's this?"

"Umm Mazin's remains."

He says, half in disbelief, half mockingly, "So she really was an enchantress."

He wraps his arm around my waist. "Saad told me that the bees had attacked you."

"Two bees stung me at the same moment, in the same place."

"Show me."

"Here, but don't touch it. It hurts."

He doesn't touch it, but he kisses it, to cool it down. He asks me, "Where's the hot water switch?"

"In the kitchen. Why?"

He heads toward it saying, "I'll tell you later."

I pick up one of the bags. "Where shall we start?"

He takes the bag from my hand and tosses it aside. The horse's jaw is coming closer to me. "How about raising some dust first?"

He moves the cacti and the thistles to one side before he lays me down on a patch covered in lavender. The grasses with a thousand holes cling to my hair. Adel laughs at the way I look. Some orange powders have splattered the side of my cheek. I push him away as hard as I can.

He lands on a Chinese rhubarb plant and his neck turns green. I pick up a sturdy branch of cedar and hold it up in front of him. "In days gone by, this wood was used to make boats."

"Enough talk," he says. His skin gives off the scent of basswood and sweat. The carpet of herbs underneath us is crushed.

We get our breath back when the map has changed and the colors of the mixture blend into one. I place my head on his chest. I am being stifled by a sneeze that tastes of carnations. His voice asks, "Dalal, when will we be celebrating your graduation?"

"At the end of the year, if I manage to keep up with the assignments."

"Is there anything that might distract you from them?"

"Nothing much; the problems between my aunt and her husband, and the madness of his bees."

I add, "But still, I'm worried."

"Why do you worry when you have me around?"

"One of my student colleagues has been expelled because he smuggled in copies of George Orwell's *Animal Farm* onto the university campus. He sneaked them in past the university guards, and handed them out to the students in the English Language Department."

"How did they find out about him?"

"One of his colleagues informed on him. He submitted a report about his actions to the National Union of Students."

"He should have adhered to the recommended guidelines. Anyway, how's your work with Saad coming along?"

"Saad is sweet. But he won't stop exchanging items from his shop for whatever he craves. He got food poisoning the other day from a tin of sardines that was past its sell-by date. He acquired it in exchange for a manicure set."

Adel laughs, my cheek picks up his chest's vibrations. His laugh has two layers; the layer closest to my ear has a clear pitch, and the other is smoky, as if it forms a lining to the first layer. He says, "I love that creature. He knows exactly what he wants. Most people don't know what it is that they really want."

"Who can decide what their goals are in times like these?"

He hands me a stick of cinnamon, and places one in his mouth. We both suck away gently. "And have you found your calling in languages?"

"At least I found a translation of my name. Dalal means 'dalliance,' an ancient word for flirtation."

I gaze at the ceiling for a while. Then I shake off some blue mint that clings to his arm, "You know, I feel that language is like a person; it never reaches completion."

After a long pause, I squeeze his shoulder. "From another angle; a person is also like a language. . . ."

He lifts his head up and follows the movement of my lips. "They're both full of common mistakes."

We don't put our clothes back on. The dust of the dried materials covers us from head to toe. I grab Ilham's nursing uniform from her bedroom and put it on. Adel finds a sheet. He wraps it around his trunk. It hangs down from his waist all the way down to his knees. We both feel the cold. We clean the room, open the windows and stack the black bags outside the flat. He then carries me over to where the hot water is. We stand and watch the dozens of different powders melt into the water. They become strands of color that flow from our bodies onto the white porcelain of the bath. The steam rises upward, taking with it the scent of spices and musk. I point to a pale red tricklet that winds its way down my leg. "Adel, this isn't pomegranate juice."

The beads of water bounce off his hair in the form of multicolored droplets. He doesn't comment, so I say, "I can feel a pain, low down in my belly."

"I'm sorry."

When the water has cooled down a little, he asks with a smile, "Would you like a bat's wing?"

I slap his shoulder; the water magnifies the echo which mingles with our laughter. "You brute! How do you know that story?"

"I live in the same area as the doctor who's nicknamed 'The Night Bat.' Some of us have heard the tale."

I pick up an old forgotten bar of soap with horizontal cracks; I try to work up some lather. "Baghdad is a small place!"

CHAPTER SIXTEEN

THE HONEYBEES DON'T CALM DOWN.

They go from aggressive to downright evil. They sting us for no reason, and we are no longer able to enter the apiary without protective suits. We start moving around on tiptoe fearing that we might enrage them suddenly. My aunt's husband is feeling very dejected. He has implemented each and every one of the recommendations for exemplary beekeeping, to no avail. He starts watching them from dawn till dusk to stop them fighting, swarming, and thieving. He sits on a podium, and keeps himself occupied by leafing through his bee-keeping booklets. He exchanges glances with the soldier across the court who whiles away his time by watching the pigeons landing and taking off from the roof of the club.

Due to recent events, the number of visits from my aunt's clients goes down. She starts going to bed early to avoid the boredom of the long evenings. Abu Ghayeb is going to stay up late this evening. He is planning to try and contact Jordan from the teacher's flat on the first floor. I say to Saad, "I can't bear it any longer."

"What's with you?"

"There's something mysterious going on."

"With Adel?"

"No, at the tennis court."

"Dalal, the sign says 'Keep Out.'"

"But it doesn't say 'Don't try.'"

"You're mad. What do you mean?"

"I've got to know what's inside that cube-shaped, khaki tent."

"What are you thinking of doing?"

"Let's sneak in from the back."

"No, you'll be putting yourself in danger."

"I grew up in that Club building. I know all the entrances and exits. I went through every gap and every opening in there when I was a child."

"But now you've grown up!"

"I can do it."

"I won't let you."

"Saad, we have to salvage the situation. If we lose the honeybees, then we'll have lost everything."

"You could lose your future if things don't go according to plan."

"My future won't provide me with an income, whereas now, we're living off the income from the honey."

Saad fiddles with his forelock. I ask, "Will you help me?"

"I'm very afraid of what might happen to you."

"If my aunt loses her clients because of the unstable current circumstances, and her husband loses his clients who buy the honey, then it could be your turn next. You might end up having to close down your shop."

He pauses for a moment, thinking. I add, "On the other hand, if production improves, we could start exporting some of our honey next year. In dollars, Saad, U.S. dollars!"

"What do I have to do?"

"Keep an eye on the soldier for me while I try to find out what's inside the tent from the back."

"What if he becomes aware of your presence?"

"I'll leave that up to you. You'd have to distract him in any way possible."

We sit down on the sofa. I pick up a pen and a sheet of paper and start sketching out a diagram for him. "We'll go in through the entrance by the kitchen wall. That will lead us to the area where they store the food. We then go round the side of the restaurant to reach the players' changing rooms. To the right is the big electric generator; you can hide behind it. In the meantime, I'll walk along the big white wall that they used to project films onto. From there, I'll go into the grove of palm trees. Just a few steps further is a medium-sized opening in the fence, on the left side. It leads directly to Court No. 2. I'll look for an opening in the tent material. I'll take a quick look inside; and then I'll come back to where I left you."

He gazes at my sketch. I ask, "Are we in agreement?"

He gathers up his courage, "We're in agreement."

It gets darker. Saad disappears behind the huge silent generator. From his position, he will be able to observe the entire scene clearly. I cautiously make my way toward the projection wall. My heart is fluttering away inside my chest in terror. There is no going back now. I try to visualize myself playing a game of cat and mouse at the age of eight. The bitter cold is pinching me. I curse the litter that has been tossed behind the wall. It crunches as I step on it. I slow down to try and minimize the sounds that my feet are making. A few moments later, I spot the soldier, hunched up in his chair, the way he always sits. His face is illuminated by the feeble glow from a lantern. I bend down as far as I can go and squeeze myself through the opening at the end of the fence that surrounds the grove of palm trees. I have finally reached my target.

A small hole in the cloth is calling out to me. A faint glimmer of light is shining out through it. It seems to be coming from a lantern that has been hung up inside the tent. The floor of the tent is slightly raised. It too gives off a dim light. I take a few cautious steps forward. Soon I am close enough to smell the odor of the khaki cloth. My eyes freeze on the spot. My God! I am unable to control myself. A scream of horror bursts out from my throat. At that moment, the soldier stands up and shouts, "Stay where you are!"

Without seeing me, the soldier starts to head toward the back of the tent. But he is stopped in his tracks by a loud din that makes him turn around in amazement. Saad has started up the electric generator, and the tennis courts are blanketed by the unexpected sounds. I am trying as hard as I can to remember the sketch showing me the way back to our building. I concentrate my thoughts, trying not to drag my feet.

I start to make my escape through the opening in the fence I came through. A creepy-crawly feeling spreads throughout my body; it is turning to goose flesh all the way down including the leather skin of my shoes!

Saad's hand reaches out from somewhere to haul me out of the darkness. The din of the machine is deafening. We emerge from the opening in the kitchen wall, and run panting, all the way back to his flat. He turns off the lights and we throw ourselves down onto the floor, trembling.

When I open my eyes, I can see his bedroom ceiling whirling around me. His face then appears, followed by the face of my aunt's husband. As soon as I see Abu Ghayeb, I throw myself into his arms sobbing like a baby. He starts caressing my forehead. "How do you feel, Dalal?"

"What happened?"

"You passed out."

"Oh my God!"

"We were worried about you. What did you see?"

"Where's my aunt?"

"Asleep."

"Does she know?"

"Not yet. Don't worry about her, just tell us what happened."

Saad starts to wipe the sweat from my face. "Dead bodies. Dead bodies everywhere!" I tell them.

My words hit them like a bolt of lightning. "I recognized two of them. They're the people from the building that was struck by the missile."

My aunt's husband holds me close to his chest. "Calm down, calm down."

He asks Saad to get me some water as I go on, "They're so many. And the children are laid out to one side."

Saad and my aunt's husband exchange glances. "And there are some soldiers there as well."

Saad asks my aunt's husband, "Why would they store dead bodies in a tennis court?"

"Maybe they've run out of space in the morgues at the nearby hospitals."

"Aren't they worried that they will start to decompose?"

"It's very cold these days."

Abu Ghayeb brings the water to my lips. It cascades onto my teeth like an icicle. "Their limbs have been severed, their legs are twisted, and their faces are deformed."

Saad comes over and holds my hand. "Saad, I saw a little girl with ribbons in her hair, but her eye . . . it wasn't there."

"Stop. Relax."

Saad asks him, "But why would they hang up a lantern to illuminate the corpses?"

"Maybe it's to enable their relatives to identify them. Maybe those soldiers were lost in a battle."

"But there are no battles going on at the moment."

"The country is full of secrets, Saad. How do you expect us to know why soldiers are dying when there isn't a battle going on?"

"Please, Abu Ghayeb, lower your voice. Walls have ears."

"That doesn't change things. We'll never know the truth about what goes on outside these city walls, or even within them."

Abu Ghayeb stands up and starts pacing up and down the room. I gesture to him, calling him over. He says, "Yes, Dalal."

"The bees, they were feeding on their blood."

The silver stars go out.

I stay in my room for two whole days. During that time, the teacher on the first floor announces that he is going to marry the woman who gave birth at home and had her baby delivered by the barber. He is going to move in with her. That way they can share their expenses between them. He can claim that he is going to adopt the boy who sells newspapers. Therefore he is entitled to be officially called "Abu Hamid." Also, the owners of Ilham's flat, who live in Cyprus, send one of their relatives to sort out the flat on their behalf. Thus the building now has three signs saying FLAT FOR SALE decorating it. The signs dangle down from the various floors, one from the fifth, one from the second, and one from the first.

My aunt follows her husband's movements from one room to the other. "I've already told you. There's no need for anyone to know."

"I can't go on pretending that I don't know the truth."

"But then our future will be over."

"You carry on with what you're doing; I'll deal with my problem myself."

"But I'm no longer expecting an income from sewing. This season isn't encouraging, and I don't know what business will be like in the summer."

"What do you want me to do? Cheat?"

"Let us at least wait and see how things turn out."

"That's too late. The insects have been tainted."

"What do you want to do now?"

"What can I tell the buyers? That the next batch of honey will be made out of human juices?"

The distress in his face is obvious. His voice is becoming more high-pitched, "Yes, I'll display the strange honey with a pinkish hue on the shelf and announce 'Just released, From Humans . . . For Humans.'"

"Don't be cynical."

"Or maybe it would be better if I brought it out at the next fair with the other flavors: Orange Honey, Date Honey, Human Honey. Do you like this idea?"

She follows him wherever he goes. "But you have no proof that the bees have been feeding on human blood."

"What other proof do I need? They went mad from the time that that tent was set up. What do you think has happened?"

"Are you sure?"

"Would you change your mind if I checked it out?"

My aunt doesn't answer him. He adds, "In order to get rid of the red bee, which is the honeybee's deadliest enemy, a beekeeper will lay out traps with rotting meat or fish in them. I suspect that my honeybees have been attracted to a similar substance."

She says to him, "But you mentioned once that bees hate unusual smells."

"In spite of that, I can't be certain that they didn't feed on the corpses. I can't risk it."

"What will you do?"

"I'll get rid of them."

"How?"

He paces around the sitting room, surrounded by the paintings. He gazes at the colors all around him. "In my own way."

"How can I convince you to change your mind?"

"I have no choice."

She shouts at him, "Yes, you do have a choice. You can keep quiet, and we can carry on with our life as before."

"At this point, nothing is as it was before."

He rubs his forehead for a while, and then pinches his cheeks between his fingers as he tries harder to concentrate. He goes up to the paintings, walks away from them, and then makes his way back toward them once again. He says, "Dalal, get me a measuring tape."

My aunt sits down on the chair to watch him. He comes and goes. She follows his movement carefully, to the right, and to the left, then again to the right, as if her head is moving in a table-fan motion. He measures each and every one of the paintings, one after the other, and writes down all their dimensions on a small piece of paper. There are so many paintings; they are hung up in three rows, one above the other, on the walls. All the rooms in the flat, with the exception of the kitchen, have paintings in them. Taking down the measurements takes quite a while. When he has done it, he says, "I have no other choice."

She waits, expectantly, and he says, "I must sell this fortune."

She looks at him as if she were seeing him for the first time. "What fortune?"

"I heard that a number of wealthy Iraqis who are now living in London and other European capitals are very keen to acquire original Iraqi works of art."

"And how are we going to contact them?"

"Through Jordan."

The look on my aunt's face changes. "You mean through Miss Psoriasis!"

"I mean with her assistance. She works in a hotel. We can get those works of art out, and exhibit them over there."

"And how will we benefit?"

"With the money that I get for the paintings, I'll acquire a new breed of untainted honeybees. After that, I'll have to start all over again, from scratch."

My aunt attempts to object. He stops her by lifting up his arm rigidly in front of her, as if warning her to keep her distance. "Don't interfere."

"I don't like your idea."

"Don't include yourself in these matters. I know you, you have the ability to insert yourself between layers of an onion skin."

"I wanted to say—"

"If what I'm doing doesn't appeal to you, then stay where you are, and don't make another sound."

"But—"

He starts to lose his temper. "Do you know what we do to the wasps that we trap, in order to protect our bees?"

She lifts up her eyebrows without saying a word when he says, "We drown them in boiling water."

❖

My aunt's husband asks us to maintain total secrecy while he finalizes his plans. He knows that getting those paintings across the border without official permissions will not be easy. Taking original works of art by well-known artists outside the country is obviously illegal.

Later on that week, he hires two laborers to bring two of the beehive boxes damaged in the battles amongst the bees, up to our flat. We no longer have the keys to Ilham's flat, so Abu Ghayeb is forced to bring them into ours. He places them on top of old newspapers that my aunt had spread out on the floor.

He cleans the hives, removing all traces of the dead bees and the dried honey discs. He takes out the white wooden frames and removes their metal grilles. He places them on top of each other, beside the boxes. Then he pulls up a chair from the kitchen to stand on. He starts taking down the smaller paintings from the walls. He treats them gingerly and lifts each one with caution. Each painting leaves behind a square or rectangle of dust that has welded itself to the wall over the years.

My aunt gives him a screwdriver, a hammer and a handful of nails. He starts to pull out the nails from the back of the paintings, separating the canvas from its frame. He dismantles each painting separately, turning them into square pieces of colored cloth. When he has separated the right number of paintings from their fixtures, he asks me to hand him the white wooden frames that are meant to hold the hexagonal wax discs within the hive. He started replacing the picture frames with the frames from the beehives! He reattaches the canvas of each painting to a white wooden frame of suitable size. He hammers the nails on the back and makes sure they are secure. Then he returns the frames to the hives. He piles up the empty picture frames to one side.

The next day, he continues. He tries to fit as many paintings as he can, of the right size, into the two boxes. When Saad rings in the afternoon asking if he can come to visit me, Abu Ghayeb says to his wife, "Tell him that it would be more convenient if he came over in the evening."

After she has hung up the phone, he asks her to conceal all evidence of his activities. She covers the boxes with a large sheet embroidered with flowers. This is when Abu Ghayeb notices the squares of dust on the walls. He contemplates the scene for a few moments, placing his hand on his back. It seems as if he is supporting a painful area that was troubling him. He says, "That'll attract attention."

He heads to the bedroom and starts rummaging through a big bag kept underneath their bed. It is full of some of his old belongings. He pulls out a long cylindrical tube made of firm cardboard. It contains a number of posters that he has kept from his days at the Ministry of Tourism. He brings them back to the sitting room and starts unrolling them. They all bear the logo of the Directorate of Antiquities. He gets a roll of Scotch tape and starts attaching the posters to the walls, covering the marks left behind by the paintings that have disappeared. He covers the walls with the minaret at Samarra, Sarsank, al-Thirthar, Salah al-Din, Haj Imran, and Shaklawa. One empty slot remains on the wall. He takes an image of Habbaniya Lake and hangs it up in that spot.

Saad doesn't notice the change in wall decorations. What attracts his attention are the items hidden underneath the sheet. He greets me, and then whispers in my ear, "Adel says 'hello' and is enquiring about you."

"I'll try and meet him when I'm feeling better. Please give him my best regards."

He then says to my aunt, "One could easily trip over something as large as this. Don't you think?"

My aunt doesn't know what to say. Abu Ghayeb intervenes rapidly to defuse the situation. "Yes, they're two old sewing machines that some friends of mine have asked me to repair."

He doesn't seem to doubt the reply, he just says, "How clever you are!"

He drinks his tea and leaves. He walks past the embroidered sheet. He has no idea that they are beehives filled with works of art, ready to travel.

Abu Ghayeb stayed up late for another two nights, finalizing his diversion plans. The hired laborers returned the heavy boxes to the separation room. He then added genuine frames that contained wax, honey, and some live bees to the hives. The sales representative for Dead Sea Products agreed to be their traveling companion. She would claim, when she crossed the border, that they were a rare breed of honeybees that would be used for therapeutic purposes to treat psoriasis.

Hopefully, none of the customs inspectors would pay too much attention to a vehicle that didn't bear local license plates. My aunt left the flat when she found out that the competition had arrived in the capital to collect the goods and travel with them to Jordan. She didn't want to face her rival, who might eventually be saving her life. She went to the cloth market and made Abu Ghayeb's mission easier. It wasn't an ordinary meeting, and everyone was tense.

In the end, Abu Ghayeb said goodbye to his loved ones: his paintings, his bees, and Miss Randa.

Chapter Seventeen

The fact that the United Kingdom and United States have been unilaterally bombing Iraq almost every other day since December 1998 has generally merited only one-paragraph notices in the *New York Times* "World Briefing" section. In a rare instance when the bombing made the front page, the *Times* acknowledged, American warplanes have methodically and with virtually no public discussion been attacking Iraq.

In the last eight months, American and British pilots have fired more than 1,100 missiles against 359 targets in Iraq.

This is triple the number of targets attacked in four furious days of strikes [on Iraq] in December [1998]. . . .

—*Iraq Under Siege*, 9

THE DAYS GO by. The phone doesn't ring. Our nightmares blend whenever we bump into each other as we move between rooms. A brief conversation between my aunt and her husband seems to me to have been going on for an hour. She picks up a magazine showing Tony Blair talking in the British parliament. His features: an evergreen eagerness.

Their paths cross. He is heading toward the phone. He picks up the receiver to make sure that the lines are not out of order while she heads toward the kitchen. He says, "I'll go to the apiary for a little while."

She gets her broom out. As he is about to close the door behind him, she asks, "Why has the Miss not called?"

"I don't know."

Then he adds, "Please don't leave the flat until the call has come through."

She sweeps his scales. "Do you trust her?"

He takes his hand out of his pocket to scratch his neck. "Time alone will tell."

Another hour goes by; even longer than the one before. Instead of the awaited call, we hear a violent knocking on our door. I exchange glances with my aunt. Without saying a word, images of jumbled up doodlings start sizzling in my head: pages of pale designs cling to each other, with beads of fire burning into them.

My aunt drops the broom and goes to open the door. When I see Adel's face, I leap toward him. Then I notice two policemen behind him. He makes his way into the flat. My head starts spinning as I try to concentrate on my aunt who is rooted to the spot. Why is Adel wearing a military uniform? I am penned in by a circle; through its middle are rows of palm trees, each the size of a pin, twirling around themselves. On the perimeter are mosques that hang in the air, dangling down from their domes. They are about to tumble, any moment now.

I am awakened by the sudden ugliness of his voice, "Where's Abu Ghayeb?"

My aunt replies, "At the apiary."

He orders the two policemen to start searching the flat. He then turns his back to us as he starts heading out. Two other policemen wait for him on the stairway. He says to them, "Let's go."

My aunt gasps in fear. She tugs at my hand, and we follow the sound of their heavy footsteps. I call out to him, "Adel!" but he doesn't reply. We leave the building. The spinning worsens; the orange minarets in my head bear no resemblance to the minaret beside the club. In the street, I can see Baghdad as endless replicas; watery layers of a city the color of dusty indigo. I call out "Adel!" once again. He picks up the pace, and the two policemen follow suit. I see them as embroidered figures wearing Abbasid turbans. We've reached the tennis courts. The tent that had been set up on Court No. 2 is no longer there, but the soldier greets Adel and his companions. He opens the door in the fence, and within moments they've encircled my aunt's husband. They do not allow us in, so we wait outside the fence. My heart is pounding; everybody around me is turning into twins.

Adel's voice descends upon us, "Abu Ghayeb?"

"Yes."

His jaws move apart, "You're being called in for interrogation."

Abu Ghayeb waits at the entrance of the separation room while one of the policemen prepares the metal handcuffs. Adel makes his way toward him, "You're being arrested."

My aunt's fingers cling to the wire fence. She cannot move. The flesh of her palms is squeezed into the shape of baklavas. Nobody is moving except Adel who is nervously coming and going. Suddenly he stops with his mouth open looking like the angry lion on the gate of Ishtar. He says, "You're charged with smuggling Iraq's heritage."

I watch my aunt's husband as he asks Adel for permission to check his bees one last time. After a moment's hesitation, Adel agrees.

❋

Abu Ghayeb heads toward the bee boxes and opens them all one after the other. He knows where his queen will be. He takes her out of the hive and crushes her head between his thumb and forefinger. He takes a few steps back and waits. A few moments later, Adel and all the others have to move back too. Hundreds of bees emerge from their hiding places and gather in the air. They start to come together gradually, all the while dancing nonstop in circles. Abu Ghayeb lifts his arms upward. It seems as if the bees have understood his signal as they all start to fly away. Our heads move backwards gradually as we watch the bees depart. A carpet drawn with dots, continuously changing its formations, as it moves away, further and further.

❋

The next day, I come down the stairs cautiously. I can no longer trust anything around me. On the pavement, I look behind to check that my shadow is still following me. Saad opens the door. He gives the impression that he is expecting my visit, even though I have given him no forewarning. He looks different. His shop is dishevelled, as if it has been burgled. I ask him, "What's this chaos?"

A dark beard sprouts from his cheeks. "It's I who caused all this."

He gestures to me, "Sit down."

"Has something happened to you?"

"Yes."

The chairs have been knocked over. I upright one of them and sit down. He asks, "How are you?"

"Time has stopped for me."

"Are you afraid?"

"I feel nothing."

"How's your aunt?"

"She can't cope with the shock. What she says no longer makes sense. She now depends on me for every little thing."

The basin for washing the clients' hair has a wide crack that splits it into two halves. "Was there a fight in here?"

"No, the fight was between me and myself. In the end, I just destroyed my possessions."

He inhales a puff of smoke, despondently. "Before you ask me about him . . ."

He puts his hand in his pocket and pulls out a thick bundle of U.S. dollars. He places it in front of me. "This is for you."

"Have you gone crazy? What's this all about?"

"Compensation for what's happened to your family."

"What have you got to do with that, Saad?"

He smokes, mercilessly. "The administrators at the Alwiya Club have sold their electric generator. I'll no longer have access to additional electricity. I'll have to close the shop. And besides, all my clients have disappeared."

"So what're you going to do?"

"I'm going to emigrate to the Lebanon. I'll join a friend of mine who has a men's hairdressing salon in Beirut."

"And what's this money?"

"It's from Adel."

It feels as if he has stabbed me all over my body. "Who is he?"

"His real name is Jamal. They call him 'Jamal Drawers.'"

He adds, "That's why he hates nicknames."

"Get on with it; explain everything. I'm tired."

"He's an assistant at the Secret Service Agency. He asked me to work for him."

"For money?"

"No."

One of the mirrors had been broken. Triangular pieces with sharp edges dangle down from it. "Don't tell me that your real name isn't Saad either!"

"My name is Saad, but it's my nickname that's more important. They call me 'Delight.'"

"Delight?"

The shelf for the boxes appears more angled. Its contents are now scattered everywhere. "Yes, because I usually bring happiness to others."

The smoke starts to snake around his forelock. He continues, "But not on this occasion, unfortunately."

He tries to hold my hand. I pull it away. He indicates that he wants me to follow him to the bedroom. He opens the door and points to the bed. "My services."

"Oh my God, you and Adel?"

"No, other men and I, with Adel's permission."

"Why?"

"In exchange for providing information about what goes on in the building."

He kicks away a dented can of hairspray. "Adel had, I mean Jamal, had been ordered to monitor Umm Mazin's activities. It was suspected that she might be attempting to corrupt society. The intention was to move her on. My job was to inform him of any unusual activity taking place in the building."

I feel in need of a chair to take the weight off my over-burdened body. He stands in front of the black painted wall. "Jamal's job was to ensure that those whose behavior corrupted society were chastised. If they persisted in their activities, he'd place one of their hands in a metal drawer, and slam it shut as hard as he could. The force of impact would break a finger or two. He punished people to stop them from reoffending."

The dizziness is rising to my head. "That's the limbs section?"

"Well, he punished them so that they don't go too far."

"So why didn't he stop you?"

He lowers his head slightly. "He made use of the information I provided about the inhabitants of the building. But now, he no longer has any use for me, so he's asked me to leave."

"And the money?"

"It was my reward when my services were terminated."

"What made you think I'd accept it from you?"

"I have no choice. I feel guilty. I'm the one who told him about the bee boxes being taken up to your flat."

"You bastard!"

He lowers his head further. "Didn't I once tell you that there's a defect in each one of us?"

"I don't understand, I don't understand."

"Calm down, and I'll explain things to you. Because of the sanctions, there haven't been enough jobs to go round for everybody. Instructions were issued to encourage more women to wear the hijab, and stay at home. As a result of that, we the hairdressers started to lose our business. That's when Adel and his colleagues stepped in. They allowed us to continue working in exchange for our services in preserving security."

"Why did you agree to work for them?"

"There was no other way I could earn a living."

I then ask him, "So how did the boxes cross the border?"

"I delayed telling Jamal about the Jordanian lady's last visit to you."

"Why?"

"I backed out of cooperating with him for your sake!"

"You're lying. You only backed out to save your salon. You needed the honey customers."

At this point, I start losing control over my questions. "And what happened to Randa?"

"That poor woman doesn't dare to make contact after what happened. I think she's waiting for Abu Ghayeb to get in touch with her when he's released."

"And the paintings?"

As far as I know, the works of art have reached the Dead Sea. They've been hung up in the hotel."

"And Ilham, what was your involvement in her case?"

"Believe me, I didn't mean to harm her. I just informed Jamal that I suspected that she was romantically involved with that butcher."

"What's happened to her?"

"She's been moved to a dispensary in the hard labor camp."

"You've ruined us all."

Saad puts his head in his hands and starts to weep bitterly. "Jamal doesn't know that I was going to confess and tell you everything."

He reaches out toward me with his hand. "Please forgive me."

As I leave, I don't know how my legs are able to support me. "Get lost."

He continues to weep incessantly, like a child. "Please don't make my predicament worse."

Sheets of herbs start blurring in front of me. "Why did Adel abandon me?"

"I think he became attached to you; but the duty to one's country is such a precious thing, Dalal. That's why Adel, I mean Jamal, works so hard for our sake."

"You still defend him even though he's terminated your service."

"There's nothing for me to defend. I'm a pragmatist. Think along with me—who'll protect you women in the future?"

"What?"

"Listen. During the past thirty years people have been leaving. The communists have fled the country, many Shiite families had to leave, the educated professionals and the scientists emigrated, and the Kurds have become independent. They're even saying that women now make up more than fifty percent of the population as a result of the wars we've been through. So what will you ladies do now, dear sister?"

"Don't call me sister! You both tricked me."

"Life is hard, Dalal."

I scream at the top of my voice, "And you claimed having spiritual vision?"

He stands there looking at me. I say, "Did you really think that you had a third eye?"

The pitch of my voice gets higher and higher, "It's your asshole that's in the middle of your forehead!"

❁

After Uncle Sami passes away, we are the only ones left in the building. I find my aunt in the sitting room. I look up at the clock on the wall. It no longer works. The nitric acid has leaked out of the battery. My aunt is standing up on a chair facing the big window. She has covered the windowpane with thin tracing paper from top to bottom. She has a thick charcoal pen in her hand and is tracing out shapes that resemble cauliflower halves. She thinks she's tracing out the clouds. Since Abu Ghayeb disappeared and we lost all contact with him, she's been trying to draw the clouds to pass time, as they change from one day to the next. The television is nearly shaking with applause endorsing the success of the elections. The president has won the backing of one hundred percent of the population this time. My aunt is babbling away, "Clap . . . clap. Monkeys clap, sea lions clap, and the first movement a child would copy is clapping." Then a program starts about the expected crash that's likely to affect computer systems throughout Europe with the start of the year 2000. Suddenly, she becomes aware of my presence. She says in a tired voice, "Dalal, you're back?"

"Yes, my aunt."

Her face has aged several years. "Dalal, what will I draw in the summer?"

I ask her to climb down off the chair. She does, crumpling into the seat beside me. "Auntie, please stop torturing yourself."

She looks at me with eyes that have lost their sparkle. "Have you graduated?"

"No."

I pat her little shoulder without its shoulder pad. "I've abandoned my studies."

She lifts up her eyebrows with difficulty. "How are we going to survive?"

"I've found a job."

She responds with a feeble smile while I explain, "I'll be working in a warehouse. They separate used and worn out items in order to recycle them. We place the different materials in separate containers. Plastics go into one bin, glass goes into another, metals go somewhere else, cloth is put to one side, wood goes into another bin, and so on."

She nods her head as if she's giving me her consent. She then gets up to pray. She spreads out her prayer mat facing the clouds that hang up in front of her, and starts to kneel.

After she kneels down for the second time, she suddenly turns toward me and asks distractedly, "Where is this place?"

"It's in the building that used to be the toothpick factory."

❁

After two years of an exhausting physical routine, I flow into my work like a machine that doesn't think. I can now differentiate between the different types of wood from their texture. I'm able to identify the different metals from their weights, and the different colors of nylons and plastics from their odors. I feel tired. I remove the mask which has become a part of my face and throw it aside. It lands on a shabby pile of old newspapers. I have to tidy them up and bind them together in bundles. My mask has settled on a picture of George W. Bush's face taken at his inauguration. A cramp in my neck is troubling me. I hear a commotion that seems to be coming from the building next door. I head toward the window to see what's going on outside.

The open space in front of the Laboratory for Analysis of Viral Specimens is filling up with large vehicles. The lab staff open the main gates as jeeps bearing the logo of the United Nations on their sides start to queue up. Groups of foreigners wearing blue caps begin to get out of the cars. They're carrying bags, instruments, and manuals. They're followed by a television cameraman. It's the inspection teams for weapons of mass destruction. They've returned.

I pace up and down the room gazing out of the window. I look around me; nobody. There's just me, the chair, and seventy kilos of newspapers that have to go for recycling today. I've got time for a short break. I drink a cup of black coffee. I turn the cup upside down in search for a sign. I whisper into the cup, "Is there going to be another war?"

❁

Someone knocks on the door. It must be Hamada. I put out my cigarette and save the stub for later. I open the door for the newspaper boy.

He comes in exhausted with a bundle of newspapers on his back. He puts them on the floor and sits on them. He takes out two cigarettes he had tucked in his socks. He offers me one. I say, "You're too young to smoke, Hamada."

"I'm not, and don't call me that. My name is Hamid."

"Indeed, you've grown so much. How are your parents?"

"Ill."

"I'm sorry."

I pay him for the stack of newspapers. He kisses the cash and puts it in his pocket. I ask him, "What's the latest?"

"It doesn't look good."

"Where did you read that?"

The thin teenager looks at the burning ember of his cigarette.

"I didn't. People are talking."

"A boy your age should be able to read a newspaper."

"You know I can't."

"Have you tried?"

"I don't want to."

"If you can't read, how will you know what the world wants from us?"

"Look outside the window."

"I did, more than once."

"It's too late."

"Nothing is too late. You still have time."

"But—"

"Listen."

"What's the use?"

"If you let me teach you reading and writing I will pay you double for the newspapers you bring in."

"I don't know—"

I interrupt, heading toward him, "Come on, I'll give you your first lesson."

I take him by the hand and lead him to the chair.

"Sit down. This is how we start."

I grab a pen and paper. "Repeat after me: *alif, baa, taa.* . . ."

Absent

BETOOL KHEDAIRI

A READER'S GUIDE

WHAT'S IN A NAME?

BETOOL KHEDAIRI

In the Iraqi society of my childhood, there was a wide variety of interesting, beautiful, and musical names, and nearly all of them had a meaning or a special significance. My neighbor was called "the beautiful one," my sister's name means "the ringing of a bell," a male friend is named "lightning," and another is "the servant of God." Kurdish girls are often named after types of flowers. My Scottish mother, whom I always thought of as the eternal tourist, would often ask me the meanings of my friends' names. I'd tell her about a Jewish family who called their daughters Iris, Valerine, and Gilda, and a Christian family who called a son Omar—a Muslim name—without hesitation. My name has several meanings. It means "the virgin," and the encyclopedia lists a Saint Mary the Betool. It also means "the believer in God." It is a name often attributed to the daughter of the prophet Mohammad, Fatima Al Zahraa Al Betool.

Many of us at school ended up in the wrong religion class simply because our parents had not told us which religion we had been born into, and therefore which class we belonged in! I remember carrying the Koran and wandering into the church in my Armenian school. One of my friends asked her father if she was Shiu'e (meaning "communist" in Arabic), thinking that this was the word for She'ie (Shiite), because the two words sounded similar to her. He scolded her for being interested in differentiating between Shias and Sunnis, insisting, "We're all the same."

When I started primary school in Baghdad, my mother took me to the jewelry market on River Street. She asked an old bearded man to carve my name in gold. She was doing what most Iraqi mothers did: cherish the name of her child. This was normally done in Roman letters, but my foreign mother, to be different, had my name written out in Arabic. So for my seventh birthday, I got a necklace with my name dangling down from it, read from right to left.

Iraqi parents take their names seriously. When a male baby is born to them, parents are traditionally renamed after their firstborn son. They take great pride in being called, for example, Abu Hassan (the father of Hassan). If they aren't lucky enough to have a son, then they will be named after their eldest daughter. It is quite unusual for an Iraqi man not to be named after a son or a daughter. If he has no children, he still has to create a name for the child he lacks. Somehow, long ago everyone agreed to call such a "child" "the absent one." So childless men automatically become "the father of the absent one," and this makes them fit in socially and psychologically.

My foreign-born mother could never understand why people would want to be called after a human being who had not yet been born. Her question lingered with me for many years until I embarked on my second novel. I named the novel *Absent* to symbolize the dilemma of the Iraqi people. They had been excluded, and were "absent," from the international scene for decades. The civilization that had invented writing was now slipping into darkness as a result of wars, sanctions, and dictatorship. For thirty-five years Saddam remained the father of the absent Iraqi people. I needed to give birth to their story.

Though I was born in Baghdad, I have lived in Amman, Jordan, for a number of years, and have traveled quite a bit. And during my travels, while getting to know more Westerners, I realized that they knew little about Iraqis as human beings. Understandably, they were taking their impressions from the Iraq of the headlines. This was another important reason to write my second novel: not to criticize the media, but rather to play the role of a diplomatic host in order to invite readers to share my seven-thousand-year-old culture, which was being destroyed by deprivation. Throughout history, Iraqis have been under the stranglehold of the Ottomans, the British, a local dictator, and now the Americans. Sometimes I can't believe that in one lifetime I have witnessed three bloody crises: the Iraq-Iran War of 1980–1988, the invasion of Kuwait, in 1990–1991, and the U.S.-led occupation in 2003. These events have been accompanied by battlefield and civilian killings, children's malnutrition, diseases, starvation, mass graves, an embargo, a forced diaspora, arrests, rape, torture, brain drain, continuous bombings, and the list just goes on. Between the exported nightmare fantasy of weapons of mass destruction and the imported dream of democracy, I concluded that black comedy was the best style for my new novel, and I took it on as a new challenge.

Absent is about Iraqi families struggling to survive during the sanctions in Baghdad. The events take place in one building; the floors represent the diverse layers of Iraqi society. Since so many Iraqi men died due to war and unstable circumstances, most of the characters are women, and they unveil the story through dialogue, chitchat, and gossip. The story shows the effects of the economic and infrastructure collapse on the social and moral structure of day-to-day Iraqi lives. I feel that when all goes wrong on earth, human beings start searching the sky for solutions, and sometimes they get lost in the labyrinth of creating their own answers. This drew me into researching the hocus-pocus underworld of the coffee-cup reader, Umm Mazin (mother of Mazin). Everybody is searching to make sense amid the chaos. The fortune-teller takes over the destiny of the inhabitants, becoming a sort of psychoanalyst for the distressed women. My novel portrays the less privileged people struggling in the back lines, suffering the toll of the political decisions made in the front lines, yet, in terms of what the world knows of them, they are absent. This is a story that talks about an "old Iraq," familiar to Iraqis but unknown to the West, and it ends with a "new Iraq," familiar to the West but unknown to Iraqis.

Yes, Saddam, the father, is finally gone, but now we have many fathers. Since the liberation/occupation so much has changed, and things are going from bad to worse. My country is actually rocking between facing the challenges of being a preindustrial state and fending off the threat of an impending, vicious civil war. In the past few months, I have received calls from distressed friends in Baghdad: "Help, some groups are threatening me because of my Sunni name," and on the other line a friend pleads, "Please find me a job; I'm being harassed because I have a Shiite name." No wonder people are lining up to change their names and have started carrying more than one identity card to avoid being targets.

Occasionally, in Amman, I order take-out dinners from an Iraqi cook who sells meals from her home. When I place the order, she asks for my name by saying, "And you are the mother of?" I don't know whether to answer with a smile or a tear, "The mother of the absent one."

This brings me back to my late mother, who ended up having three names: Sophia, her registered Christian name when she was baptized; Hazel, her domestic name when she lived in her country; and a Muslim name when she converted to Islam to marry my father. On her wedding day, a friend of hers suggested that she adopt an Arabic name similar to her English name. The friend came up with Hadeel, which means "cooing of the dove." My mother said, "I like it, it's peaceful."

QUESTIONS FOR DISCUSSION

1. On the first page of *Absent* we learn that Dalal's uncle "didn't follow the custom that dictates parents be named after their firstborn child. . . . Instead, he insisted that he should be called Abu Ghayeb, the father of the absent one." What motivates this unusual choice, and how does it affect his adopted "daughter" Dalal? What examples of "absence" and "the absent one" can you find in the novel, and what is their significance?

2. Aspects of *Absent* are profoundly universal, such as the depiction of the fractious marriage between Dalal's aunt and uncle, Dalal's uncertainty as she ponders what to do with her life, and the resilience of her friends and neighbors who manage to stay hopeful and make a living under dire circumstances. What other aspects of the story and the characters did you find yourself identifying with?

3. *Absent* is set in the 1990s, after the Gulf War, but the exact time period and the conflicts described are intentionally left ambiguous. Why do you think that Betool Khedairi chose to do this, rather than setting it during the war itself, or during a particular postwar event?

4. How would you characterize Dalal's and Abu Ghayeb's relationship, and how does it evolve over the course of the novel?

5. What role does the fortune-teller, Umm Mazin, serve in the novel? Is she there for comic relief? What else might she represent? Why do so many people take comfort in visiting her? What would you ask her if you had a chance to visit her?

6. Dalal's uncle, a former artist, places a high value on aestheticism. When he asks Dalal how she would measure beauty, she responds, "If things aren't distorted, they may be more beautiful" (p. 64). What does this tell you about Dalal's feelings toward her facial disfiguration? How do you think her physical appearance shapes her as a character? How does it affect her romantic relationship with Adel?

7. Unlike many of her friends and neighbors, Dalal and her uncle have spent time in Western countries. How does Dalal's family feel about the West, and the Allied nations in particular? How does this compare with the impressions of other characters? Were you surprised by their reactions?

8. Why does Dalal choose to study French literature? Is there special significance in the fact that Dalal is reading Flaubert when she first meets Adel?

9. The characters in *Absent* spend a lot of time reminiscing about the Days of Plenty. In what ways are the clashes between the new and old Iraq apparent in the novel?

10. Abu Ghayeb tells Dalal that there is much to learn from the bees that he keeps, a lesson that she passes along to Adel and Saad. How does this wisdom become particularly profound? How might the bees serve as a metaphor for life in Baghdad?

11. Three of Dalal's most intimate relationships in the novel are with Ilham the nurse, Saad the hairdresser, and his exciting friend Adel. What does Dalal gain from getting close to each of these people, and what does she lose?

12. Do you think the novel ends on an optimistic note? How, if at all, do you think Dalal will be able to play a role in the reshaping of her home city?

BETOOL KHEDAIRI was born in Baghdad in 1965 to an Iraqi father and a Scottish mother. She received a BA in French literature from the University of Mustansiriya and then traveled between Iraq, Jordan, and the United Kingdom, working in the food industry while writing her first novel, *A Sky So Close,* published in Arabic in 1999 and published by Pantheon and Anchor in 2001/2002 to wonderful reviews. She currently lives in Amman, Jordan.